The Midnight Mile

by

Denis W. Flood

Word Association Publishers
www.wordassociation.com

ISBN: 978-1-59571-393-3
Library of Congress Control Number: 2009926128

Word Association Publishers
205 Fifth Avenue
Tarentum, Pennsylvania 15084
www.wordassociation.com

What was the pain I suffered, Johnny,
bringing you into this world
to carry you to your cradle,
to the pain I suffered carrying
you out of the world to your grave.
Mother of God, Mother of God,
Have pity on us all.

Sean O'Casey
Juno and the Paycock

For the Gold Star Mothers,
and for my hometown.

Coming
Home

The nuns of Saint Joseph's Home were on their mark the day Corporal Jackie Carroll's body came back from Vietnam. In solemn procession, they walked down the long series of steps from their convent to the Peekskill train station. A long column, maybe thirty in all. Mother Superior led the march. Not one of the Sisters said a word. Their procession moved quietly and quickly to the edge of the tracks where they prayed in silence with rosary beads.

A few of them stole looks southward, peeking for an early glimpse of the Albany-bound train that today was making a special stop in Peekskill to deliver the latest war casualty. It was hot that morning and some of the nuns were perspiring. In Catholic school one never saw a nun perspire even when in full gallop on the school grounds heading to catch a smoker or break up a fight. Nuns never perspired, and never cried (even when Pope Pius XII died). But on this morning, they did both.

Along with the suffocating mid-morning heat, heavy humidity had settled over the train station. Vinnie Sereno, the local cabbie, was busy wiping condensation off the windshield of his dilapidated station wagon. He wore a smashed up pork pie hat and wide suspenders that were barely holding up his pants over a beer barrel gut. Sereno, a fixture at the train station since the end of World War II, was the only cabbie that would drive passengers to the "colored" parts of town day or night. He liked to say he had the knots on his head to prove it.

Out across the railroad tracks, the mighty Hudson River appeared as calm and still as a painting in the Field Library. It was as if the river had stopped. Years later, people would remember that morning for its absolute stillness. They would also remember it for what happened after the train arrived.

Near the train station, Sorentino's Italian restaurant was already open for business. Normally, it catered to the commuting crowd late in the day coming in for shots and beers after the train ride home from the city. But today was different. This morning the monsignor might be there. The postmaster. Surely, the mayor.

Some of the locals were already drinking and talking about what a good kid Jackie Carroll was. How he set all the high school running records, worked in the post office and still found time to drive the good nuns to JC Penney, Woolworth's and the religious store. There they would buy soaps, shampoo, bags of candy and items like mass cards and Virgin Mary bookmarks.

Around 10 a.m., an immaculately detailed hearse pulled up to the station and those gathered cleared a lane so it could back up to the loading dock. A gruff-looking little man drove the hearse. He sported a flat top and looked like a tough guy, but when Mr. Huffman spoke, he had the voice of an angel. He always stared straight ahead when driving his hearse, like he was in a trance – so much so that he was T-boned a number of times around the town and funeral home, one time even losing a casket that came to a stop in front of the Modern Bakery on South Street.

The slain Marine's parents, Mickey and Marie Carroll, sat frozen in the front seat of the hearse, lost in time. No one spoke. A few local high school kids approached the hearse, stealing glances inside, but saying nothing. Everyone knew Mickey Carroll from CYO youth leagues. He coached every sport and looked like movie actor Fred McMurray who starred in the *Flubber* movies, one of which was currently playing at the local theater. Mickey had big jowls and a hangdog face and wore his whistle everywhere he went, some said even to bed. He got in trouble once when some of the high school girls he was coaching told the monsignor that Mickey's female assistant was playing with his trouser snake on a bus ride home from a volleyball tournament in Albany. The monsignor was outraged.

He sternly cross-examined the girls. "How do you know what you saw in a darkened bus?" the priest demanded. The girls cried and cried but stuck to their story. And Mickey got a three-week pass to a special retreat where the priest who touched an altar boy went to pray and repent. Mickey was back coaching in short order and better than ever, what with all the prayers and meditation he did.

Fewer in town knew his wife Marie, who mostly stayed home and drank vodka while listing to Johnny Mathis records. Her kids ran wild all over the place, with one of them, son Mike, running so fast that he was the new state champion in the mile. She must have been really pretty at one time, with angel's kisses that blended into a soft-freckled tan, long statuesque legs and a figure that still attracted stares while she shopped at the A&P. She had dark brown eyes and plucked stylish eyebrows and wore the most gorgeous clothing that one could find at a discount store.

Meandering around the train station, five other Carroll kids moved among the crowd, desperately grieving in small groups with some of their friends from grammar school. Mike Carroll, Jackie's younger brother and running partner, stood apart from everyone, speaking not a word and staring down the tracks.

The sadness, the humidity, the stillness and then the whistle of an approaching train hung in the air. Long and slow, like the whistle one hears late at night, then a sharper sound as the approaching train rounded the final Buchanan curve pulling into "P-E-E-K-S-K-I-L-L."

This was no commuter train.

It was way long and had three big diesels pulling the heavy load. At first, the engineer didn't know exactly where to stop. He idled his freight train at the station, then with a belch of black smoke and noise, moved the train forward so that only the caboose remained near the temporary platform. After some hand waving by the crew, the train backed up so a dull-green mail car was flush with the platform. The train was square now.

None of the gathered spoke a word, but a chorus of sobs began to sweep through the station like a wave at a sporting event. In full view, the grief-stricken parents and funeral director walked slowly from the hearse to the large sliding door of the mail car. The train hissed and bumped. The morning sun beat down.

After a few moments, the big door clanked open revealing a large mahogany casket covered by an American flag. A U.S. Marine corporal, dressed in a summer Class A uniform with tie and ribbons, stood at attention. Only stillness and the hissing of the train could be heard. The Marine moved first. He saluted and then spoke softly, barely above a whisper to the dead Marine's parents, Mickey and Marie Carroll. "I'm so sorry," he said as tears welled up in his eyes. "I haven't left your son's side since we left Quantico, Virginia."

The Carrolls approached the casket, their arms outstretched, first touching the flag. Mickey trembled as he tried to steady himself by putting two fingers on the casket. Mrs. Carroll rolled her head back in grief as she ran her hands along the flag.

An angry scream broke the silence as the punch hit Mickey squarely in the face, breaking his glasses. Stumbling back, he grabbed the casket for balance before punches number two and three put him on his knees.

"You killed my son, you son-of-a-bitch," his wife shrieked. "You killed my son." Falling to her knees to meet the wounded and confused man face to face she sobbed, "All he wanted was some money for college, and you wouldn't give it to him. You killed him for seven hundred dollars." She spit in his face.

A split second passed before the Marine guard dove in to separate the two. Mrs. Carroll grabbed the corporal's tie, choking him while all three fell to the sawdust floor of New York Central Mail Car #2455. Monsignor Healy jumped into the fray, his face beet red and large hands pulling and pushing. With the help of the disheveled Marine, they pulled Marie away from her husband. The monsignor tried to calm her. "The Lord took your son. He's in a better place now."

Getting her second wind, Mrs. Carroll used a wrestling move she had seen on TV to break away from the Marine. She turned her wrath on the monsignor. "Shut up," she screamed, "I got six kids and three miscarriages because of you and the Church… and now," she said between sobs, "I've only got five."

The Town Moves On

After Jackie's military funeral and Mickey's punch-out at the train station, an inexplicable sadness set in around Peekskill that made the summer days move as slowly as big Rupert, the 50-year-old black man who collected shopping carts for the A&P on Main Street. Rupert was big, bald and heavy and moved along on tree trunk legs. In the evening, kids would line Rupert's sidewalk route and blast him with BB guns.

His eyes were covered with cataracts. He couldn't run; he could barely walk so he absorbed hit after hit as BBs pelted his head and body. The only thing he'd ever say was, "I'm going to tell your mothers on you." Sometimes, if Rupert was lucky, an adult would shoo away the kids.

When the harassment got especially bad, he'd go into Ladder #12, where the volunteer firefighters would scream, "Get those damn carts away from the fire truck!"

Mostly, the firefighters treated Rupert pretty good. They'd offer him a soda and chase the kids away, threatening to kick their asses, which they never did because they couldn't catch them.

But there were other things on the firefighters' minds these days. Eddie Feigner and his barnstorming King and His Court softball team were coming to Peekskill to play the fire department All-Stars. In a town crazy about summer softball with everyone over the age of twenty-one playing on an organized team, the news couldn't have been bigger.

In fact, it was monumental. The charity event was to finance a major expansion of the Peekskill War Memorial on Division Street. It was still only the mid-1960s and already the Vietnam casualty numbers exceeded those from the Korean conflict. City fathers knew how much effort the new memorial would require. Years ago, when the city decided to build a suitable memorial to General George Washington who crossed the mighty Hudson River at Peekskill (King's Ferry) in order to confound British forces, the project fell through for lack of money and lack of interest.

Many in the town wondered aloud, if the first president couldn't even get a memorial, what chance did the Vietnam veterans have?

This time would be different. Mayor Di Gregorio put out feelers to Albany, checking to see if the state would contribute to the project. He knew the state capital had written Peekskill off as a dying river town as its industry bee-lined to the non-union south. But Peekskill still had voters in the general election.

The mayor established architectural and design committees, and put together a consortium of city workers and local contactors to move the project along. But money was the big hurdle, and this King and His Court softball game was bound to be a financial winner. He just knew it.

Eddie Feigner was the most famous softball player who ever lived. A pitcher with a throwing arm the size of a redwood oak, he fired the ball at over 110 miles per hour. No one could see the pitch, much less hit it. He needed only three others to "whip any team, anywhere." The King and His Court was comprised of a pitcher, catcher, first baseman and shortstop. Feigner could pitch from the pitcher's mound, second base and center field. He struck out batters wearing a blindfold, throwing between his legs and behind his back. At Chavez Ravine in Los Angeles, he struck out the entire Dodger World Championship team in an exhibition.

In fact, no one even fouled off a ball. New York Yankee centerfielder Mickey Mantle was the King's friend. And the Court traveled. Like the Harlem Globetrotters, they played in every hamlet, city and "berg" in America. They played in Pakistan and Egypt and ultimately wound up with a USO tour firing the hot fat one somewhere along the Ho Chi Minh trail. During the traveling season they played two to three games per day.

Fliers showing the famous flat-topped ex-Marine Eddie Feigner firing softballs began appearing on telephone poles, phone booths and windows of local retailers such as Tuller's Department

Store, Chuck's Grill, Mary's Tavern and Grill and The Big Embo soda shop. Kids were promised $1.00 an hour to carry sandwich boards advertising the upcoming charity event.

On the Peekskill side it was announced there would be tryouts for the big game. The twelve area volunteer fire departments would hold a weeklong practice session to select the 27-man team. To make sure there was no hand jiving with the selection process, the head baseball coach (and full colonel) from nearby West Point would have the final say.

Peekskill's volunteer fire department was split between the RIPs (Rotten Irish Pricks) who tended to be located in the suburbs and the Italian Americans ("my girlfriend has bigger tits than yours") who worked downtown or "down street" as the locals said. And young or old, no one was better looking or stacked higher than Honey Sanders.

Summer School
Commandos

The prettiest girl in summer school was painting her nails cherry to match her lipstick in French III class while browsing some dated stories in *Paris Match* magazine, when she came across a track article about Frenchman Michel Jazy setting the world record for the mile run.

> *Rennes, France –Frenchman Michel Jazy broke the world record in the mile run tonight with a time of 3:53.3. The old world record belonged to Olympic Champion Peter Snell of New Zealand. Jazy, France's premier distance runner, was denied an Olympic medal, finishing 4th. In tonight's race, Jazy, who at times trains barefoot, used a combination of fast pace and endurance to set the new record, which most people believe will be difficult for anyone to break.*

Never missing a chance to bust balls, Honey flipped her hair back, pursed her lips and said to classmate Mike Carroll, "Monsieur Michael, how fast do you run the mile?"

"Fast enough to win," he said.

"No, mon ami," she protested, "Répondez en français." (Answer me in French.) "How fast do you run the mile?"

Carroll, an acne-faced string bean who looked like a piccolo player in the band but ran like a gazelle answered, "Four minutes, ten seconds."

"Monsieur Jazy runs the mile in three minutes, fifty-three seconds," she said. "Vous n'êtes pas très rapide." (You are not very fast.)

Carroll began frantically thumbing through his book, looking for the response in French. Summer school had been a blessing for

Mike since his older brother's death in Vietnam. He cried for a week straight, and then one night broke out all the windows at Mary's Grill. That's where the despised Galer clan hung out. They were the local tough guys who beat him and his brother to a pulp after the Carrolls got caught sneaking into the Verplanck movie theater.

The cops caught up with Mike a mile down the road. The town police had been at the train station when his brother's body came home and knew the terrible times the family was going through. They gave him a pass on the broken windows.

Mike had lived in the shadow of his older brother since the boys were tots. Jackie played baseball, Mike played baseball; Jackie played hockey, Mike played hockey. When Jackie began long training runs to prepare for the hockey season, Mike followed. And after a while, they were zooming all around town and setting running records in every race they entered. In cross-country, their performance was off the charts as they finished first and second in most championship events.

Brother Jackie was the faster, tougher and older of the two. He was a grinder who set a fast pace and dared anyone to stay with him in a race. Mike was fluid, simply a beautiful runner whose feet barely touched the ground. It was as if he ran on a cloud. At the end of each season, his running shoes hardly had any wear on them, while Jackie's shoes looked like they had been through the Battan death march.

Honey Sanders, cheerleading captain and the prettiest girl in the city, had it in for the track team and all the skinny troublemakers on it, including Mike Carroll. She didn't care anything about his winning races. She thought Carroll and his friends were a leering bunch of homos who couldn't get girls on their own. And they were troublemakers, too. Always bringing heat on the football and basketball teams and cheerleading squad with their sophomoric humor and locker room antics.

Because they had to rake and line their own cinder track before meets, the runners declared war on the "lazy" janitorial staff at the high school, writing filthy cartoons and painting pictures about fat, bald men porking each other in the boiler room behind the cafeteria. The school's football and baseball fields were meticulously groomed by the janitorial staff, but they wouldn't touch the track, which was always a mess and needed much attention.

The janitors doubled as bus drivers so keys and bus numbers were mysteriously switched around from time to time, leaving snarling traffic jams out in front of the school at 3 p.m. On more than one occasion, bus drivers tried to run the distance runners off the road and into a ditch on Route 6. It was an ongoing war.

Honey only dated football players – the guys who had nice cars and wore cool threads. She let everyone know it. Rumor had it she was secretly seeing a twenty-one-year-old University of Rhode Island halfback whom she'd met at a college dance. She passed for 21 in order to drink beer and bump and grind with the big kids.

Honey had the brightest blonde hair, big blue eyes and the most startling figure anyone had ever seen. "No bra could hold 'em," was the rallying cry of half the school's athletic teams whenever Honey cheered. She was the sexy dream of the entire male population of the school and probably half the faculty too.

A solid "A" student, Honey made one big mistake during her junior year and it wasn't even her fault. She happened to be in back of the athletic bus making out with a football player when a large paper banner depicting two naked characters was unfurled from the bus window: "MR. MURTLE WAKES UP AT THE CRACK OF DAWN." Silly high school stuff.

That happened one late Saturday afternoon coming back from a football game against Sleepy Hollow High School. Monday morning, Principal Murtle's new wife – math teacher Dawn Griffin – sat in his office crying her eyes out, so he sentenced a dozen football players and cheerleaders to a summer school class of their choice.

There was much whining and crying by the athletes but the principal wouldn't budge. No letters of recommendation for college would be written unless the summer school classes were completed.

The principal had a flattop, big nose, and huge balloon lips. He was strictly "by the book" and a prick at heart. A bad combination for wayward teens with senioritis. Even the latest Vietnam War casualty Jackie Carroll, who got along with everyone, couldn't stand him. During June's hot days when her friends were getting tanned at Blue Mountain Lake, Honey spent a hard time in French class repeating audio phrases in language lab and cursing the wimps on the track team who had made the filthy poster that put her in this fix.

Fast
Ball Inside

The softball diamonds around Peekskill were busy morning, noon and night with the best players in town practicing for the twenty-seven spots on the All-Star team that would face the spectacular King and His Court softball team. Tavern owners reported a drop in revenue as hard-drinking Irish firefighters hit the base paths instead of the whiskey shots and Piel's draft beer.

"My take is off by thirty percent," said the owner of Duffy's, cursing "this softball nonsense."

Another owner said his weeknight business was off close to fifty percent.

"And then they ask me to sponsor the team," he said. "They can have this joint and I'll play softball."

Italian firefighters took a break from tuning up their hotrods and girlfriends' chests in order to run faster, throw harder and find some way to hit Eddie Feigner's 100 miles per hour softball pitch, which they couldn't even see at that speed. Many of the young firefighters had been good high school athletes and lifelong friends. They played every sport together – football, basketball and baseball.

Fire departments tended to be located in the same areas as the local high schools. For many, the competitions that began in peewee ball as kids continued through high school sports and into the fire departments' summer softball and winter basketball leagues.

Not many athletes played college ball. A few really smart kids went off to Ivy League schools. Sons of area professionals, doctors and lawyers. And a few might get in a college game now and then. But it was no big deal. Peekskill was a blue collar town and starting for one's fire department softball team, with a wife at home, a union job at Indian Point power plant and a cold beer after the game, was about as good as it gets.

Having a chance to beat The King and His Court on their home softball field in Peekskill's Depew Park was even better.

Some of the engine companies were famous – Continental Fire, Hook and Ladder 51, Engine Company 11 – and had been in existence for well over a hundred years. Some of the Peekskill fire department personnel and equipment were used in New York City during the draft riots of the American Civil War. (And it was often joked in town that much of the equipment belonged in the Civil War.)

During cold winters when fires ravaged Peekskill's wooden tenements, firemen crashed through doors, rescued trapped occupants and dragged them to safety through fiery infernos while all the time breathing superheated toxic smoke and air. They threw babies from the inferno into the arms of waiting firemen and pulled victims off of rickety fire escapes. A number of brave firefighters lost their lives and many later died from smoke-associated cancers. Peekskill's firemen were hugely celebrated at the annual Fireman's Parade, an event no one missed.

They were heroes of the town. Pride, balls and the ability to throw from third to first base off either foot was what made a good fireman, and Peekskill seemed to have them all. And during those summer days and nights they were swinging for the fences, figuring a hit off the King that made it to the outfield was a surefire homerun.

Eddie
Redlight

Eddie Redlight knew that the fastest high school runner in the nation, maybe in the world, was living right there in Peekskill, though he hadn't seen him much lately what with all the commotion about the upcoming softball game.

When he did, it was usually late at night with the Galer boys chasing him through the darkened streets. Sometimes, Eddie Redlight saw Mike Carroll scooting through town after finishing his shift at the post office.

Before Vietnam, it was older brother Jackie racing through the darkened streets. Redlight thought Jackie Carroll was the fastest person he'd ever seen in his ten years of standing on Peekskill's street corners, until his younger brother Mike came along. He was even faster.

No one in Peekskill knew where Eddie Redlight came from. He was seen mostly at night and not a soul in town knew his real name or where he lived. Some said he stayed at the Union Hotel near the train station, but this proved to be a false lead after kids from a high school newspaper went there to interview him for a column they were doing on town oddballs. The Union Hotel said they never heard of him.

Eddie couldn't be found during the day and he didn't have much to say at night, especially to kids who had belted him with snowballs during the winter, and eggs and tomatoes during the summer.

He was mostly a nice, kind man who barely said a word. He was also an easy target for teenagers with nothing to do—a strange, little fellow who stood near the traffic light at the corner of South and Division Streets, illuminated only by the colorful hues of the changing lights. What was known about Eddie Redlight came mostly from rumors and a few tidbits from the cabbie, Sereno, who had given him taxi rides on occasion.

For twenty-four years, it had been Eddie's job to signal the right-of-way for New York Central trains coming and going along the Harlem/Hudson river corridors. He was a signalman, hence the moniker "Redlight." He'd give trains a green or red signal, depending upon who was in the slot to take the line. Trains then proceeded at approved speeds.

He was about fifty-five years old, thin as a rail with a face that looked like one of the suffering saints in Assumption Church. His neck and hands appeared discolored, though it was hard to see at night. He had thinning black hair with a perfectly combed wave in the middle, matted in place with some type of pomade. He always wore clean clothes, along with work boots and a light jacket in the summer and a Navy pea coat in the winter. It was as if he was on his way to work. He had a lit cigarette between his fingers at all times and stood on the same corner every night.

Soreno said Eddie told him that he worked the late shift during his years with the railroad, sleeping away the days in old hotels along the rail line. As far as anyone knew, he was never married and had no family. During his railroad days, he'd head out to the small brick signal shacks that were barely heated in the winter and sweltering in the summer and were scattered along the high-speed rail line between New York City and Montreal. It was before automation, so Eddie's job was an important one. He was working near Sing Sing prison in Ossining when Ethel and Jules Rosenberg were put to death in the electric chair. Eddie told the cabbie that the lights dimmed in his little rail shack.

Eddie Redlight worked the signals for President Franklin Roosevelt's private train that would take him from Washington, D.C. to his summer retreat in New Hyde Park, a beautiful swath of land along the Hudson River. Because FDR's travel plans were classified, Secret Service men showed up in his signal shack prior to the train's arrival, always late at night, making sure it was Eddie Redlight hitting the signals and not Eddie Von Bismarck.

Those were the good days, Eddie confessed to the cabbie.

It was rumored that late in his career Eddie Redlight took to warming himself with a drink or two on cold nights, though no one in Peekskill ever saw him with a bottle. The rumor was that *he* was the signalman whose responsibility it was on an especially cold February night to warn the hard-charging Montreal-express that a southbound freight train from Rutland, Vermont (carrying quarry products and wood) was making its way at a very fast pace along the right of way.

Eddie hit the signal switch the way he always did. First the green, and then the red – then green again for the southbound train. No — the red! The trains collided with a horrendous roar. People living near the tracks said they thought it was a Russian A-bomb going off.

Hundreds of sleeping passengers were seriously hurt, twenty-five killed, four missing. Pullman cars spilled into the frozen Hudson River in the darkness.

From Eddie's perch he could see the collision and the awful flames a half-mile to his south. He took off running down the tracks faster than he ever thought possible, slipping and sliding on the frozen ice to reach the flaming crash site. He was first on the scene to witness the carnage of his mistake.

Surrounded by critically wounded and dying people, Redlight dove in the frozen Hudson River and swam out to a Pullman car that was floating down the river. Covered in oil, his hands and face burned, he pulled himself up on the car and crawled along the top to reach some stranded and near-frozen passengers.

"My baby!" a woman screamed and Eddie Redlight saw a child slip from the grasp of her mother and fall back into the icy Hudson. He dove back in and swam out to where the little baby was, but she had disappeared beneath the darkened water.

Eddie Redlight screamed and cried and moaned louder than all the wounded people together, "Oh, my God! Oh, my God!" He dove deep into water again and again and again, but he couldn't locate her.

A week later, the body of a baby girl was found thirty-five miles to the south, washed up at Peekskill.

Holy Cross,
Holy Christ!

Recruiting letters began pouring into the Carroll household, urging son Michael, who was New York state champion in the mile run, to apply to their schools. They came from Ivy League colleges such as Harvard, Columbia and Brown, and top-notch Catholic schools like Notre Dame and Boston College. Letters also came from College of the Holy Cross of Worchester, Massachusetts, which was the darling of the parish and the undergraduate college attended by Monsignor Healy.

This was some of the best news the monsignor had heard for quite a while. Because he, too, had been a runner of note at one time – participating on both the mile and 440-yard relay teams for that great university. Healy was originally from Boston and had run with a tough crowd until he fell under the tutelage of a wise old priest who encouraged his study and participation in sports. Monsignor Healy was going to make it his business to see that Mike Carroll was running for the Purple and White, by hell or holy water.

In any household in America, such letters of interest from these top-notch universities would be hailed with the greatest of joy. At Sunday mass, the priest mentioned the Carrolls' good fortune to parishioners. But in the Carroll household, the recruiting letters and scholarship offers were barely noticed and piled up on a living room table. There was no talk about college. Actually, there was no talking about much of anything. Vietnam was still too fresh and painful.

Mickey laid low from the town's sporting events, staying around the house as the monsignor suggested, "helping Marie deal with her grief."

He piled the little ones into the car, taking them to the Carvel ice cream stand any time night and day, whenever they asked, spending more money on ice cream and frozen custard then he did on household food.

Before Jackie's death, Mickey would never get Carvel ice cream because it was too expensive. Mickey took the kids to the Hollowbrook Drive-In Theater, which they all enjoyed, him included. There, they lay on the hood of the car propped up against the windscreen, eating popcorn and hot dogs from the snack bar.

The kids would run all around at night bothering people and playing grabass while sucking down orange and grape soda by the gallon. No war movies though. Only comedies – lots of Dean Martin and Jerry Lewis and Peter Sellers and Pink Panther movies. Some of the kids still believed Jackie would be home for Christmas like he said in his letters from Vietnam. They'd talk among each other like his death didn't happen. Like they didn't bury their brother two months earlier.

Mickey thought to himself, Who did the kids think was in the coffin we buried at Assumption Cemetery?

Mickey avoided the subject all together.

Besides work, Mickey got out of the house when he could and sat on the bleachers in the late afternoon timing son Mike in his repeat 440s and 220s at Depew Park. The quarter-mile track in town was everyone's favorite, unlike the awful oval setup at the high school. The backstretch was shaded by huge oak and maple trees that reached up to the heavens. Behind the bleachers near the finish line was a beautiful lake full of geese and ducks. Kids fished there from sunup to sundown, pulling in small pan fish along with varieties of bass and perch.

The park was home to an entire flock of peacocks whose beauty was surpassed only by their temperament. Newcomers who got too close to the birds were chased right into the pond.

Two ball fields were located at either end of the oval. Depew Park had been built by the Civil Conservation Corps (CCC) and the Works Progress Administration (WPA) during the depression on land donated by Chauncey Depew, former U.S. Senator from Peekskill.

Many out-of-work locals had built horse paths, lakes, tennis courts, cross-country courses, pools, softball and baseball fields and the fastest 440-yard cinder oval in Westchester County.

Though it was only six lanes wide around the turns, the cinders were tightly packed, holding runners spikes tightly to the track as they ran. It was eight lanes on the main straightaway where sprints were held. The track sat in a slight bowl that protected it from wind coming off the Hudson River. If records were ever to be set in Westchester County, Peekskill's Depew Park would be the place to do it.

Like his brother before him, Mike Carroll liked to run at the park and it showed. In June, he won the state high school mile in four minutes, ten seconds (4:10). He floated along in that race, through the first half-mile in two minutes, ten seconds (2:10) and raced home in two-minutes even (2:00). He finished ten yards ahead of his competition and said he "never felt tired."

Most high school track coaches thought Mike capable of a four-minute mile, but thought he lacked the motivation to be "a great one." He had heard those rumors and thought they were nonsense. He was practically undefeated on the track, setting new records every time he ran, be it the Northern Interscholastic League or the Westchester County Championships. He won the state meet easily in a great time, but no record. What was so bad about that?

On this summer evening, Mike ran a hard five-mile run along the park's cross-country paths. He finished with four fast 440s all timed in fifty-four to fifty-five seconds.

He was barely breathing at the end of the workout. Mickey had never seen anything like it. Even at his fastest, his older son Jackie couldn't touch the times Mike was turning in. It was as if he had moved to another level. Mike had always had tremendous endurance and now his speed was off the charts.

Sneaking into the Movies

As early as grade school, the Carroll brothers began their running careers trying to escape ass whippins administered by security ushers at the Verplanck Movie Theater and Dance Club, a large venue that held a theater and dance floor under one roof. It was common during those days for kids to sneak into the movies in order to save a buck or two that could later be used for candy – and much later, for a marijuana joint.

If one had a date, both might try to sneak in, and this was often accomplished by walking backwards as the crowd exited the theater. It's an optical illusion of sorts and should be practiced in order for one to blend smoothly in with the crowd. But it succeeded, and with movies such as *Sinbad, 20,000 Leagues Under the Sea, It's a Mad, Mad, Mad, Mad World* and *The Ten Commandments*, the system never worked better.

The theater owners soon caught on and hired a few local toughs, including the two Galer brothers, who doubled as ushers, to keep the non-paying crashers out of the theater. At first, this was accomplished by intimidation. The offender might be grabbed by the collar and escorted out of the theater through a back door and given a kick in the ass to send him on his way. One might be embarrassed, but that was a small price to pay for a free movie.

If the same individual was caught two times by the Galer brothers, an ass whippin in the alley behind the theater would likely take place. Depending on how much beer the Galers drank at Mary's Grill prior to assuming their shift, the beatings might include smacks, kicks, and heads slammed against brick walls. Violators were even spit and pissed on.

Since Mickey Carroll's cheapness was ledgendary and his boys spent most of their free time involved with sports and summer school, there was little time for working and, sadly, no money for the movies and dance club. So sneaking in became a way of life.

Jackie and Mike worked the scam in pairs. If one of them got into the movie, he might lie low for a short while, then open the back door for his brother when the coast was clear. Often, they created diversions by screaming there was a fight in the line out front, which would draw the Galers away from the back door.

Black people tended to sit in the movie balcony, though there was no segregation in town, and every so often someone would write "Nigger Heaven" on the stairwell and all hell would break lose. "Do rags" and popcorn boxes would rain down on the people below with a bunch of "motherfucka this" and "motherfucka that" thrown down for good measure.

The Galers were expected to keep the peace in these instances as well. And for the most part, they did.

However, sneaking into the movies was becoming harder for the Carroll kids. Much harder. Sometimes, the boys made it in and sometimes they got caught and beat up.

And sometimes, they ran like hell from the Galers, covering the mile distance from the theater to the safety of the woods near their home in five minutes if running in the snow. Four minutes or so during the summer.

The Galers were from Lake Mathews, an area containing a number of summer homes built by Jewish people from New York City who vacationed there in the 1940s and 50s. A number of the cottages lacked winterization and stood as cold, dark shells during the long winter months. The Galers lived in the biggest, dirtiest, wreck of a haunted house on the lake. It was scary to drive by the place during daylight hours. It was mind-boggling at night.

Newspapers from that time reported the elder Mrs. Galer disappeared one cold winter day and was never seen again. Some said she fell through the ice while trying to get away from her drunken husband, Tony. He was a local pervert who shoed horses when he wasn't exposing himself to kids walking home from the ball fields.

"You know where I can get this thing straightened out?" he'd yell, as he flailed his anaconda back and forth in his hands. Startled kids would gasp and run like hell at the sight of his mean-looking machine.

The Galer boys, Richard and Robert, were in their mid 20s and looked very much alike. They were as feared and despised throughout town as their old man. Richard was heavily pockmarked, six-feet two inches tall and strong as an ox. He had some type of Navy tattoo on his right forearm, and word in town was that he killed a shipmate during a fistfight while deployed on a U.S. destroyer.

Robert, younger by a year, had done time for burglary, car theft and some type of sexual perversion. He was about the same height with a strange look about him, and had a long red scar on his forehead where his old man cut him with his horseshoeing knife. Some said he looked like Richard Speck, the murderer from Chicago who killed all the nurses.

The Galers drove around in a dented red Ford Galaxy with a foxtail on the antenna. They had a 15-year-old sister named Lilly who had dropped out of school. People who knew the family said she wasn't right in the head, and that she mostly walked around town talking to herself. Now and then, the Galers would bring her to work and she'd sit in the back row of the movie theater, eating popcorn and drinking 7-Up.

Marie
and the Sergeant

It was before noon on a June morning that Marie Carroll, the newest Gold Star Mother in Peekskill, set out a plan to even out the score with Navy and Marine Corps recruiters on South Street.

She'd been gearing up for a fight since Jackie's body came home from Vietnam. Marie still hadn't forgotten the recruiter's sales pitch to son Jackie, telling him that because of his running ability, he'd be a shoo-in for the Marine Corps track team at Quantico, Virginia. The recruiter also told Marie and Jackie that he'd probably get an appointment to the Naval Academy and a free education, sparing her husband Mickey the cost of tuition.

Mickey, of course, was all for it. Marie kept asking the recruiter, "What about Vietnam?"

The staff sergeant's response was always the same, "With Jackie's test scores and running ability, he'll wind up in an officer pipeline and be on the Marine track team in six months," he said. "All that will be settled when he gets down to Parris Island for boot camp training."

Marie knew that the only record Jackie ever set while in the Marine Corps was getting to the front lines. Six months and six days after leaving Peekskill, Private Jackie Carroll, 0311, was walking point for the second platoon of November Company in the An Hoa Valley of Death, traipsing through unexploded napalm and praying harder then he thought he ever could. Even with the Galers chasing him.

After her son's funeral, neighbors began to notice a pronounced change in his mother's selection of music (as if they could avoid it, with her windows wide open) from soft and smooth Johnny Mathis, to boisterous Phil Harris, "Brother, Can You Spare a

Dime." Lately, however, there was very frightening and incredibly loud "Jungle Music" – some type of Gregorian chant sung by Zulu warriors together with drum beats and hysterical screaming. Someone had sent the record to Marie during her time of mourning and now it blasted on her LP all day, driving the neighbors crazy. Sitting in the living room downing vodka and tonics under the pounding jungle beat drove Marie even crazier.

On this particular morning after getting Mickey out the door for work and the younger kids ready for day camp, Marie turned off her music and softly chatted with son Mike, who had just finished a long training run through the trails of Blue Mountain State Park.

"That was Jackie's favorite spot, you know," she said, trying to gauge his reaction. She continued, "He just loved running through that park. He'd come back and talk about all the animals. There were packs of deer, raccoons, foxes—and remember when he saw the black bear?" she asked. "He really ran fast that time," she said with a smile.

Mike came over and put his arm around her. She continued, "Your brother loved the birds too. He'd listen to them call out when he was running. He'd come back to the house just like you did today and say he saw the most beautiful bluebirds or cardinals. I wish, just once, I could have run with him and seen the world through his eyes," she said as her own began to tear up.

"Mom, my brother's always with me," said Mike. "...I feel him near me wherever I go, whatever I do, whenever I'm running. The nurse at school said I'd have lots of dreams about Jackie for a while, until the shock of his death wears off. And the monsignor said I'd be dreaming about Jackie in heaven… But Mom, this is different. This is real. It's measurable. The other day at the track, I was doing quarter-mile repeats and Pop was timing me. It felt like my legs were barely touching the ground.

"Running through the park this morning, I was just cruising along looking at the scenery like Jackie and I did and when I came to the timed mile portion, I decided to go for it. I wasn't even pushing, and I ran it in four minutes, eighteen seconds. That's way faster than I ever ran before," he said. "I'm happy because I'm so fast, and sad because I'm so lonely."

She steered her still sweating second son towards the backyard above-ground pool – the biggest in the neighborhood, according to Mickey – where he did his best imitation of Russian Olympic high jump champion Valeri Brumel. He leaped over the pool's edge with a perfect western roll. Water cascaded over the sides, knocking the cylindrical filter off its stand and onto the grass, something that always pissed Mickey off, but made Marie laugh.

Marie then began to plan her revenge. She knew that shortly after one p.m. the military recruiters would eat at the luncheonette at Tellers Department Store, across from where Eddie Redlight hung out. There would be two of them, the big Marine staff sergeant and his Navy buddy who was a first-class machinist mate.

They always ate lunch together and later at night, drank rum and cokes at Charlie's Grill, an old rummy hangout where local kids would never go. Actually, the two recruiters were inseparable.

They passed off "leads" to one another, making sure the Department of the Navy (including the USMC) got its pick of able-bodied high school graduates before the Army scoffed them up.

The big Marine often boasted how he never failed to meet his quota of fresh recruits for the Vietnam gristmill. "Who in the fuck would want to join the Army?" he'd ask after a few rum and cokes. "Who in the fuck would want to get drafted and serve with a bunch of dope-smokin' idiots?"

Putting his arm around his drinkin' buddy, he would say, "Hell, I'd rather join the Navy and get blowjobs from queer sailors than put on that Army hat and wrinkled khakis and call myself a soldier.

"You know a Marine can shoot the dick off a dog at five hundred yards, and throw a hand grenade the length of a football field. He has women moist between the legs whenever they see that beautiful dress blue uniform."

Raising his glass high above the bar for everyone to see and with enhanced oratory he said, "A good Marine's got the balls of Chesty Puller (legendary Marine) and the piety of Saint Thomas Aquinas. Here, here." And he'd toast to the muffled cheers of the lost souls of Charlie's Grill.

Marie took the late afternoon bus into town with a 12-gauge shotgun under her summer coat. Her kids wouldn't be home until late, as this was a campfire night. She sat stiffly in the back, trying to avoid being goosed by the long barrel of Mickey's prized

Remington. She talked to no one. Marie stationed herself across the street from Chuck's Grill, nearest the second hand store where she could browse unnoticed for the longest time. Under her coat, Marie fingered the safety mechanism on the gun, repeating to herself again and again, "Back is safe, forward is fire, back is safe, forward is fire." She was going to blast the big Marine first. She would shoot his Navy buddy for good measure next, if she had the time.

Like clockwork, the two recruiters approached Chuck's a minute before happy hour began. It was now time. Marie took a few steps towards the bar when it suddenly dawned on her. *She hadn't loaded the weapon.* God, she thought, I must be dumb drunk.She looked down at her feet and cursed.

It was as if someone's guardian angel was looking out for her on this day. The next bus back home stopped right near her on the street. She took the bus home and began her evening cooking, as if nothing whatsoever had happened.

That night, Marie made the biggest pan of macaroni and cheese ever. She knew the little ones would be hungry after a day of swimming and running at day camp. She cut some wieners up and sprinkled them throughout, sliced real thin the way Mickey liked them.

She and Mickey hadn't slept in the same bed since that awful day in May when the telegram came telling her that the 8.5-pound baby boy she delivered at the Peekskill Hospital in July 1945 was dead "of multiple gunshots to the head and body, in the vicinity of An Hoa, Vietnam… your anxiety and great loss is realized."

Marie hadn't remembered attacking Mickey at the train station. She remembered being on the ground, rolling around in the sawdust, and a frightened young Marine trying to pull her to her feet.

And the monsignor, always lecturing, always siding with Mickey and the men of the parish. God forbid a wife has something worthwhile to say. Like the time after her second miscarriage when she received a lecture by the holier-than-thou Father Sarno, an Italian exchange priest.

"Father, forgive me for I have sinned," she said in an act of true contrition befitting the Virgin of Guadalupe. "I have let my husband use a rubber on me."

Father Sarno, who occasionally smoked smelly cigars in the confessional, blurted out in the darkness. "He beat-a you with-a rubber what?"

"No Father," explained Marie. "He used a birth control device on me."

"It's-a you birthday. Why-you-no-say? Happy birthday. Baby Jesus loves you so much."

"Father! My husband had sex with me using a rubber birth control device so-I-won't-have-any-more-BAMBINOS."

"In Saracusa, we call-a women like you, 'whores.' It's a not possible to do what you do. No more birth a control for you or I'll tell the monsignor to excommunicate you from the Catholic Church."

Duty, Honor, Country
& Baseball

Colonel Miles D. Parrish, professor of military history at West Point and full time varsity baseball coach, was fifty-two years old and one year away from mandatory military retirement when Salvatore "Freckles" Fraggo, steward for Laborers Union #1224, showed up unannounced at his modest brick home on officers' row. Fraggo was assistant softball coach and all around cheerleader for the Italian firefighters in Peekskill and wanted to get the feel of the man picking the all-star team.

Col. Parrish was drinking his second mint julep of the night (fixed extra strong by his lovely bride of thirty years, the former Mae Van Ardsdale) as "the sun was dropping from the sky like a big orange wafer," just like in *The Red Badge of Courage*. Colonel Parrish loved that book and used it in his history classes as a testimony to the perils of the foot soldier.

The Colonel had been baseball coach at the Academy for four years and had a win-loss record of about .500, not bad for a school that couldn't recruit. The only scholarships offered were for dodging bullets at Normandy, Korea, and now Vietnam. Lovely wife Mae came from Southern aristocracy, "Ma people are from Culpepper," she'd answer in a heavy drawl, referring to the horse riding capital of the Virginia Commonwealth.

Freckles's people came from East 225th Street in the Bronx, and many sat on plastic-covered couches in the living room when they weren't playing kick-the-can in the street. His mother was a stay-at-home mom who cooked pasta all day while screaming at the kids; his father had been a city fireman who mostly steered the back end of the giant hook and ladder, until a terrible accident claimed his life during a five-alarmer when young Sal was only ten years old.

Little Salvatore then went sideways in school and fought anyone who joked about his light-skinned freckled face, which was especially odd since both his parents were dark-skinned Sicilians.

"I'll kick your fat ass," he'd say, as he chased kids around public school, PS 78.

Eventually, Salvatore got tired of fighting and adopted "Freckles" as his moniker, which became a gangster nickname after he and his crew hi-jacked a million-dollar fur shipment from Kennedy Airport. Along with a few other big paydays, Sal was on his way. In the mid-sixties, Sal Fraggo wormed his way into the coveted steward job with Union Local #1224, the biggest union hall in the state.

He had six hundred men working under him on the giant Indian Point nuclear power plant which was owned by New York City's behemoth Consolidated Edison (Con-Ed). Half the workers were from the city of Peekskill. The Indian Point project was continually plagued by labor strife and always behind schedule, especially with construction of Reactor Number 2.

If a worker crossed Sal, he didn't work. Ever. If Westinghouse (builder of the reactor) or Con Ed crossed Sal or the union, there was a work stoppage. Salvatore "Freckles" Fraggo was the most important person in Westchester County and when he pulled up to Colonel Parrish's brick home in his imposing stretch limo, wearing aviator shades, he looked as important as any general in the Army.

"I'm here to make a donation to the West Point baseball program," he said to the surprised colonel who met him at the front door. After brief introductions, the two men retired to a lovely screened-in porch that overlooked the mighty Hudson River. In short order, Mae had a "toddy" for the guest. "It's sure beautiful here," said Sal, surveying the scene.

"It's the prettiest place on earth," said the colonel. "I've been everywhere with the Army – Germany, Austria, Lybia, Morocco, Australia, Vietnam, Alaska, but this is primo. Best place ever."

"Ah second that," chimed in Mae, who was eyeballing Fraggo with a suspicion reserved for a bible salesman who shows up on a soldier's doorstep after the death telegram has arrived.

"Colonel, we – our union that is – admire what you do up here," said Fraggo. "You know... with the baseball and all. Everyone understands the funding problems you must have with all that money going to the troops in Vietnam."

"You got that part right," said the colonel. "As a matter of fact, our baseball team gets much of its practice equipment from the New York Yankees, if you can believe that." Fraggo, a super Yankee fan, took notice.

"The Yanks come up here every other year to play an exhibition game. Right up from Florida before their major league season opener. They play the cadets and then have an intersquad game where they divide up the sides, just like we did as kids. They leave us all their equipment used in Florida: catchers' masks, first baseman's gloves, bats, balls, bases, fungos, and you-name-it. And it's all practically new.

"Ole Casey puts 'em in the barracks for a few days and restricts the team to the post. They're allowed to go to the officers' club and we go out of our way to show them a good time," said the colonel as Mae lightly touched her husband's arm to interrupt, "Sometimes, too good a time."

"Oh," said the colonel, "things get outta hand once in a while, and Mickey, Whitey and a few others sneak off to the local gin joints in Highland Falls, but it's not a big deal. They're great partners and winners, and we hope they're success rubs off on the kids."

Fraggo suddenly interjected: "But your baseball bleachers are fallin' apart. The wood is rotted through. It's only a matter of time before some of your fans fall to their death over at your field over there."

"Sadly, that's true," said the colonel. "We were supposed to get new aluminum bleachers and press box and refreshment stands, but the money has gone to advanced summer training in the mountains. Our superintendent is trying his best to get these young soldiers ready for Vietnam, and well, it's an expensive proposition," he said with a heavy sigh.

"Are you selling bleachers, Mr. Fraggo?" said Mae.

Standing up to face the colonel's wife, Fraggo squared himself, saying, "I'm not *selling* bleachers. I'm offering to *buy* all the bleachers, press boxes, whatever this great baseball team needs. Consider it a gift from the patriotic men of Union Local 1224. We have as much as a hundred and fifty thousand dollars to give ya, and there's more where that comes from. You know, we also lost a lotta guys in Vietnam."

Colonel Parrish, who had twenty-nine and a half years in the military, two bad knees from parachute jumping, and twelve hundred dollars total in his bank account for retirement, said he'd have to inform the athletic director as well as the superintendent (a three-star general) of this great gift to his baseball program.

As they walked to the car, the colonel presented Salvatore Fraggo with a small statuette of Saint Crispin, the patron saint of foot soldiers. It was the greatest gift the colonel could give. He then went inside and asked lovely wife Mae for another toddy.

After leaving West Point, Fraggo had his driver stop in the nearby town of Highland Falls at the very same gin mill that Mickey Mantle, Whitey Ford and even the great Joe DiMaggio frequented. Pictures lined the walls: Generals Douglas MacArthur, Robert E. Lee, and Dwight Eisenhower. Lots of athletic team photos of football greats Blanchard and Davis, Mr. Inside, Mr. Outside. Army coaches Red Blaik and Vince Lombardi, and the amazing Army runner, Pete Dawkins. Team photos of undefeated seasons and train trips to Philadelphia. And there, in the corner of the bar, a photo of West Point baseball coach Colonel Miles Parrish drinking a cold one with all the AWOL Yankees. Fraggo touched the frame and studied the photo for a long moment.

A few enlisted soldiers were seated at the bar and over in the corner. Some underage girls from Ladycliff College were drinking beer and doing homework. Fraggo took a seat close to the back wall, a habit he had gotten into while working the docks in Brooklyn. Nancy Sinatra was singing "These Boots Are Made for Walking" on the jukebox. He ordered a scotch and milk and watched the news of the army fighting in the Iron Triangle north of Saigon, where "U.S. forces have sustained heavy casualties while uprooting an NVA Regiment."

Fraggo thought about the last time he was at West Point, which seemed like forever ago – it was a big, winter indoor track meet during his sophomore year at Cardinal Spellman High

School. He was leadoff runner on the 440 and mile relay teams that won both their heats, placing high in the overall standings.

His times were the second fastest on the team, which was great for a sophomore, so impressive in fact, that the head track coach at West Point told him to keep up his grades and remember West Point when time came to apply to college.

He remembered it very well because it was the first time since his father's death that an adult male had said anything positive about his performance.

In the afterglow of these comments, young "Freckles" Fraggo then made a serious mistake, one that would keep him from attending West Point under any circumstances. When the team bus stopped at the base commissary to pick up food for the trip back to the Bronx, Fraggo and his teammates went on a shoplifting frenzy, stealing food, pennants, sweaters – anything that said, "West Point."

Before the bus got to the main gate, MPs had it surrounded, forcing its occupants to brace on the side of a frozen access road. Fraggo's pockets were stuffed with stolen goods from the commissary.

Along with a few others, the MPs took down Fraggo's name and told him he was banned from setting foot on Academy grounds for ten years.

Fraggo finished his drink at the bar and left a generous tip for the bartender.

After a while, it was time to head back to Yonkers. He said very little as his stretch limo crossed over the Bear Mountain Bridge, plowing southward along the banks of the Hudson River.

"Stay Away From That Young Stuff"

On a warm summer night, Mike Carroll was putting on quite a show at Depew Park's cinder oval, turning 220s and 440s with such speed that softball players and guys shooting hoops stopped what they were doing to watch. Carroll glided effortlessly around the track, never tiring. His long strides dug so hard into the cinders that occasional sparks flew from his half-inch spikes.

"Y'see that shit? You see what that motha-fucka did?" said Peekskill's legendary high school basketball star Cookie Reams to his hoop mates as he watched the speed and power of miler Mike Carroll in amazement. "Holy shit, there he go again. That be one fast motha-fucka... Whew! Sparks flying all over the place. Can you believe this shit?" Reams asked.

"Oh, you could beat him Cookie," said a heavyset black man sporting a goatee and sweating up a storm. "You beat 'em all in your time."

Cookie wasn't listening to his blabbermouth friend. He was watching this runner who could have destroyed him in any race on the track. Cookie still looked like a young kid despite his age: Six-feet two inches tall, 170 pounds, long arms and powerful legs. He had short hair, a thin mustache and a large moon pie face, with eyes spread far apart. On the athletic field, he could see things shaping up around him with those big eyes. Things that no one else could see.

Cookie was Peekskill's greatest athlete ever, averaging thirty-nine points a game in basketball and winning every race in track from the 100 to 880. He ran cross country only one year and placed third in the New York state finals. As a high school freshman, he scored seven touchdowns in a JV football game but gave up football because he didn't like the coach.

Cookie Reams had graduated five years earlier and received a scholarship to a small, all-black college in North Carolina. It was a segregated South that he lived in, much different from upstate New York.

There were no mixed dances in the Carolinas, no Salt and Pepper Clubs, no Harlem, no protective nuns of the Franciscan order who would always watch out for a brother. There were rednecks, German Shepherds, and totally separate and unequal classrooms and training facilities.

Cookie persevered. As a college freshman, he placed second in the cross country conference meet. And he was running just to stay in shape for basketball. Hoops was another story. Cookie led the freshman basketball team to a 20-3 record, averaging eighteen points and seven rebounds per game. The freshman team regularly routed the varsity in practice games. Local newspapers touted his "New York-style fast break and ball handling abilities." Cookie was every bit as good as the famous cross-town star from Winston Salem, Earl Monroe.

And when Cookie came home to Peekskill during school breaks and visited his friends on lower South Street, he was treated like returning royalty. At first, he let them all go on about how lucky he was to be away from Peekskill and how the women down South were "so fine they'd take a brother's breath away."

But Cookie was only foolin' like a feint in basketball where your head goes one way and ball and lower body goes another. The greatest athlete Peekskill ever produced was miserable.

He didn't tell his friends that his college was so poor that it held practice in a tobacco warehouse and played its home games in a local high school gymnasium. Or that the college track was a large grass field marked in an oval shape with road cones ("How am I goin' to make the Olympic Team running on this piece of shit?"). Or that he shared textbooks in class, that there were four guys living in a two-person dorm room, and that his big scholarship was just a series of EOGs (economic opportunity grants).

Cookie knew that in his lifetime he'd never set foot on a basketball arena at Duke, North Carolina, Clemson, or Kentucky. And if his school's converted airport limo held up, he might make it to Alcorn A&M, Maryland State, Tuskegee or the North

Carolina Correctional Institute in Greensboro where some mean hoops were played by some mean men.

"What about all them fine singin' groups that jam at your college?" his friends would ask, "Like the Platters, Temptations and Dion Warwick."

"Oh yeah," answered Cookie. "I seen 'em all."

Yeah, right. Cookie knew those famous black groups only played on the big white campuses, the same places where he couldn't play basketball. The only groups Cookie had ever seen in concert were "Redd Foxx," "Doug Clark and the Hot Nuts," and "Rudy Ray Moore" – black comedians who recited offbeat prose:

…Now, some folks say that Willie Green,
Was the baddest motha-fucka the world's ever seen.

I want you to sit back, take a real good shit, and screw your wig on tight,
And let me tell you about this bad motha-fucka named Dolomite.

By his junior year, Cookie was a college dropout and in the Army playing hoops on Fort MacArthur's service team in California. He was a Spec-4 postal clerk and laying up with a woman in Long Beach. Before long, they had two kids. After his enlistment was up and he was armed with a postal clerk MOS (military occupational specialty) and five extra civil service points for being a veteran, he was delivering mail in Peekskill and shooting nightly baskets back where it all began.

Turns out it was a good night for a track workout after all as the beautiful Honey Sanders broke away from her softball playing friends to watch Mike run, probably out of boredom.

Her eyes followed his movements for a long time. Honey was standing at the 330-yard mark wearing a madras blouse, blue skirt and penny loafers. Her blonde hair danced in the soft evening breeze. She looked around Depew Park and saw all these people looking at the runner circling the track. Softball players stopped batting and throwing to watch Mike Carroll fly through the turns. Black guys shooting hoops paused as Carroll bolted by them on the straightaway. Even the little Italian man herding up his peacocks stopped what he was doing to watch the kid run by.

A few moments later Honey was holding two beers, compliments of the softball crew.

"I've got a brew for you after your workout," she hollered as he circled by.

Carroll, who always had trouble hearing splits in a race, had no trouble with Honey's reference to a beer. He finished his interval and jogged over to her side. "Are you trying to get your boyfriend jealous?" he asked in a light-hearted way. "Or do you need help on the French final?"

"Help from you?" she laughed. "I *understand* French, remember? I heard Mademoiselle Plante say that you and Brown were the two dumbest students in the language program."

Carroll laughed. "I'll drink to that," he said. "But I really think Brown is dumber."

Honey proceeded to tell Mike that the softball players were only going through the motions tonight because word on the street was that the all-star team was already selected. The fix was in. City administrators were hyping the event, and even forking out five thousand dollars for lighting Depew Park so the game could be played at midnight – precisely when The King and His Court would arrive from Danbury, Connecticut.

"There's been about three or four heart attacks since this King and His Court thing started," said Honey, who added, "Seems every week, another volunteer fireman keels over running the bases."

Honey moved in closer to Mike, who was now sitting on the grass swilling beer while changing his spikes. Her perfume floated slightly ahead of her.

"Now, you're really trying to get your boyfriend jealous," he said.

"I'm not dating anyone," she answered.

It was dusk now, and the softball players were leaving. Honey stretched flat on the grass looking up at the sky, which was fast losing its light. A slight breeze kicked her skirt up around her panties. She made no attempt to pull it down. Mike tried to look away but after a few moments stared directly at her beautiful and revealing body.

"Why don't you run a mile race?" she asked, "You're the state champ. Get all your running friends together. The spotlights will be up, and the town is ready for a big event. Run a track race. Fuck these firemen."

Mike Carroll was barely listening, and running any distance was the last thing on his mind at this point. Honey slid her hand down between her legs and began to rub herself and softly moan.

"Rizzo told me you track guys can't get girls. Is that so, mon ami?"

"It's hard to get dates when you got no money and no car," said a now embarrassed Carroll, who was growing pudgy under his running shorts.

From across the track where the basketball game was finished, Cookie Reams was rubbing his tired dogs, gulping down water and taking in the show between the two lovebirds across the field.

Sizing up the situation and giving the best advice he possibly could, Peekskill's greatest athlete shouted across the athletic field: "Hey, champ, stay away from that young pussy or you'll wind up on the mail route with me!"

Point
Man
(the Spring Offensive)

No one in Marine Corporal Jackie Carroll's November Company knew where the Abco Study Guide came from. Some said it was from Division Special Services; others said it was from the base library. Rumor had it that a Marine's parents sent it to him in Vietnam so he could brush up on civil service examinations prior to discharge. The Abco Study Guide was an enlisted Marine's chance for a better life – a way to even the score with officers who in most cases served only six months in combat. (The other six months were spent in the rear area pasting up charts for the battalion commander.) The average enlisted trooper dodged bullets for a full thirteen months, if he lived that long, which he seldom did.

With a little study preparation and not five but ten additional points on a civil service exam (five points for being a veteran, ten points for being wounded), an average GI might get the edge he needed to get a decent job and a better life. And in November Company, everyone got wounded so they earned an automatic ten points.

The Abco Study Guide was easy reading and geared to those with GED degrees. The guide contained hundreds of practice tests that allowed Marines to prepare for a future in civil service – the post office, customs, police departments, and forest management. In the latest edition, they could prepare for a career as an accident investigator, though this was not technically civil service. This last one attracted the most attention from the Marines in November Company because it had a photo of a beautiful girl wearing a hiked-up mini-skirt.

The girl appeared as if she was hanging on every word of an accident investigator who was jotting in his notebook while looking over her dented automobile. Like a former gunnery sergeant now wearing civilian clothes, the investigator had a flattop, dark pants, a short-sleeved white shirt, thin black tie and penny loafers. He was buffed from years of working out and three squares daily, courtesy of Uncle Sam. You could imagine him driving a company car and having an expense account in addition to his military retirement.

He exuded confidence and sexuality like only a combat veteran could. The perfect life. He's seen the shit and lived to tell about it – and now he's making money and has the absolute attention of the best looking women in Beverly Hills and West Palm Beach. And, because he's a Marine, he's ballin' them too. The Abco Study Guide was every grunt's dream because it provided a positive vision for the future, if they lived that long.

The study guide in reality was the kiss of death to any sane person who was mildly superstitious in November Company during that terrible spring offensive. It had been thrown away numerous times, even tossed down the shitter where no person on earth would go fetch it. But it kept coming back to November Company. The study guide didn't come from the base library or Special Services – it came from Ho Chi Minh himself. Every Marine who had read the book was now dead. Only when the practice tests were discovered by an administrative corporal packing up "last effects" of the deceased and the correlation made, did the horrible reality of the study guide set in.

It revealed a paper sarcophagus for Santori, Cheeby, Ramos, Ricks, Madden, Maltby, Donovan, AJ and CC Jones ("CC come from DC to kill the VC"), Top Jenkins and even Lt. Cink who browsed through it on radio watch when he told his PFC runner to "go find me something to read."

It was the book from hell, meant to punish any person foolish enough to think he could cheat death or plan for the future. There was no future in November Company just like there was no future in the 351st Communist NVA Division—which was hunkered down waiting for the Marines in the hills of Antenna Valley hard along the Song Thu Bon River.

"Corporal Carroll, get up on point!" barked Sergeant Don Zoeller as November Company snaked its way along a mountainous ridge twenty miles west of An Hoa, South Vietnam.

It was springtime and heavy rains made the trail almost impossible to navigate. Large stretches of trail had disappeared ahead of the advancing column, washed out by earlier torrential rains. One misstep and Marines would fall to their deaths down a thousand feet or so to the valley floor where the bodies would be picked over by villagers until the rescue party arrived.

Jackie Carroll, 19, didn't mind walking point, which was the most dangerous position on the modern battlefield. Carroll was "salty" now, having been in Vietnam a few months. He was also emaciated, standing six feet one-inch, and weighing 135 pounds. He had sandy blonde hair, a razor thin face and a three-day-old beard. He had big sores on his hips and shoulders from the heavy equipment he carried colliding with his bones. A common ailment among infantrymen. Each morning, the corpsman would change rotting bandages on his hip and wonder how Carroll could keep going.

"It doesn't hurt," said Carroll. "Smells like shit, but doesn't hurt," he said while tossing his nasty, blood-soaked bandage onto the helmet of a fellow Marine.

The Marine ducked and shouted back: "You're fucked up, Carroll."

Carroll moved to the point position. One would hear a lot of nonsense about enemy ambushes letting the point man through so it could annihilate the main column behind him, but that was mostly nonsense.

The first guy in the enemy's gun sights got drilled through the 10-ring every time, along with anyone near him. If you walked point in Vietnam during that terrible offensive, you were a dead man if the enemy was set up ahead in an "L" or "V" shaped ambush. Gone.

To make matters worse on this day, a Marine spotter plane, traversing the same path as the men of November Company, had sighted a column of seven hundred or so North Vietnamese soldiers earlier in the day. Seven hundred enemy soldiers added up to a couple of regiments – probably from the 351st Division that had left Hanoi a few months earlier.

Far across the hilltop, three other Marine companies had been dropped off and were marching at rout step to seal off enemy escape routes and force the North Vietnamese soldiers into a pitched battle. A "text book battle" as they liked to say back at headquarters.

"Watch your step, dammit!" shouted the squad leader as Corporal Jackie Carroll momentarily lost his footing and slipped off the path, coming perilously close to falling down the side of the cliff. Other Marines in the column latched on to his shirt and rifle to keep him from dropping. They tugged and struggled mightily to pull him up from the abyss. They screamed and cursed as their feet slid closer to the edge, threatening to pull the rescuers off the cliff as well. A full squad was now involved.

"Michael the archangel, please protect me," Corporal Carroll prayed as his legs dangled a thousand feet in the air.

He tried desperately to find traction on the cliffside, but his rotted boots slipped down the muddy wall. Skin on his hands was ripped off as the rifle he was grasping grinded against the rock cliff.

"Don't drop me! Please don't drop me!" he screamed.

"Michael, *my* archangel, protect me," he repeated as his comrades struggled to drag him back to safety. And suddenly, he was pulled back up on the trail.

In the chaos, Carroll lost two canteens, a gas mask and some extra ammo. And when he finally pulled himself together, he was confronted by his company commander, Captain Lucian Oates, a short, stocky Citadel graduate.

"What the fuck is going on up here?" shouted the captain, his face drenched in sweat. Addressing Carroll, he said, "Son, we got between six hundred and a thousand gooks up ahead of us. They walked up this *same* mountain trail a few hours ago wearing two-ply tires for shoes, and they made it *without* all this slippin' and slidin' and fuckin' around."

Turning his wrath on Sergeant Zoeller, a 24-year-old pipsqueak with a tiny head that seemed lost in his helmet, Captain Oates yelled, "Get this column moving! We need to make a click an hour (1,000 meters) until sundown."

The captain's PRC-25 field radio crackled: "Mike Six, this is Red Rock Six (Battalion Commander). State your position. Over."

Captain Oates whipped out his plastic laminated map:

VIETNAM 1:50,000, 6640.III, QUAN QUE SON/QUAN HEIP DUC. He began to feverishly assess his location. Around him, Marines were gabbing and the radio crackling with heavy static.

"Everyone, shut the hell up!" yelled the captain. He continued, "Radioman, can you get rid of the static on this thing?"

Captain Oates, along with a platoon commander and company gunny, studied the map. It was quiet along the column now. The three leaders went back and forth and hemmed and hawed about their position while the radio continued to crackle in the background. The radio operator tried his best to muffle the noise.

"I think we're here," said Gunny Martin, pointing to a spot on the map.

"No, no we're here," insisted Lieutenant Behring.

Captain Oates studied the map carefully and then said to Lt. Behring for all to hear: "Four years in college and you can't even read a combat map. You're a hundred meters off, Lieutenant. A hundred goddamn meters! You'd kill every one of us if you called in artillery."

Lt. Behring, a truly gentle and miscast man who began his career as an *artillery officer*, took the affront in stride and tried to put on his best face as the company commander continued to humiliate him in front of the enlisted troops. After a while, the lieutenant walked away from the map reading party, sat down on the trail's edge and drank water from his canteen.

Back on the radio, Captain Oates responded to the battalion commander.

"Red Rock Six, this is Mike Six. Over."

"Mike Six, go ahead."

"Our position is... uh, from Target Hopscotch, down three point six, right, one point five. Overall, we're about three clicks (3,000 meters) from End Zone."

"Three thousand meters!" the battalion commander shrieked. "Captain, move your company at once. You're falling behind the attack plans."

"Repeat. MOVE YOUR COMPANY AT ONCE!"

Captain Oates wiped his forehead, as his radio operator looked away. "This is November Six. Copy your last, Red Rock. Over."

Bypassing the lieutenant altogether and turning to the company gunny, the captain said, "You heard 'em, Gunny. Move this column out... and fast."

Gunny Martin turned to Sgt. Zoeller, "Donny boy, take the point. Put a corporal in charge of the squad. You're the only one who can get us there."

The Marines moved out and continued to climb the mountain trail. Carroll, now relieved from his point position, took a spot directly behind the M-60 machine gun team. He was given four boxes of machine gun ammo to hump.

After a while, Carroll took the 7.62 mm-belted ammo out of the pouches because the straps were cutting off circulation to his shoulders. He strung the ammo "poncho villa"-style across his chest. This usually pissed off the machine gunners who wanted clean ammo for their weapons. But Carroll didn't care. Carrying ammo "poncho villa" style could result in debris and dirt stuck in the belts, which could jam the weapon. But the gunners needed their ammo, and they'd take it any way it was carried.

"Just don't fall down on that shit," said machinegun team leader Corporal Larry "the retarded Polack" Pulaski. Carroll liked Pulaski and always humped his ammo when in the field.

The big machine gunner was the first to befriend Carroll when he arrived as the FNG (fuckin' new guy) in Vietnam and they played cards together whenever they could. At six-feet three inches, 220 pounds, Pulaski was the biggest man in November Company. Because of his size, he'd carry long-march dropouts on his big shoulders until they could pull themselves together, or be evacuated to the rear. From boot camp forward, everyone in the Marine Corps liked Pulaski. When he arrived at November Company on a rainy autumn morning, his life changed.

Pulaski, "the retarded Polack," got that name from Gunny Martin, who watched him almost shoot down a U.S. helicopter the first time he was in combat.

After the battle, the gunny had a heart-to-heart with Pulaski.

"What the fuck is wrong with you?" said the gunny.

"Nothing. I was just scared," Pulaski answered. It was then Gunny Martin made the discovery. Pulaski was cross-eyed.

Amazed, the gunny shrieked, "Look at you! Look at your eyes!

They're goin' all over the place. How in the fuck can you hit anything?"

Pulaski began to stutter. "They're… they're… they're not that way all the time. Only once in a while, when I'm… I'm under stress. My eyes 'wander' when I'm under severe stress." Gunny Martin buried his head in his hands.

Pulaski continued, "Navy doctors examined me and gave me a waiver on my eyesight," he said. "I'm fit for everything except… uh, nighttime flying."

"Oh. And why's that?" asked Gunny.

"Because," he hesitated, "I'm also color blind."

The gunny laughed his ass off.

He loved to tell that story to his drinking buddies back at their base camp hooch. In reality, Gunny Martin wasn't much older than the troops he commanded. Only twenty-nine years old, he had the look of an old man. Gunny's face, aged by premature wrinkles from a smoking habit that began in grade school, was the first thing Marines of November Company saw when they fucked up. No matter how hot the battle, if a Marine wasn't pulling his weight or somehow screwing up, Gunny Martin would come on the scene in full gallop (sometimes in full view of the enemy) his hands flailing about.

"Didn't they teach you anything in training?!" he'd yell, "Get your shit together, Marine!"

In due time, the retarded Polack became the surest machine gunner in November Company, maybe all of Vietnam. He was the Gunny's greatest success story.

"This is truly a miracle," the gunny would proclaim to anyone listening as Pulaski poured hundreds of rounds dead on target. His tracer rounds went straight up Charlie's ying-yang. At 450 yards, Pulaski didn't need to adjust fire. Everything was right on target from the first shot. He never wasted a single round.

Gunny Martin figured that Pulaski was able to hit his spot so accurately because rather than focus in on a specific target like most people with normal vision, Pulaski's eyes (looking as they did, all over the place) acted as a scanning radar which gave him range, movement, and size of mass. Gunny Martin was a smart man and tried to explain these facts to the surgeons at Medical Battalion, but they just blew him off.

Gunny also knew Pulaski was anything but retarded, and now was saddened he had given him that name in the first place because it stuck with the troops.

With the "Retarded Polack" hauling his M-60 in front, Gunny Martin to his rear and Sgt. Zoeller leading the Company up the mountain, Corporal Jackie Carroll relaxed as best he could after his near-death fall. He carefully put one foot in front of the other, moving with his comrades to their rendezvous.

On this day, the heat and high humidity were stifling. No air, not a breeze of any type could penetrate the dense overhead canopy. Around him, the Vietnamese jungle was suffocating. Looking to the side, Carroll spotted unexploded mortar rounds wedged tightly in the jungle canopy. Their ominous presence frightened him.

"Saint Michael the archangel, please protect me," he whispered to himself.

There were lizards, snakes, giant spiders and a monkey or two jumping around in the trees as well as noises he had never heard before.

Though others in the column were tiring from the steep climb and cursing life as they moved along, Carroll handled the forced march well. He was down to only one canteen after losing the others in his near-death fall, but he didn't drink that much water anyway. It was probably because of his cross-country training, he thought.

The entire mountain climb reminded him, on a good day, of running through Blue Mountain State Park back in Peekskill. His coach had a sign posted in the locker room: *"You ought to have to pay to run on a day like today."*

Coach was right.

Especially in the fall, when trees began to turn bright hues of orange and red, and leaves dusted the winding trails. Trees of all types: maple, oak, spruce and white birch, in addition to evergreen trees that grew out of cliffs and cracks in the rocks.

It was so enjoyable to run in the mornings, brisk as it was, because there were animals on the park trails – deer, foxes, raccoons, and once, a big bear. Later in the day, with Indian summer bringing the temperature to the mid-70s, Carroll would marvel at all the birds. Big red robins, bluebirds, cardinals, and woodpeckers. Lots of woodpeckers.

And on long runs along the banks of the Hudson River, a stiff breeze would hit his face as he turned north and sprinted as hard as he could for as long as he could.

It's right here, he fantasized, right in the middle of this war zone. He could feel it as he humped the heavy machine gun ammo. The beautiful cross-country trails, the rabbits and foxes, the sweet-sounding songbirds of upstate New York.

Two clicks (2,000 meters) up the trail, the North Vietnamese Army feverishly dug their fighting trenches to make a perfect "L" shaped ambush. Five hundred enemy soldiers would line the high slope only forty yards above the main trail and run it for a quarter mile. Directly in front of the ambush site, three hundred and fifty heavily camouflaged soldiers would stop the Marines from getting through at all costs. The NVA had fifteen light machine guns with their troops.

The NVA commander knew the Marines couldn't use flank security because the narrow trail was the only passable way up the mountain, and judging by their cadence, knew the Marines were in a hurry. NVA 82mm and 60mm mortar crews set up their aiming stakes to cover the trail with deadly projectiles. And the NVA commander kept one company as his reserve force to be used in a rear flanking movement to close off any escape routes by the Americans.

About a dozen North Vietnamese company commanders met for one last time with their division commander. He issued his orders: "The Marines will be here by four o'clock. At three o'clock, cease all digging and movement of any type. All forces must be in position at that time. Absolutely no more movement.

"Do not smoke or open any canned fish as the wind is blowing in a favorable direction for the Americans. The leading elements on the trail will open fire first. As the battle progresses, move in as close to the enemy as possible as their bombers will soon arrive.

"Kill all the wounded Americans, as we can handle no prisoners. A green flare will signal the end of the fight. At that time, all remaining Peoples' Forces will move 1,000 meters down the trail and wait for the American relief forces.

"To our great leader, Ho Chi Minh, and please have everyone write a letter to their uncle."

Softball
Tryouts

All around Peekskill and Cortlandt, softball players were getting ready for final tryouts. In the Peekskill area, firehouses with names like Continental, Hook and Ladder #1 and Main Street Fire were teaming up with bars like Johnny P's, Sally & Dino's and Richie's for All-Star preparations.

Sal Fraggo was at the tryouts and assured his goombahs the majority of players facing the King and His Court would come from the Italian parts of town. After all, blood was thicker than water, and many of the players and players' relatives were members of his union. So this was an obligation – and Fraggo took his obligations seriously.

At St. Peter's School on ball fields high above the Beach Shopping Center, the majority of RIPs (Rotten Irish Pricks), the Harps, Micks and a lot of transplanted Bronx troublemakers held their tryouts. They, too, had affiliated wateringholes: Duchy's, The Grasshopper, and Carney & Phil's. It was decided that twenty-seven players would make up the overall roster, along with six coaches and two managers.

West Point's Colonel Parrish would visit each practice site watching the players hit, field, run and slide. He directed that each player stay in the position he was trying out for during a series of practice games. Then, after seeing everyone perform, he would pick the team.

Those trying for coaches would get their shot along the base paths at first and third where the colonel encouraged them to give clear, concise instructions to base runners.

On the Peekskill softball diamonds, players fielded hundreds of ground balls, pop-ups, fly balls and foul pops. Out-of-town pitchers who could throw heat were brought in to help prepare hitters for Eddie Feigner. During one practice, Steve Cirillo rigged up a crude batting machine with two spinning truck tires powered by a giant electric motor he got off the GM assembly floor in Tarrytown to fire balls from the pitcher's mound.

Because the tires were not exactly synchronized, the balls boomeranged to the batters box at ninety miles per hour, hitting players in the head, feet and nuts. Just the act of standing up at the plate and waiting for a pitch from this lethal contraption should have been enough to get one selected to the team.

"Balls!" yelled Fraggo from bleachers. "You got to have balls to play this game!" But after three days of nearly crippling everyone that mattered, the batting machine was taken down.

"We ain't playing against no machine anyway," said one disgruntled player.

"Oh yes you are," yelled Fraggo. "When you see that big flat-topped bastard throwing from the pitcher's mound, you're going to see the biggest machine ever."

Practice wasn't all work. Wives and girlfriends showed up with protruding bellies and holding onto little kids in order to cheer their men from the sidelines. The daytime heat had given way to cooler evening breezes.

The gals brought food and drinks, though players were careful not to get drunk during tryouts. For a while, it was like being back in high school when all things seemed possible before shingling a roof or humping a heating oil hose became the reality of day-to-day life.

Preparing for the King and His Court softball team during that summer in Peekskill was a highlight of many people's lives, though they didn't realize it at the time.

"I was there. I was at the tryouts. The ball from the tire machine hits me right in the mouth, right here, chips a tooth," said an old timer some years later as he pointed to a broken tooth and balanced himself on his stool in Chuck's Bar. "My wife, when she gets the cancer and she's delirious, all she talks about is that ball hitting me in the head and saying 'who's going to pay the bills?' I'm trying to tell her not to leave me, that I love her."

While up at the St. Peter's field with the RIPs, Colonel Parrish couldn't help but do a little coaching. Looking smart in his West Point practice uniform — blouse, pants, leggings and spikes — Parrish went to the shortstop position and demonstrated proper fielding techniques. Down in a squat, glove on the deck (it's easier to bring the glove up then bring it down), body square to the playing field. In the outfield, the West Point coach showed how to angle one's body to the left or right depending on batter's stance. And again, to keep the glove down near the deck to keep the ball from going through on a hard hit shot.

He had a few tricks for the catcher too, like setting up inside then moving outside when the batter faces the pitcher. In fast pitch softball, there isn't a lot of time to adjust, he noted.

"One has to be in position," the coach said. "From that point on, good things will happen."

Sal Fraggo's $150,000 labor union donation to the baseball program arrived at the West Point Athletic Department on a Friday afternoon. It came in regular postal mail and was almost thrown away by an athletic department temp because it did not have a proper return address.

The envelope looked like it was typed on an old Royal manual typewriter with very uneven font. It contained the wrong zip code:

West Point Baseball Program

West Point,

New York 10566

10566 is the Peekskill zip code, not West Point.

It was summertime and many department staffers and officers were on leave. Only incoming plebes were around, and they were getting screamed at by a cadre of upperclassmen. Most of the Corps of Cadets were on summer maneuvers away from post. The temp worker opened the envelope and saw a check made out to Colonel Miles Parrish for the amount of $150,000 from Union Local No. 1224, signed by Salvatore Fraggo, President. There was no note of any kind with the check.

As there was no one of authority around at the time, the temp worker put the check in the baseball team's inbox where it sat along with unanswered phone messages as well as advertisements for non-slide pitching rubbers, Rawlings gloves, and deep penetrating salve called "Atomic Balm" for sore and aching pitching arms.

The temp locked the office for the weekend and drove to a bar in Highland Falls where she met her enlisted boyfriend for happy hour drinks.

Shots and
Beers

The late Friday night show was over, and after locking down the movie theater, the Galer brothers moved to Mary's Grill where they swilled Pabst Blue Ribbon beer and drank shots of rye whiskey.

The Galers always had money, most of it stolen from the snack bar at the theater. They had crumpled dollar bills and sometimes even a five spot. But it was mostly change that weighted down their pockets, and tonight they had as much swag as ever as they bellied up to the bar.

Mary's Grill was a shot and beer joint located not too far from the Peekskill Cemetery. It was near the center of town and catered mostly to old pensioners, a lot of whom were down-and-out rummies.

Mary's had dark, knotty pine walls, a large mirror behind the bar and the usual array of beer signs: Miller High Life, Pabst Blue Ribbon, Piels, and Rhinegold Beers. There were jars of pigs' feet, boiled eggs and racks of Slim Jims. And seemingly everyone smoked two cigarettes at a time.

A half-dozen tables with stained red-and-white-checkered tablecloths were scattered around a warped dance floor, but no one could recall having dances there. There was a Nickelodeon in the corner, and one of the drunks always played, "Auld Lang Syne."

Robert and Richard Galer took prime seats along the center portion of the bar where they often got loud and drunk and sometimes beat up old men who bumped or somehow annoyed them.

They were "big men" in Mary's Grill, that's for sure. On this night, they laughed about some kids they beat up who snuck through the back doors of the theater.

"They won't do that again," said pock-faced Richard who showed off his skin-scrapped knuckles. "I might have broken the kid's arm tonight," he boasted.

"And his scared buddy tried to run, but I caught him," said brother Robert, who added, "I kicked his little balls right up through his throat." Robert then held up three one-dollar bills. "And those kids had money on them. Can you believe this shit?"

A few of the old-timers at the bar gave the Galers some atta-boys and thumbs up but most just listened to scratched records playing on the juke box.

Around midnight, a stranger entered the bar and went directly to the men's room. No one noticed except for the Galers, who followed his movements very closely.

They were pretty drunk but sobered up immediately at signs of trouble, and unknown persons entering their bar at this late hour had to be trouble.

A few moments later, a pizza delivery kid from Sorentino's Italian restaurant busted through the door making lots of noise and wanting to know who ordered the "large pepperoni pie and calzone."

No one owned up to ordering it.

"Come on," chatted the pizza guy. "I wanna go home."

The Galers gave the pizza guy a look, but then stared back at the men's room door, which was on their left.

Very calmly, the pizza guy took out a cigarette and put the food down on the bar. "Well then, all the food's free! I'm not going back to the restaurant tonight," he said, leaning across the bar.

"Bartender, you got a match?"

As everyone went for the free grub, no one saw the pizza guy light a big red cherry bomb and drop it into a pitcher of Pabst Blue Ribbon beer in front of the Galers. Out of the corner of his eye, Robert Galer saw the beer begin to fizzle, but it was too late.

The explosion was deafening in the small gin mill. Robert and Richard fell to the floor, their faces covered with imbedded glass. Blood and beer oozed from the cuts on their faces. Some of the old timers got a beer shampoo. Smoke filled the room. Everyone was holding their ears.

"What happened?" said one of the rummies.

"Dunno," said another. "I think the calzone blew up."

Mike Carroll ran out the door, scooting down the street running a four-minute mile pace, his delivery cap and thick glasses flying onto the sidewalk behind him. He waved to Eddie Redlight on the corner of South and Division Streets. He had done it again. And he would continue. He felt very close to his brother Jackie at this time, and it was a good feeling.

"Where's Mom?"

Asked one of the Carroll kids as she came home from summer camp to an unusually quiet and empty house.

"Don't know. Maybe she's up in Jackie's room," said another. The kids moved swiftly up the stairs sensing trouble but finding none. She was not anywhere upstairs. Jackie's room had become a shrine since his death. His letterman's jacket hung on his bedpost, where he had left it the day he traveled to boot camp at Parris Island. The bed was made and a few schoolbooks were piled at the foot as if someone was going to read them soon.

There were trophies, medals and running photos all around the room, along with some old Wild West cowboy pictures on the walls. In one corner, there was a team photo of the 1961 New York Giants football team, as well as individual photos of Charlie Connerly, Frank Gifford and Roosevelt Brown.

Then there was the Yankee wall. Team photos of the Bronx bombers and individual shots of Mickey Mantle and Roger Maris, the M&M boys. Stubs to Yankees versus Cleveland, Detroit and Baltimore were scattered about, along with official programs advising fans to meet at the Yankee "Stadium Club," where "the most important New Yorkers can be found."

Suspended from the ceiling were plastic Revell model airplanes: B-24 Liberators, B-17 Flying Fortresses, and (leading the pack) P-51 Mustangs with their lethal .50 caliber machine guns glistening from silver paint.

It's apparent the planes were on a mission. Deep into Germany, maybe even Berlin. Stacked neatly on a desk were a dozen or so envelopes from university athletic departments, NYU, Fordham, Penn State and Ohio University.

"Mom! Mom!" the kids shouted as they searched the house. But Marie was not answering. She was nowhere to be found. The second car was still in the garage. This was not unusual as her nerves were so bad she couldn't drive.

The kids looked in the basement where piles of dirty laundry sat near the washing machine. A bad sign. It wasn't like their mother to leave dirty laundry around. She always did the wash, even when she was "sick with the blues." The kids looked in the closets, outdoor tool shed and one of them even peeked in the above-ground doughboy pool (the biggest in the neighborhood), but she was nowhere to be found.

"Maybe she went for a walk," said one of the little ones. After an hour or so, the kids were panicky, and when they were unable to reach older brother Mike, they decided to call their father, who worked at the telephone company.

"Accounting. Carroll here," said the voice on the other end of the phone.

"Dad, it's Megan. Mom's gone," said the ten-year-old.

"What do you mean, she's gone?" said Mickey. "Mom's got to be around the house somewhere!"

"We've been home two hours and looked everywhere," said Megan. "We also checked with the neighbors, thinking she might be in someone's house, and no one's seen her."

"How about the car?" asked Mickey.

"We checked it," said his daughter, who started to panic. "It's still in the garage and Mom's not around, Daddy. We've looked everywhere."

Getting agitated, Mickey asked, "Have you talked with your brother Mike? Is your brother around?"

"No, Dad. We don't know where Mike is," said the girl as she began to cry.

"Now, don't cry, Megan. Please don't cry. I want you to do me a big favor and don't tell the other kids. Go into the cabinet near the stove where the liquor is and the bottle that says vodka, spelled V-O-D-K-A, tell me how much is left."

"What do you mean, Daddy? What does that have to do with Mom being gone?"

"Just do it, Megan. Do it for me and don't tell the others. I'll hold on. I love you, Honey."

The little girl put down the phone and Mickey could hear background noise of chairs being moved, cabinets banging and bottles clanking.

"There's none left, Dad. The vodka bottle is empty."

"What do you mean, empty?" yelled Mickey, "There's got to be something in it? It can't all be gone, young lady."

"Don't get mad, Daddy. The bottle's empty. The bottle that says V-O-D-K-A is empty."

Mickey's voice was quaking now. "Daddy's not mad, Honey. Daddy loves you. He loves all of you, and I'm coming home now. I didn't mean to yell at you, Darling. Daddy's worried like you are, but things will be OK. I'm coming home right now and we'll find Mom.

"Now, call some of Mike's friends and see if you can track him down. The phone numbers are in the address book by the lamp. You're such a big girl, always helping Daddy. Helping everyone. I'd never yell at you Honey," said Mickey as he closed his eyes and pushed away the monthly billing statement of the Peekskill Stove and Foundry Works.

Blueberries

Soon after Mickey got home, Mike and his friends showed up and, together with some neighbors, fanned out in the woods with everyone moving into a different search quadrant. Clouds had gathered late in the day. The dark ones moved in across Blue Mountain, the highest point in the state park. There were only a couple of hours of daylight remaining.

Mickey confided in Mike before he headed out. "The vodka's gone. She drank at least half a bottle by two p.m., probably more. Anything's possible, Son. Do your best."

Overhead, skies continued to darken. Thunder cracked in the distance, and Mike's younger brothers and sisters began to cry.

"It'll be alright," he said to them. "We're going to find Mom."

After giving directions to his friends, Mike took off running faster than any race he ever ran. Marie had talked recently about the fishing hole where Jackie caught the 10-pound bass a few years back. She also talked about the time they picked blueberries in fields behind the mountain. She knew where both places were but hadn't been there in years and could have lost her way. He'd head to the fishing hole first. It was two miles away along the main path in Blue Mountain State Park. If she wasn't there, he'd head up and over the mountain to the blueberry fields on the other side. That was all he could think to do.

Drops of rain began to fall as Mike Carroll bolted through the fields, over old stone walls built in the mid-1800s and down the forest road to the state park.

Carroll knew the area well. He and his brother and fellow teammates ran along these same paths in training runs. But this was no training run. It wasn't even close. His feet barely touched the ground as he plowed along. There were no problems with his breathing or arm swing or anything else. Only movement and motion.

He was trying to save his mother, but from what he couldn't possibly know. Why had this happened to the family? What had they done to have a son and brother come home from Vietnam in a casket?

Hear me Lord,
For I am weak, and I am humble.
And I want my brother back.
Please Lord, bless our mother,
Don't take her from us.

Mike Carroll arrived at the fishing spot, only to find it deserted. It was two miles from his house, and he had covered the distance in exactly nine minutes, which would have been a state high school record in the two-mile run. Rain was coming down very hard now and thunder shook the heavens. It began to darken so that he could barely see across the small pond.

"Mom! Mom, if you're here, answer me!" Mike screamed, trying to compete with the thunder.

"Marie Carroll! Marie Carroll, come home!" he screamed again and again.

"For Christ's sake, answer me." But there was no answer, only the continued torrent of rain.

It was no use. She wasn't there.

After getting his bearings, Carroll bolted from the pond to the path that would take him over the top of Blue Mountain. But this was dangerous, and he knew it.

Whenever storms came in, he would watch lightening hit the peaks of the mountain from his upstairs window at home. And there was no bigger summer storm than the one he was running through now. He charged along the path to the top of the mountain, grinding it out the way he did in races. He stopped to duck his head into an old, abandoned stone cabin.

"Mom, Mom are you here?" he shouted.

Empty.

Hitting the trail again, he raced past a rock outcrop that

overlooked the valley, and then past a sign that said: "No Horseback Riders."

Crash! A lightening bolt hit three hundred meters ahead. It was an explosion – a giant flash of light with a green, purple and blue core. And it was superheated. He could feel the rush of hot air. He smelled the smoke from the lightening and it reminded him of the puffs of smoke from his brother's Lionel train set during Christmastime. "Surely lightening wouldn't hit in the same spot twice," he thought as he plowed through the burned area.

His brother Jackie would have continued to charge forward, he thought. Nothing ever stopped him. Not in a race and not in Vietnam. They had to kill him to stop him. THEY HAD TO KILL MY BROTHER!

Less than a half-mile to the blueberry fields, all downhill now. He ran faster than a sprinter in a short dash.

Suddenly, as he turned the corner he could see someone up ahead through the heavy rain, trudging along the trail and hauling something. There she was!

"Mom! Oh, Mom! Where have you been?" he asked, as he hugged and kissed her wet face. Her light dress was soaked through, and she was missing a shoe. Her mascara was running down the sides of her face.

"Mother, you're very sick, and need help, and we're going to help you."

"No Jackie, I'm going to help you. Look at all the blueberries I picked," she said as she held out the half-loaded bushel.

"I'm Mike. Jackie's not with us anymore," he cried.

"But I picked them as a surprise for you. I know how much you love blueberry pie, and it's for your birthday, too," she said.

"Mother, you're not alone, I miss Jackie too. Remember when we ran at the state meet? You were right there at the finish line. Jackie said we couldn't have done it without you. You should have gotten the awards, not us. All we did was run around a circle… We love you, Mom. Jackie's in heaven now and he loves you too. The little ones love and need you."

"No, no!" Marie shrieked as she smacked her son across the face. "Jackie's not in heaven. He's home, and I'm bringing these blueberries for him."

"Jackie's not here anymore! He's gone!" her son screamed. And then more softly, "We're going to help you, Mom. I promise to help you."

He began to cry as the rain pelted both their faces, while thunder and lightening continued to savage the skies.

"Don't ever leave us again," he sobbed. "The family can't take anymore."

Marie put her blueberries down and wiped the rain from her face. Looking directly at her son Mike, with eyes as bright as the berries she picked, she asked, "OK, then, from now on, will someone help me with the laundry?"

"You bet, Mom," said Mike Carroll, as he hugged his mother and carried her blueberries along the trail back home. "We'll do all the wash from now on."

The Good Nuns of
Saint Joseph

Sister Claire Marie was the first one to spot Eddie Redlight hit the ground. As a half-dozen or so nuns were exiting JC Penney's department store on Division Street, they saw an object fly from the window of a beat-up Ford Galaxy and hit Eddie Redlight squarely on the noggin. Eddie went down in a heap.

Thursday evening was shopping night for the nuns, who looked forward to this simple pleasure all week long. On this night, they carried with them a few bags containing the simple, life-sustaining things they needed: soaps and shampoos, toothpaste, a hairbrush or two and some pajamas for the drafty convent that sat beside the Hudson River.

They rushed across the street and cradled Redlight's head in their laps, trying to stop the bleeding with their black cotton habits. Near where he had fallen, they found the remains of a large melon. Pits and slimy vegetable matter covered Eddie's face.

Eddie had cracked open his skull when he hit the sidewalk. His eyes rolled around in their sockets like they were disconnected and the cigarette he was smoking had fallen into his jacket, starting his shirt on fire.

"His clothes are smoking!" yelled one of the nuns, who reached into Eddie's jacket and pulled out the burning butt. Then they patted his chest to make sure the fire was out. Eddie wasn't saying anything. He was just moaning and groaning. The nuns noticed large scarring burnmarks on Eddie's neck and the backs of his hands.

Like everyone else in town, they didn't know his real name, and called him "Redlight." They, too, had seen him over the years, often waving to this small man as they passed him by. He, too, was a child of God.

"Mr. Redlight, are you OK?" they asked.

"Mr. Redlight, we're going to help you," one of the nuns said, as she rubbed his face, neck and hands.

A few locals happened on the scene, and one of them provided information on Eddie's attackers.

"I saw Robert Galer throw something out the car window," said a man in his mid-30s who happened to witness the attack from across the street near Weeks' Jewelers.

"Richard was driving. I know the car real well," he said. "It's got the fox tail on the antenna and mud flaps on the wheels. Those two have been picking on Eddie for years."

The nuns waved down Cabbie Sereno, who happened to be driving by, and loaded Eddie Redlight in the back seat of his beat-up station wagon. They took him to the hospital off of Bay Street. Sister Claire Marie and Sister Imelda ministered to Eddie while the cabbie did his best to run lights and avoid drunks who were leaving bars after the end of the Yankee game.

Sereno tried to speak to his delirious friend. "Well Eddie, they finally got you," said the hard-driving cab driver with the pork pie hat. "What did they hit him with?" the cabbie asked the nuns.

"A pumpkin," answered one of the Sisters.

The cab driver explained that over the years the Galers, along with local kids, had pelted him with "eggs, rocks, firecrackers, baseballs, beer bottles and, one time, even a toilet seat."

"Eddie's gotten real good at ducking," said Sereno. "He told me once that he looks at the kids' hands as they drive by. If he can't see both of them, it puts him on alert."

"Why does he take this abuse?" asked one of the Sisters.

"Dunno," said the cabbie. "He's been standing on that street corner for a dozen years. It's all he knows anymore."

"Where does he live?" she asked.

"Wherever he can," said the cabbie. "Over the years, he's lived in the Union Hotel, the train station storage shed, abandoned signal shacks, and even in Sorentino's Restaurant. He'd clean some pots and pans and Vince would put him up for a while in an empty room upstairs. Mostly in the winter. In the summer, as far as I know, he sleeps outside."

Arriving at the hospital, Sister Imelda ran in the front door to summon help, and after a few moments, two orderlies arrived with a gurney. One of the orderlies, a black kid about nineteen or twenty years old, recognized Eddie.

"That's the cat that stands up on the street corner," he said. Turning to Sister Imelda, he asked, "What happened to him?"

"Someone hit him and hurt him very badly."

Eddie received twenty-five stitches, two pints of blood and was hospitalized for three days. Doctors cautioned that Eddie be closely watched over the next week as he had suffered a concussion.

In the morning, the nuns brought him clean clothes and some brand new Joe Lapchick sneakers because his old clothes were covered with blood.

Upon exiting the hospital, an administrative type presented Sister Imelda with a bill for $260.00. The sister took the bill and said it would be paid within thirty days.

What were they to do with Eddie?

"Just drop me off by the Peekskill train station," Redlight said to the nuns.

"Nonsense," said Sister Imelda. "You're coming back to St. Joseph's Home with us for a few days of observation. The doctors said you have to be watched and we'll put you up in the dormitory. It's empty nowadays. Nothing fancy, but the food's good and the place is clean."

Still in a daze, Eddie didn't much argue.

St. Joseph's Home began taking in orphans sometime after the American Civil War. In 1875, the Home reached its high water mark as old photographs revealed a giant fortress-like brick structure, complete with towering spires surrounded by high walls. St. Joseph's was built on a hill above the Hudson River at Peekskill about thirty-five miles north of New York City. Some said it reminded them of a prison.

Rumor had it that St. Joseph's also served as a Catholic insane asylum and a home for unwed mothers, but this information could never be confirmed, as the high walls prevented interlopers and the nuns seldom spoke.

St. Joseph's was also a convent that housed the good Sisters of the Franciscan order. The Sisters taught academic subjects and maintained discipline at the Home, which at one time housed as many as five to seven hundred orphans from pre-school through high school age.

The nuns also provided classroom instruction at area Catholic schools and worked free of charge at the Peekskill Hospital, serving as nurses, aides and orderlies.

During the great influenza epidemic, which lasted from 1914 to 1920, it became the final stop for children from New York City who had lost both parents to the Spanish flu. During that period, relatives took in some children, but the homeless and abandoned were just as likely to be shipped off to an institution. Many children were simply left on church steps with peanut butter sandwiches and a note asking the church to take care of them: "And may God forgive me for what I've done."

St. Joseph's Home was supported by funding from Catholic Charities, New York City Department for Orphaned and Homeless Children and the Society of Prevention of Cruelty to Children. And anyone else who could spare a buck.

The holy Sisters invited Eddie Redlight to eat dinner with them and that commenced exactly at 6 p.m., after evening prayers, of course.

Eddie was asked to pray with the nuns at evening chapel. Father Damon Meade presided over mass and gave communion to the holy Sisters. There must have been seventy-five or so in attendance at evening prayers. A packed house, Eddie thought. With incense wafting through the air, an organist played beautiful music and some of the nuns sang along.

Kneeling at his wooden pew, Eddie tried his best to blend in. He studied the holy chapel. First, he saw the Stations of the Cross and tried to imagine hundreds of jumpy little kids praying in stone silence before these tortured paintings. Next, he noticed the unusually large statue of St. Joseph, baby Jesus's earthly father.

This seemed appropriate because this was, after all, St. Joseph's Home.

Dear St, Joseph, Please grant me one wish. Let me see my father and sister again. I know Momma is in heaven, but Pop said he would get me before too long. I continue to wait, and in your

*good graces, I hope to stay. I pray to you St. Joseph that I've been
a good boy, and not taken your Heavenly son's name in vain nor
have I stolen from others, or lied in any way to the Sisters.*

Eddie looked at the painted-over carvings etched in back of
the wooden pews. Some gave initials and dates but little else.

"EC – NY
—1915"

"TP and MJ
—Yonk. 1921"

"Richie/Brooklyn/1919"

Surely those who had defaced this sacred chapel never had
wishes granted, he thought.

Eddie didn't receive communion but lip-synched many of the
prayers. He also followed along in Latin, lip-synching the
appropriate responses. This was not lost on the good nuns of St.
Joseph.

Eddie thought he must be a sight to look at – a 55-year-old
man, head swathed in bandages, wearing kids' sneakers and his
hands pointing straight to the heavens.

And the whole time, all he really wanted was a smoke.

Sister Imelda had thought of everything. After observing
Eddie's nicotine stained fingers, she thought he'd go sideways at
the Home without his cigarettes, so she had stopped at the grocery
store and offered to pick up (not purchase) a couple cartons of
cigarettes.

"Thank you, Sister. Thank you," said Eddie as he handed her
a five-dollar bill. "With the change, please buy yourself something."

"No need of that," replied the Sister.

Dinner was simple. The nuns first assembled in a waiting area,
then walked in silence to a large cafeteria with three long, linen-
covered tables. The walls were painted white and a huge crucifix
hung in the center. After the Sisters were seated, prayers of thanks
were said. Then, older nuns, along with a few novices, began serving
the food. The mood changed from somber to joyful and the Sisters

chatted among themselves, enormously at ease.

Pieces of meat, cut potatoes, green beans and baskets of bread were the fare for the evening. Iced tea was plentiful and it appeared that Sister Agnes, the head nun, was drinking a glass of wine (though Eddie couldn't be sure).

Eddie Redlight sat between Sister Claire Marie and Sister Imelda in the center of table number three. They were proud and happy that they had done a good thing for this man and were sure that acts like these would not go unnoticed by the Almighty.

Redlight was feeling pretty swell himself. His appetite had returned after being force-fed macaroni and cheese in the hospital, and he helped himself to generous portions of the Sisters' food.

As Eddie reached for the food, one of the nuns noticed the terrible burns on the back of his hands.

"What happened to your hands?" one of the Sisters asked, before being shushed by the others.

"That's okay Sister," said Redlight. "I burned my hands in a railroad accident about fifteen years ago. I thought they would have healed by now, but never have."

The Sister who asked the question said that before he left the Home she would provide him with their special holy water to bathe his hands, and that would surely do the trick.

Eddie thought how kind the nuns were.

And when Eddie Redlight was tucked in for the night – the only occupant in a giant dormitory that had once housed two hundred and fifty orphaned and unwanted children – he fell immediately to sleep.

At about two in the morning, Eddie woke up with a terrific headache – residual effects of his concussion. He got out of bed, put on his pants and new Joe Lapchick's and walked out to an empty ball field where he lit up a cigarette and breathed in the night air. The moon was high in the heavens, and the stars shone brightly.

He felt a little better already. He walked directly to a spot in far center field where he could see out over the wall and looked down on the Hudson River. In the distance, he heard a train whistle before spotting the oncoming light of a big locomotive. He felt a thrill all over. Nothing had changed.

Racing in Yonkers

"In lane five, representing the Peekskill Striders, Mike Carroll," said the announcer as he rolled through the list of entries in this annual summer track meet held in Yonkers, New York.

Tonight's 880-yard run was the top event that brought together collegians, club members and even an Olympian from Canada, William McKenzie.

McKenzie was, by far, the class of the field. A member of the 1960 Canadian Olympic team who finished ninth in the Games, he had the second fastest 800-meter time in the world this year. Actually, he was only participating in this race in hopes of doing a little speed work prior to his upcoming attempt at the 1000-meter world record.

Last year, he had missed that middle distance record by only four tenths of a second. Newspaper reporters showed up at the Yonkers meet seeking interviews with McKenzie. Most couldn't understand why a runner of his stature would show up at a bush meet like this.

"Actually, my wife's relatives live here in New York City. So I thought I'd drive up for the race," he offered.

The New York Times, The Herald Tribune, The Daily News and *New York's Irish Press* all sent reporters.

"What happens if you get beat?" asked one of the reporters.

McKenzie smiled. "I don't think that's going to happen," said the Olympic finalist.

McKenzie would be in lane one, wearing, of course, number one on his racing singlet.

In lane two, Willie Goins, IC4A champion from Penn. He was a local favorite, having attended nearby New Rochelle High School.

In lane three, from St. John's University, Pete Passi, sixth place finisher in the NCAA Division I finals. Passi was also the IC4A champion in the indoor 1000-meter race.

Lane four was Jimmy Wagner, the former New York state high school 880 and mile champion, now a sophomore at West Point. Wagner had set most of the Blue Mountain cross country records until both Jackie and Mike Carroll broke them. He was also an IC4A champion.

Ron Dearborn from Manhattan College and three local high school standouts, including Mike Carroll, rounded out the field.

One of the high school kids had dual citizenship with the country of Germany and was an absolute burner on the track. He was already positioning himself for a place on the next German Olympic team.

Up in the bleachers, Mickey, Marie and a few of the Carroll kids watched the meet. Marie was calm, sitting back in a rickety wooden seat like she was on tranquilizers, which she was.

Mickey was fidgeting. Always fidgeting at track meets. Full of self-doubt for himself and everyone around.

The beautiful Honey Sanders had talked her date into driving from Peekskill down to the Yonkers meet, where she took up position at the 220 mark on the backside of the track. Earlier in the day she had stopped by the Carroll house, making small talk with Marie and reading letters from son Jackie written while he was in Vietnam. Honey was drinking a soda and holding a stopwatch, her beautiful hair, like always, blowing in the evening breeze.

"You know, this is not a good event for Mike," said an exasperated Mickey. "His race is the mile and two-mile. I don't know why he wants to run this distance with all these college coaches around. He might run himself out of a scholarship offer."

Since Carroll had won the New York state high school meet in the mile, he'd had a steady stream of interest by higher education institutions for his running services. Monsignor Healy was always making cracks that should Mike decide against the great College of the Holy Cross, he might as well pack his bags and go directly to hell.

Carroll laughed off the monsignor's comments. He didn't care where he went to college, as long as he received a scholarship.

Cookie Reams drove down in his Buick 88 to watch the race – a race that he himself had won two years in a row.

But Cookie didn't run against this field, and he knew that "sparks be flying" or not, Carroll would have his hands full with this bunch.

Cookie walked over to where Carroll was warming up.

"I know you don't need any advice from this over-the-hill brother, but I'm giving it to you anyway. And listen up boy, because I won this race a few times myself. The 880 is the fastest track race not run in lanes. Race strategy counts most in a two lapper.

"Don't get boxed in on the last turn. These guys are tough and fight hard. They aren't the high school kids you're used to running against. Be in front or behind, but not in the middle of the pack. And that Olympian, he's a rocket at the end.

"I seen you run; you a fast motha. Blow by them with half a lap to go. Make them catch you," said Reams.

Cookie high-fived him and went to join a couple of his partners. Carroll walked to the starting line.

The official was an old timer from the Westchester Coaches and Officials Association. Carroll had seen him at other track meets and, for some reason, this made him feel more at ease.

"Runners, I'll give you two commands," said the official. "Set, and then the gun. Good luck."

With that, he held his arm up. The starter fired his pistol.

Pete Passi from St. John's bolted to the lead with Manhattan's Ron Dearborn and local favorite and IC4A champion Willie Goins following closely behind. Olympian William McKenzie was in the middle of the pack with West Point's Jimmy Wagner on his shoulder. Carroll trailed the pack slightly, with the two high school runners behind him.

"Get 'em, Willie!" shouted Goins's cheering section from the bleachers.

"Smoke 'em, Willie!"

There was a slight breeze on the track, and nighttime temperatures were in the mid-70s. Perfect weather for a race, Carroll thought as he ran.

But Carroll always felt tired in the 880, and tonight was no different.

It's why he never ran great times in the event. He thought of himself as a distance runner, although he was getting faster as his 220 and 440 practice times indicated. He knew he just had to relax at this fast pace and stay out of trouble. The pack passed the 220-yard mark in 27 seconds with the group still in roughly the same order: Passi, Dearborn, Goins and the rest. Carroll heard Honey Sanders yelling, "You're going to beat these guys! Relax!"

As the runners thundered into the straightaway before the viewing stands, Carroll heard his father yelling, "Don't get boxed in! Don't get boxed in!"

Wagner shot to the lead at the quarter mile mark, as McKenzie moved up on his shoulder. The high school kid from Germany bumped Carroll hard as he tried to pass him when the gun lap fired. It pissed Carroll off.

Carroll's time at the 440 mark: 54.0 seconds. The runners circled the third turn and Olympian McKenzie made a big move, lengthening his stride and moving into the lead ahead of Wagner. Carroll was in fourth place, the middle of the pack, with much bumping and pushing going on.

Carroll watched McKenzie stretch his lead, pulling away from the runners. He decided it was time to move out. He bolted out to lane three, bypassing the entire pack and moved squarely behind McKenzie, who was barreling along.

"Go motha-fucker! Go now!" shouted Reams at the 660 mark. Carroll could see Honey, but couldn't hear her. He missed his split time. Some of his senses were shutting down, as he knew most of the oxygen was going to his leg muscles.

McKenzie was ten yards ahead of Carroll, with 200 yards to go in the race. The college runners had moved up on Carroll's shoulder. It was time.

From up in the stands, Mickey was the first to see it: The sudden leg pumping and the slight tilt of his son's head in an inboard manner. Taking in the sight, Marie sat up in her seat.

In a split second, Mike Carroll closed the gap on the Olympian and was even with him as they rounded the final turn. McKenzie looked to his right to see the fresh faced teenager running stride for stride with him. He'd give this kid a lesson. The Olympian dropped a gear and began his final sprint to the finish line, a powerful sprint that would surely crush this high school kid.

Carroll stayed right with him stride for stride, knees and arms pumping, before pulling ahead.

He crossed the finish line with arms extended – something he seldom did.

And then it was over. The PA announcer:

"Winner of the 880-yard race, from Peekskill, New York, Mike Carroll, with a time of 1:46.1, one minute, forty-six point one seconds."

The PA announcer abruptly broke off. A moment later, he continued. "The time tonight in the 880 is the fastest time recorded in the United States this year. Although unofficial, it is a new Westchester County, State of New York and national high school record. It also betters the U.S. Olympic qualifying standard."

High up in the stands, Marie hugged Mickey for the longest time. The younger Carroll kids watched this unusual display of affection.

One of the little ones asked, "Mom, you're not going to pop Daddy in the nose, are you?"

"Money, Money Everywhere..."

On an overcast weekday morning, Mae Van Ardsdale Parrish, the great horse lady of the South, was opening up "guard mail," which had been delivered to her home on officers' row.

It was all the usual official stuff from the bureaucrats at West Point – fall class schedules, upcoming ceremonies, newly-remodeled officers' club hours, West Point Ladies' Club announcements and reminders to remove trash barrels from the street no more than six hours after pickup. Two violations would get the occupants a hearing before the provost, as "West Point is always on display as America's premier military academy."

At the bottom of the pile was Colonel Parrish's monthly paycheck for $806.00, which included a twelve-dollar raise, for which they were both thankful.

And another check made out to Colonel Parrish for a much larger sum, that of $150,000.00. It was signed by Salvatore Fraggo.

She held the check in her hand for a long time, trying to imagine what it would be like to have that much money in a bank account. She could buy a horse of her own – maybe two – and a trailer to pull them in. They could own a house in Virginia with a big porch and giant lawn, and it would be theirs to leave the garbage cans out in front if they wished.

The Parrishes could send some money to their children. One, stationed at Fort Bragg, could buy a house off base for his new young family and move out of the dilapidated junior officer housing that his mother and father once lived in.

Their daughter in college might have the funds necessary to join a sorority, a beautiful thing for a young girl, maybe pledge Tri-Delta. And a coming out and graduation party and a new car for everyone.

Mae Van Ardsdale Parrish had a wish list a mile long, but she also had her share of Virginia horse sense and knew that any check signed by Salvatore Fraggo was trouble for her husband.

She folded the check, put it in her pocket and began the long walk to West Point's baseball field, where her husband was overseeing the repair of the large screen backstop with the help of base engineering. He did everything at West Point, she thought to herself.

"Honey, honey, I need to speak to you," she said in her slow Southern drawl, as she approached him.

She was wearing black capri pants, a pink blouse and white chiffon scarf, and, at that moment, she reminded the colonel of movie actress Doris Day. He got a little aroused, and pulled her towards him.

"We can't do it right here, Honey. Then again, maybe we can," the colonel said, as a half-dozen maintenance workers looked on.

She pulled away, embarrassed. "I don't know what's become of you. You're beginning to talk like those second lieutenants on prom weekend."

"Remember our prom night?" he said.

"Right over there, remember?" he said, and pointed to nearby "Flirtation Walk" where the beautiful Mae Van Ardsdale had surrendered her virginity on senior weekend over two decades ago. And up against a tree no less.

"Ah remember," she said. "Never trust an upperclassman. But Honey, I'm not here to talk about your horny memories of yesterday." She handed him the check. "Here, this came in the mail today."

The colonel studied it carefully. "It's sure a lot of money."

"There's something about this Fraggo fellow I don't like. Why did he pick the baseball program for his donation? Everyone always gives money to football and basketball. All you've ever gotten are a few bats and balls from the Yankees." She paused. "And he's always looking around. Like someone's after him. Maybe some mob guys would like to rub him out."

"You've got a great imagination, young lady," said the colonel. "West Point is an open base. Anyone can come up here and walk around and do whatever they want. Nobody would pick this place to hide ..."

"What are you going to do?" Mae interrupted.

"First of all, I'm taking this check to the athletic department and giving it to the director. He can deposit it in the general account and parcel it out to the team, as needed. I don't want personal control of this money any longer than I have to. Next, the superintendent will write a thank you note on behalf of the sports department. And, your little buddy will probably get some free football tickets and be put on the VIP list."

"Oh, ma God," said Mae. "He'll be sitting right up there next to Jimmy Doolittle and Mr. Dulles."

Later in the day, Colonel Parrish went back to his office at the athletic department and presented the $150,000.00 check to his boss.

Whew! Safely out of my hands, he thought. Tomorrow, he'd be traveling down to Peekskill to observe more tryouts for the softball game.

Colonel Parrish was no one's fool and had determined early on that nothing is free in this world, including "free" donations.

He had only seen Fraggo once since their initial meeting and that was at the softball field in Peekskill where firemen were running, batting and throwing. Nothing unusual there, he had thought. Fraggo had been standing on the sidelines commiserating with players and wives. Everyone seemed to know him. He had seen Fraggo's big stretch limo parked on a side street with his driver polishing different spots on the hood. Again, nothing of concern.

What was it? he mused. What was it about this man that didn't square up?

There was a war on and being patriotic was normal, and that was a good thing, with hippies burning flags and shitting all over Uncle Sam. Patriotism was OK, he thought. Fraggo wanted something, that's for sure—but what?

The colonel knew all about subversion and trickery – it was part of his craft. He taught it at ranger school and lived it in the jungles of Laos and Cambodia where he worked with insurgent teams that mounted armed raids against the communist-controlled Ho Chi Minh trail.

Back in those days, he had paid tribal chiefs hard cash to recruit, train and deploy a small insurgent army to attack the North Vietnamese forces along the trail where they were most vulnerable. And everyone in the loop had their hands out, cheating and scamming him at every turn.

Irregular battalion commanders and Laotian tribal chiefs lived like kings in their villages, all courtesy of Uncle Sam. Chiefs were paid for numbers of recruits brought into the program. Maybe five thousand piasters per head. Once a month, the village chief would give the colonel a list of new recruits. If the number was a hundred, then the chief was given money to feed, clothe and train the men.

Colonel Parrish checked his forces on a regular basis, flying unannounced to distant outposts to see what was going on. Most of the outposts seemed almost deserted with only a few stragglers hanging around cleaning their M-2 carbines and chewing beetle nut.

"The troops are on combat patrol or out training," was the answer he usually got from his local commanders.

"I'm paying for seventy-five men on this base. Why do I only see twenty-five?" Colonel Parrish asked one day.

"Beaucoup VC! Beaucoup VC!" said an excited village chief, as he pointed to a series of distant mountain ridges. "VC number ten. VC number fuckin' ten," he continued, as the colonel prodded him for more information.

Parrish also noticed that when his irregular forces didn't want to answer questions, whatever grasp they had of the English language seemed to vanish.

Nobody at the base camp seemed to communicate when the scam was going strong. They just repeated something the Americans always like to hear: "Beaucoup VC! Beaucoup VC!"

Peekskill was a long way from Southeast Asia but in the back of his head Colonel Parrish kept hearing the same voices whenever he watched Sal Fraggo's softball practice.

"Beaucoup VC! Beaucoup VC!"

Just
Desserts

About the time the nuns of St. Joseph decided to file an official police report over the beaning of Eddie Redlight, a bad thing happened in town to a truly bad man.

Tony Galer had been caught at Drum Hill School, airing out his Anaconda while girls practiced volleyball on the outdoor courts. Only this time, someone with a badge was watching him. The incident is contained in an official police report:

At about 1000 hours, Peekskill Detective Danny Cantoro, Badge Number 18, observed a suspicious white male driving a late model green-colored Dodge Dart automobile back and forth in the parking lot of Drum Hill School, 616 Bennett St., Peekskill, NY. The school was empty for summer vacation, but a dozen or so teen-age girls were practicing volleyball on the Southwest outside courts. The vehicle appeared out of place, giving this officer PC (probable cause) to run the license plate.

According to New York State DMV records:

Registered Owner, R/O Anthony 'Tony' Galer
    Address: P.O. Box 1468
                Lake Mathews, NY

DOB:	9/9/17
HT:	6"1"
WT:	200
HAIR:	Black
EYES:	Brown
RESTRICTIONS:	None

The police report also stated:

At around 10:10 a.m., suspect vehicle stopped and a male wearing cowboy boots, blue jeans, black sweatshirt and otherwise described above exited the car. He walked over to a series of benches located immediately north of the court where he sat down and lit a cigarette. The Subject never appeared to take his eyes off of the girls playing volleyball.

After about 15 minutes, the Subject stood up and walked to the edge of the chain link fence. The Subject unzipped his front fly and pulled out what appeared to be a flashlight. I was facing the Subject about 75 yards away looking out of my unmarked police car using binoculars.

After a few moments I noticed that it was a male penis, hanging from the front of his pants. Not a flashlight. My error was that I had never worked a case like this, and also that the binoculars were old and somewhat cloudy. Almost immediately, the girls began to yell and scream and run off the playing court.

I immediately activated my siren and headed to the location. Upon hearing my siren, the Subject was startled and attempted to pull his now enlarged penis back through the opening in the chain link fence.

When I arrived at the scene, a few seconds later, the Subject appeared to be stuck and unable to free himself from the fence. He was somehow impaled on a sharp piece of metal.

Subject was cursing and screaming mostly at the girls, who by now had run to the other side of the courts. He kept repeating, 'Look what you did to me. Look what you did to me.'

I immediately called for police backup and an ambulance. Approximately four minutes later, K-9 Officer D. DeLuca, badge 26, arrived on scene with his working German Shepherd dog, 'Sweetie.'

Officer DeLuca found a loaded .45 caliber pistol on the front seat of Subject's vehicle. K-9 dog Sweetie then began to sniff Subject's feet and legs.

I'm going to kill this dog if it doesn't stop! Subject shouted. Subject then kicked Sweetie in the face and chest.

At this point, the Subject was told additional assault charges would be filed against him, to which he replied, 'Fuck You.'

At approximately 10:28 a.m., an ambulance siren could be heard in the distance. Officer DeLuca temporarily lost sight of his working dog. After a moment or two, we both observed Sweetie inside the chain link fence running toward the Subject at great speed.

An instant later with the ambulance pulling into the parking lot, Sweetie lunged at Subject's exposed penis, biting it completely off, and running with it back across the volleyball court, and into a wooded area.

Subject began hemorrhaging blood and passed out falling to the ground.

He was driven by ambulance to Peekskill Hospital where he was admitted to intensive care. Additional officers responded to the scene taking names and obtaining witness statements (which will serve as an attachment to this report). Additionally, officers spent numerous hours searching the area for Subject's appendage but nothing was found.

Working dog Sweetie was re-acquired at 11:15 a.m. by Peekskill Police. The dog was transported to an area veterinarian where it was given a series of shots and then placed on temporary leave.

Officer Dan C. Cantoro
Badge #18

Mort Pour La France

(Died for France)

"You've done it now," said the beautiful Honey Sanders, touching Mike Carroll's arm as he entered language lab to recite common French phrases ad infinitum.

Mademoiselle Plante spoke first to the class, not about which page to turn or phrase to repeat, but to congratulate Carroll on his great track and field achievement. She had brought with her the latest copy of the *The New York Times*, which was the only readable newspaper snooty teachers dared look at. And the mademoiselle was about the snootiest.

"Mr. Carroll," she said. "*The Times* said you beat an Olympic runner Wednesday night and that you are, at present, the fastest half-miler in the country. Is this so, monsieur?"

"Oui."

"You're certainly quite the French conversationalist," said the teacher. "Congratulations, and let's get your vocabulary ready so your can run track at a great university."

Carroll waited a moment, gathered his thoughts and responded. "Merci beaucoup, Mademoiselle Plante. Je suis très rapide." (I am very fast.)

"Oui," said the teacher.

"Mademoiselle Plante, you are quite the French conversationalist," said Carroll, as the class cracked up.

"Oh, you're such a kiss up," said Honey before she turned very quietly to him. "Like your basketball buddy from Peekskill says, 'you one fast motha-fucker.'"

Carroll responded, "My buddy from Peekskill said something else."

"What's that?"

"Stay away from that young pussy."

Honey cracked up and Mademoiselle Plante told her to quiet down so "the champ" could study his lessons without distractions. The Champ! How the tables have turned, she thought. One minute she was making out with Louie Mistro on the athletic bus coming back from Sleepy Hollow. Next, she's standing tall in front of the principal, accused of something she didn't do.

Then, she finds herself in class with one of the guys that caused her problems and who she vows to get even with. Watching him train for the track meet while "motha-fuckin' sparks be flying" and then watching him win, she comes to realize that she is somehow attracted to him. Drawn to him and his complicated and screwball life. And he doesn't even own a car.

Honey Sanders wasn't reciting "voulez-vous," or "je ne vais pas" on this day in class. She was well beyond that. She was thinking of a way to get classmate Mike Carroll and French world record holder Michel Jazy on the same track together in a mile race. And that was a *real* French project. Honey liked challenges, and she liked research. Only a year before, she had completed a French term paper on the fall of Dien Bien Phu, a horrific battle that was won by the communist Viet Minh and lead directly to the French exodus of Vietnam. Her paper was so good the university press of New York published it.

After French class, she went to the library to read up on runner Michel Jazy. She learned he was a great French athletic hero and had run in two Olympics.

He often trained barefoot and was a premier distance runner, meaning he could run any event from 800 to 10,000 meters. On a given day, he could both win and set a world record in an event, if the pace was fast enough.

Earlier in the year, Jazy had broken a world distance record and now stood atop the heap as the greatest runner in the world.

Honey began reading old copies of *Track and Field News*, which were stored in the library archives – a creepy place with no circulation that sweltered during the summer. She studied past running performances, who was winning distance races, and by how much.

She learned that most of the world's best distance runners were from "down under" – Australia and New Zealand—but that great runners were spread all over the globe. France, England, Tunisia, Kenya and America had its greatest stars.

The latest *Track and Field News* listed Michel Jazy's summer competition schedule and she found out that he would race in California in late August after his European circuit was over. Honey hit the books, studying up on French culture, war, diplomacy, sports and even the value of the French franc. She virtually memorized her term paper on French combat experience in Indochina.

Using her near-perfect French, Honey contacted the French consulate in New York City and set up an appointment to see the consular general. A week later, dressed to kill in a tight skirt and form-fitting sweater, the prettiest and smartest girl in Peekskill (3.9 gpa) waltzed into the French consulate on 5th Avenue and knocked their Parisian dicks stiff.

The Chargé d'Affaires, Monsieur Claude Lambeau, mistook Honey for a high school teacher and entertained her for lunch, which included some crèpes and the finest Chardonnay wine.

He gave her a tour of the facility, even the communications center where encrypted messages were sent back and forth to Paris. The consulate was a magnificent building with wood-paneled walls, deep luxurious carpets, Louis the XIV furniture, and magnificent chandeliers.

The exquisitely dressed senior diplomat who resembled actor David Niven explained the love-hate relationship between the French people and the Americans.

"You Americans are much more like the English, than the French. You are historically mostly Anglo and Saxons, while we are Celtic and Latin with Teutonic."

He pointed out that the French supported America in its Revolutionary War against the British, providing the colonies with men and material at great cost to the French government.

"The English never forgot," he noted. That Benjamin Franklin lived for a long period in Paris, as did John Adams, both getting support for their cause.

Monsieur Lambeau went on to say that the Americans paid back their debt to France in the First and Second World Wars.

He showed Honey paintings of U.S. Marines fighting the Germans at Belleau Wood and Chateau Thierry in France during the First World War, and the Marines being presented the croix de guerre by a grateful French government for the heroic battle. He talked about the D-day landings at Normandy and showed her a photo gallery of grateful French citizens liberated from the yoke of German occupation, kissing and hugging the Americans. Mr. Lambeau was clearly more at ease talking about military matters than waltzing the likes of Coco Chanel up and down 5th Avenue in staged photo ops.

"My job is one of liaison," said the diplomat. "Before this assignment, I served for twenty years in the 14th Paratroop Regiment: Bleu, Blanc et Rouge. Mort pour la France," (Blue, White, Red/Died for France).

"I learned fluent English and Vietnamese during my military career, and that's how I ended up in the diplomatic corps. When our VIPs and diplomats visit New York, which they do on a regular basis, I make all the serious arrangements," he said, and then turned to Honey. "Now, what can I do for you, mademoiselle?"

She pursed her lips, brushed back her hair, and squared her shoulders to the questioner. She responded in perfect French.

"Monseiur, one of our students, Michael Carroll, recently lost a brother fighting communist forces in Vietnam. Your government has come out against the American involvement in Southeast Asia. C'est la vie. (Such is life.) The boy was a brave U.S. Marine and wore the French croix de guerre that was presented by your government to the fighting 5th Marines, to which you've already alluded.

"His death was at the hands of the North Vietnamese 324th and 351st Divisions, the same forces that inflicted heavy casualties on the French garrison at the Battle of Dien Bien Phu – especially units of the 6th French Colonial Parachute Regiment and the 5/7 Algerian Rifles in battles involving sectors Claudine and Dominique."

A flabbergasted Monsieur Lambeau stepped back and said, "Mais oui! Comment savez-vous ceci?" (How is it you know about this?)

Honey continued in French: "This same 351st Viet Minh

(North Vietnamese Regiment), after the battle was involved in the systematic slaughter of almost 4,000 French enlisted soldiers who surrendered under the terms of the Geneva Convention, of which the Viet Minh were not a signatory to, but promised to abide by.

"In a way, my friend's brother died fighting communism just like your comrades," she said. "He died for the United States and in a small way for your country as well. Mort pour la France."

"Mais oui!" said the startled diplomate once again. "Mais oui!"

Honey hadn't even gotten around to asking the diplomat about Michel Jazy and the mile race when he suggested that the French consulate do something honorable for the slain Marine's family.

"Monsieur, that's why I have come to visit with you. Our hometown of Peekskill is building a memorial to those who have died in the defense of our country.

"We don't want your money. What we want is for world record holder, Michel Jazy, to run an exhibition mile race in Peekskill in September against our great high school runner whose brother was killed in Vietnam. Admission will be charged for the race, and with the money we will build a suitable war memorial."

The attaché said, "Yes, Monsieur Jazy will be in California to race and in New York for a couple of days on his way back to France. I already have my staff working on his arrangements. But Jazy is an Olympian and world record holder and will embarrass your high school athlete."

"Monsieur, we are willing to take that chance," said Honey.

The Attaché continued, "Jazy and his coach love to shop and see the sights like the Empire State Building, Radio City Music Hall and the Statue of Liberty, which, as you know, was constructed by the French."

"Monsieur Lambeau, the Statue of Liberty is one of your country's greatest gifts to us. Now, we need one more," said Honey. "Do you believe Michel Jazy will take part in our race?"

"Possible, very possible. Monsieur Jazy is a fine athlete and a wonderful man, but more importantly, he had an older brother who fought at Dien Bien Phu."

Eddie
and the Sisters

Saint Joseph's Home for Orphans was suiting Eddie Redlight fine when he decided to take the good Sisters up on a caretaker position they had offered him.

He didn't need much money, as he had a small poke from railroad retirement. Over the years, the pension supplied him with enough money for food, clothes, and cigarettes—though it was never enough for lodging so he just stood around on the street corners for as long as he could before finding a place to sleep, usually under a tree or in an abandoned car. It had been that way for years.

That had been Eddie Redlight's life for so long a time that he couldn't remember much else. The doctors at the Peekskill hospital who patched Eddie up after his beaning told the nuns that Eddie had "a case of the slows." He was pretending to be asleep when the doctors briefed Sister Imelda on his condition. The slows? Now what the hell is that? thought Eddie.

And what was wrong with standing on the street corner at night? He had no family, no car, no place to go, and had sworn off liquor. And he never caused problems. Sure, people threw things at him, but they didn't hit him much. On occasion, you know, on occasion. And the cops and firemen all liked him, and now the Sisters too.

Three years ago, Eddie had become a mascot for one of the city fire departments. He was in their Christmas photo, wearing a Santa Claus hat while sitting on the big hook and ladder. Not bad for a guy with "the slows."

On his street corner, Eddie watched kids grow up, moving from bicycle to hot-rod to station wagon. He watched the victorious high school football and basketball teams come streaming back into town late at night after victories. The kids yelling and cheering out the bus windows. "We're number one! We're number one!" This always made him smile.

Eddie saw desperadoes, too. Bank robbers who hit the town bank late at night and blew the safe with enough black powder to bring down the two-story building.

And he got along with the black people in town. Eddie didn't see any difference in white or black. They were all the same to Eddie, who had worked with lots of black guys on the railroad, and yeah, he even dug their music.

At Saint Joseph's Home, he could smoke all he wanted, which is something he really liked to do.

Sister Agnes, the head nun, briefed Eddie on what this job would entail.

"First of all, painting. Lots of painting." Sister Agnes asked Eddie if he had problems with heights or standing on a ladder. "This place was built right after the Civil War. It's old and dry and sucks up paint by the gallon," she said. "A couple of years ago, we hired painters from town. The monsignor said he got us a deal, but it almost busted our budget, so we had to let them go. And then, we had a lovely little Italian man named Uncle Patsy," she blessed herself. "He fell off a ladder and killed himself."

The good Sister continued, "In the spring and summer we have hedges to trim. The place was over-planted for years and is now completely overgrown. Some of the students help with that chore, but they do a poor job without supervision. In the fall, we try to repair the walls, sidewalks, and steps. This is the freezing and thawing capital of New York, and everything cracks, splits and breaks. So Eddie, if you take the job, you'll have to be good with mortar and cement."

"How much does the job pay?" asked Redlight.

Moving her hands quickly around her desk like some kind of Ponzi dealer, Sister Agnes said, "Room and board, plus seventy-five cents an hour."

"Sister, there are a couple of things I'd like to ask about," said Redlight.

"Go ahead, sir."

"I like to walk around at night, off property. I go up on Division Street, you know, where I got hurt. And sometimes I walk down along the railroad tracks, and other times, when I can't sleep, I just look over the walls and out at the river and railroad tracks."

"What are you looking for, Mr. Redlight?" she asked.

"I don't know."

Batter Up

Colonel Parrish decided to have a scrimmage between the two entities vying for spots on the All-Star softball team. The game was to be played in the evening at Depew Park.

Sal Fraggo was sitting in his office in Yonkers, jawboning with a cutie named Marci that he was interviewing for an executive assistant position. The job entailed not much of anything. Sal made all deals in the back room and never had any witnesses around, and that included executive assistants. But Sal needed a larger entourage and this good-lookin' Sarah Lawrence College graduate might just fit the bill. Plus, she could help with correspondence and correct his misspelling and punctuation errors.

"What are your long-term plans?" Sal asked the well-built brunette who bore a striking resemblance to a famous movie star.

"I'm going to graduate school in a year or two, after I get some work experience," she offered. "Maybe I'll get a teaching degree or go into sales and marketing. Don't know for sure."

"I travel to a lot of construction sites," said Sal. "Some of the men we deal with curse and use the Lord's name in vain and don't know how to behave around a lady. It's always 'fuck this' and 'fuck that.' Would something like that bother you?"

"Not in the least," she responded. "My boyfriend works the docks on the West Side and you know how they talk," she said.

Fraggo picked up his ringing telephone.

"Yeah, yeah... oh, shit... yeah, yeah, fangoule! OK... see ya." He turned his attention to the young girl sitting in front of him. "You've got the job if you want it," he said. "Start you out at two hundred dollars per week and you'll begin Monday."

"What's my job? What will I do?" she asked Fraggo, as he was sailing out the door.

"Whatever I tell you to do."

Fraggo walked across the street and roused his driver, who was reading the morning newspaper and drinking a cappuccino.

"Get the car. We're heading up north," Sal said, as he browsed the *New York Daily News* headlines.

G.I.s Storm Hill 566—
Entrenched Enemy fights to Death

Sal Fraggo was as patriotic as the next man, but there was something about this war that didn't jive with him. Losing all these boys in a muddy shithole, half a world away, because Lyndon Johnson and a few of his cronies said there was a threat.

What in the fuck is Ho Chi Minh going to do to us? Where's the threat? he mused. Where's the threat?

At Johnny P's place, plans were made for the big softball game. Annihilation of the Micks was the first order. The game would have to be a rout.

Sal and Johnny would hand-pick the starting lineup and have ready to go the best pitcher in the county in Stevie Mazacco. Mazacco was a super athlete at Hendrick Hudson High School who made all-everything while playing for the Sailors. He cold toss a softball with the best of them, throwing strikes and curves and brushing back batters who got close to the plate.

Lil' Trenton Jackson, a black kid from Queens, would be brought up as a ringer. He was on Fraggo's payroll at Indian Point as a laborer at the new reactor and could hit the ball across the Hudson River if he got a hold of one. And Jackson was anything but little. He stood 6'2" and weighed 230 pounds.

"After we get a big lead, we'll play some of the other guys," Fraggo said to Johnny. "But we got to get a big lead first. At least ten or twelve runs up before we put in the subs."

Johnny was OK with that, but asked Fraggo, "What happens if those Irish pricks suit up Ivan Martin?"

"Then, we'll ask Colonel Parrish to throw his ass off the field."

Ivan Martin might have been called "Ivan the Terrible" in another era. He was of Russian origin, and his family had stowed away on an American Liberty ship bearing that name. After the ship had just delivered lend-lease armaments for the Russian army in 1941 and left the port of St. Petersburg, it was struck by torpedoes fired by a German U-boat. The family of six struggled in the frigid waters for a day, floating along on top of giant wooden crates that held airplane tires that were, fortunately, fully inflated.

They were rescued by another Liberty ship and transported back to New York. The family eventually settled in the Peekskill area where it operated, of all things, a dude ranch.

The family was serious about making a buck and refused to let any of the kids play high school ball. The old man built the dude ranch up from nothing. He and his hardworking kids ripped up trees with their bare hands, moved boulders and carted them away on their backs, if necessary. They were tough people.

Ivan Martin wasn't a kid anymore, but a six-foot five-inch, 275-pound man among men. When Jimmy Dean's popular song "Big John" hit the airwaves in the early 1960s, it was quickly renamed "Big Ivan" by anyone who knew the Russian. On and off, he was recruited for softball games by the Irish pricks up street.

One time, he knocked out a short fielder with a line drive that hit him in the head. The paramedics took him away on a stretcher. Ivan also hit a foul ball once that decapitated one of the park's peacocks. A few more incidents like that caused Big Ivan to lose his taste for softball, as he had for all sports, because he always wound up hurting people. And in his heart, Big Ivan was really Big Softie.

"They better not play that Russian bastard," screamed Fraggo.

"How you going to stop 'em?" asked Johnny.

"Those Russians aren't citizens. I'll call the State Department," he said. "They're probably commie spies and have transmitters up those horses' asses. I don't know. I'll think of something."

The mayor of Peekskill suggested charging admission to the game and hawking all the refreshments and souvenirs they could. He figured to pull in every bit of $15,000, and with that he would pay for the war memorial's granite slabs, the bill for which sat on his city hall desk.

On a warm Saturday night, five thousand people – more than had ever gathered for a sporting event in Peekskill – jammed the bleachers to watch the "practice" game. Among the honorees were area Gold Star Mothers, a dozen ladies who had lost their sons to America's wars. Among those were five younger mothers whose sons had been killed in Vietnam. The women held hands and some cried. They were presented one by one, with Marie Carroll being introduced last.

She held together well and waved to the crowd. People were happy to see her spirits improved, since many had been at the train station when son Jackie's body came home. The good Sisters of St. Joseph had driven to the match in their rickety old bus and were granted free admission to bring in fifty or so orphaned and abandoned children. And driving the bus without a license? None other than the late-night waving man himself, Eddie Redlight.

And then the procession began.

On the Italian side, it started with the Catholic Knights of Columbus marching around the track and onto the center of the playing field. They wore their long black robes and tasseled Napoleon hats, and looked slightly tortured, like they were saying the stations of the cross.

Behind them, four super-sized altar boys carried a huge statue of the Madonna, which would bless the event. The statue had been recently repainted, and those in attendance thought the Madonna looked exquisite.

Fraggo, together with his beautiful new aide-de-camp, Marci, followed the altar boys. He waved to everyone as he walked, a true celebrity who employed half of the town. From up in the stands, people shouted at Marci, "Annette Funicello, Annette Funicello! Sal brought Annette Funicello!" Fraggo smiled to himself. He never disappointed.

Now, it was the Rotten Irish Pricks turn.

Coming onto the track from an opening in the fence, blowing for all to see was the glorious sight of the giant emerald green flag of the "Sons of Erin," the Civil War banner of New York's Irish Brigades. The flag was trimmed in red and contained a large gold harp in the center. The flag was carried by a soldier who wore an old red Zouave uniform and a low-crown cap.

The Irish Brigades were the most famous fighting units in Lincoln's Army of the Potomac, and thus, the entire Civil War.

The Brigades fought in battles from Bull Run to Antietam and were made up of mostly Irish immigrants from scattered New England regiments.

Following closely were thirty or so slightly inebriated infantry officers wearing the smart Civil War uniforms of the "Fighting 69th" New York militia.

And then came the bagpipers playing the "Garryowen" so loud that it made the entire herd of peacocks run to the woods and hide.

Quite a show, thought Colonel Parrish.

"Ma God," said his wife Mae. "This is as big as the Army-Navy game."

Standing more than a head above their teammates, Ivan Martin and Lil' Trenton Jackson gave each other the high sign.

Colonel Parrish gathered team captains Tommy Duffy and Tony Sarno and went over the ground rules.

"I'm from West Point, as you know, and tonight we won't have any fighting or name calling. No leading off first or any other bases. And I don't want your pitchers throwing at anyone's head. There are lots of little kids up in the stands tonight and your behavior on the field will determine how they view competition. I don't want any overt drama and cursing.

"Remember, we're here to pick the team that will represent your town – all of your town, not just a select group," said the colonel as he looked over to where Fraggo was standing. "Play your best guys for the first half of the game and after that, win or lose, put in your substitutes. I want them all to play tonight. Now let's have a good game and get ready for the King and His Court. What do you say, fellows?"

"Fuckin' A," one of the players answered.

As His Honor prepared to throw out the first pitch, the peacocks emerged from the woods storming the field. Agitated and crazed from too many verses of "Garryowen," they began to attack and bite everyone they could find.

When the mayor tried to corral one of the big birds, it grabbed ahold of his nut sack and wouldn't let go. The good Sisters of St. Joseph turned their heads away and tried to shield the young orphans' eyes as well but four thousand others laughed hard enough to be heard in the town of Croton, which was ten miles to the south.

The game was predictable, with the lead changing hands back and forth throughout the early innings. Peekskill's pitcher threw some serious heat, but Ivan the big Russian got ahold of one pitch and sent it into space to visit that other Russian, Sputnik.

"Fuck that guy!" screamed Fraggo from his front row seat. "I swear to Christ, his sorry ass is getting deported even if I have to pay off everyone in the State Department."

Lil' Trenton Jackson had a present for the Rotten Irish Pricks when he belted a ball that landed in the outdoor swimming pool.

"My God," said Colonel Parrish. "He hit that softball as far as anyone's ever hit a baseball. Never seen anything like it."

After five innings and another frontal attack by the peacocks, the score was deadlocked – six all. Those watching the game realized the Italian side probably had the better players. No doubt. Good pitching, slick infielding, fine base running and they played together as a unit. And they had a few big bats too. Fraggo was licking his chops knowing that he had the best players on the field. And now everyone, including Colonel Parrish, knew it.

But never doubt Irishmen, especially ones who've been off the juice for a few weeks. They played tough, running out every ground ball and beating throws to first base. And they made great catches in the outfield to rob sure homeruns from the guineas.

All the while, the emerald green flag of Erin waved in the evening breeze, bringing with it all the good fortune it never brought to its Civil War soldiers who were slaughtered at Manassas, Bull Run and Mary's Heights high above the Rappahannock River in Virginia. Brave, yes. Lucky, no.

As the fifth inning was about to get underway, Colonel Parrish called captains Duffy and Sarno over and told them to begin wholesale substitutions. He had seen enough of the first string guys and had taken copious notes on everyone's performance. Now, he needed to round out the team with the remaining players, a few of whom were also very good.

Fraggo broke away from his little Funicello cutie pie assistant and stormed over to where the coaches were meeting.

"What's going on here?" asked the frazzled union steward.

"We're playing the rest of the team for the next two innings," said the colonel.

"But the score's still tied. We haven't officially won yet!" yelled Sal.

The colonel, using a tone reserved for Laotian village chiefs, explained that the purpose of the game was to pick out top players, not to see which team was better. The score was tied going into the sixth inning and that was perfect for the fans and town.

"What could be better?" asked the colonel. "Now, let's suit up the subs."

Fraggo was in a delicate spot and he knew it. There were too many people around for him to make a big scene. Even Monsignor Healy was eyeballing Fraggo, wondering what misdeed he was up to.

The West Point man was selected for his integrity. Donations or not, he was standing on his principles.

Fraggo had a side bet of $10,000 on the outcome of the game. He didn't know how a tie in softball would be handled by the bookie. Maybe he'll just roll the bet over, thought Fraggo. "You know, you're right, Colonel. This is the right thing to do. We've all seen who the better players are. Let's have some fun and get everyone in the game."

The substitutes took the field and play resumed. After a while, those in the stands couldn't tell the first team from the second. Subs always played their hearts out, and in a lot of ways, were more fun to watch.

Eddie Redlight stood off to the side smoking his cigarettes. Marie and the other Gold Star Mothers continued to hold hands to dissipate their personal grief. Fraggo's new assistant was signing autographs "Best Wishes, Annette Funicello."

The Irish Brigades were now hitting the grog, and the Knights of Columbus were passing their big Napoleon hats up in the bleachers, trying to collect more money for the war memorial. A breeze had come in off the Hudson River and the sun was now setting on this beautiful picture post card evening.

Over in Lake Mathews another breeze was blowing. Old Mrs. Galer, who had returned home from Cato, New York after two years of hiding, was fixing her wounded husband, Tony, a sandwich with peanut butter and of course lots of grape jelly – just the way he liked it.

The
Abco
Study Guide

First Sergeant Rudy "Top" Simmons was doing a rear area inspection of empty tents and hooches that belonged to recently deployed men of November Company. It was standard operating procedure (SOP) to do walkthroughs of the dozen or so tents that housed the troops. These tents would be vacant for the next month while the company was out hunting Charlie, and sometimes malingerers broke in and stole things or plain hid out from the first sergeant.

From a distance, "Top" Simmons saw the Abco Study Guide and recognizing it early may have saved his life, he thought. He knew the death curse that went along with this study manual and thought it was crazy but dared not go near it.

Because everyone was needed for fighting, only a few people stayed in the rear during these large combat search and destroy missions. The executive officer and first sergeant usually stayed behind, along with a couple of enlisted clerk typists, and then there was a small assortment of fuck-offs and sickbay commandos, but not too many in November Company because the company commander simply wouldn't allow it. If you could breathe and walk, then you were fit to dodge bullets.

Actually, the "Exec" and "Top" had very big jobs, especially if the company hit the shit and took casualties. It was up to them to visit the hospital morgues and make sure, with absolute certainty, that the bodies that were shipped home were properly identified. And this was no easy task.

When a Marine was killed in the field, an identification tag was tied around the casualty's wrist or leg – or in some cases, whatever body part remained. Sometimes, the dead would lie where they fell until a counterattack could push the enemy back. This could be anywhere from twelve hours to a couple of days, and in the terrible tropical heat, bodies would rapidly decompose and become unrecognizable. Marines under fire had to carry, sometimes drag, bodies long distances to a helicopter-landing zone. The Marines always recovered their dead, no matter how long it took or how difficult the task.

There were no body bags in the field, and often an entire helicopter would be loaded with the mutilated remains of American servicemen – each sprawled out in his own death scene. Helicopter door gunners who took part in these evacuation missions were often haunted for the rest of their lives.

Fallen Marines did not go back to their company area, but to an assortment of temporary morgues associated with transient field hospitals that were scattered all over I Corps. Many of these morgues were simply standard green holding tents, and casualties were lined up on the floor. Not out of disrespect, but that is what happens in combat.

Body tags were sometimes inadvertently ripped off the deceased during transit. It happened all the time. Bodies might then be misidentified, unless someone made a positive ID at the morgue, and that was no simple task.

Even November Company's rear area was located out in the remote jungle, nowhere near hospitals, morgues or anything resembling civilization. The executive officer, first sergeant or someone they anointed, had to track down the KIAs (Killed In Action) and make sure they were properly identified. It had to be done with great speed.

They were the jobs nobody wanted, but were as important as any in the infantry. And if an exec or first sergeant wasn't sure of a casualty's identity, he had to go through hospital wards looking for wounded Marines who might have known the deceased.

This was a double whammy for the wounded man because he had to view the gruesome remains of a friend, and looking into his death mask, he inevitably saw his own.

Top Simmons was satisfied with his walk around. He loved neatness and order. All personal effects of the deployed Marines were neatly stored on top of their cots to keep them out of the onslaught of rain and mud when the summer storms hit. Neatness was a Marine requisite.

But one poor son of a bitch had the Abco Study Guide, the black dahlia itself on top of his cot. Top Simmons couldn't bear to look at the name on the bunk, but knew that it was someone from the second platoon.

The
Poker

Marie's nerves were on the mend, said Dr. Gilcrest, who gave her the OK to drive. But he also cautioned her in the strongest terms possible. "Do not drink and drive, and never mix alcohol and your prescriptions." The doctor knew what he was talking about.

It was a beautiful day to get out and about in the car and with the kids at camp Marie decided to go for a drive. The humidity of late had disappeared and a high translucent sky gave no hint of foul weather. Today, Marie felt happy all over and thought to herself that the veil of sadness might slowly be lifting. It was a good feeling.

She put on a fresh face, a pressed cotton summer dress, matching scarf, and big sunglasses. She thought she resembled Audrey Hepburn.

"Where was Cary Grant?" she opined.

Then again, Audrey Hepburn wouldn't be riding around in a car like this – Mickey's second-hand 1949 rust-over-white Ford coupe with a standard on-the-column shift and four mismatched tires.

First gear didn't work so Marie had to take off in second with the engine rpms racing like hell to get the vehicle moving. It made a racket and the kids were self-conscious about riding in such a crappy car, especially around Assumption School, where their friends teased them.

"Here comes that pile of shit!" yelled a fourth grader, as Marie roared into the parking lot to drop off the kids for Sunday mass.

Marie was a good driver and adapted to the transmission problems with ease. Mickey said it would cost more to repair the transmission than the car was worth. His friendly mechanic told him to drive the car until it died, then take the plates off and leave it on the side of the road. So Marie was stuck with the car that wouldn't die.

But that was only part of it because in the back seat of the old Ford, hidden beneath a worn cushion and unable to be located under any circumstance, was "the poker," a broken piece of steel spring, sharp as a tack, that poked anyone in the keester who sat on it. The poker was famous around Peekskill for after a person was stuck, he or she had "the pokes." Sometimes, the poker drew blood. It was that savage. And most people who knew the Carrolls had had a case of the pokes.

Marie laughed to herself as she drove along Route 6 reminiscing about Jackie's friends piling into the car after track practice, and then a howl from the back seat: "Oooh, shit!"

All the kids would crack up as a new member of the group got poked.

Not everyone who sat in the back seat got stuck. One had to hit the spot at a certain angle before the little rascal popped through the seat cushion.

Even one of the good Sisters of St. Joseph got poked in the rear when Mickey gave her a ride home from church. And yet no one could find the poker.

Mickey took out the back seat of the automobile, but could not locate the errant spring. Like they said in the Church, it was one of those mysteries. Probably right up there with how the Holy Ghost could be everywhere at the same time.

Marie drove through town, briefly shopping at the A&P where she waved to big Rubin, who was lumbering down Main Street, shopping carts in hand.

Years ago, with six crying kids in the car and snow coming down, Rubin had changed her flat tire in the store parking lot. When she tried to give him three dollars for his effort, he wouldn't take it. The poorest man in Peekskill wouldn't accept money. She thought Rubin would one day go to heaven.

Marie drove to Assumption Cemetery, where she prayed over the grave of her departed son, Jackie. She tried to visit the cemetery every day and often had to wait for Mickey to return home from work. But with her driving again, she could make the trip anytime. And that was another cause for celebration. She did some housekeeping chores on the grave, cleaning up old flowers and placing new ones. She noticed how the dirt was still shifting around the gravesite and she was still waiting for the large copper plaque from the Veterans' Administration to be placed at the foot of the grave. Jackie's plaque would list his military awards:

> Corporal Jack C. Carroll
> USMC
> Killed in Action
> Vietnam
> Silver Star
> Purple Heart

She sat back and looked around. This was certainly a beautiful, peaceful place. High above Oregon Road in Peekskill, surrounded by hills and forest. This is where she would join her son, she thought. After the little ones were raised, of course. Marie knew she'd been shortchanging her other kids since the death of Jackie, but she just couldn't stop being sad. She just couldn't snap out of it.

"Oh Lord, how long will it take," she prayed in all sincerity.

Marie thought about sins she committed during her life – sins that would have led to the death of her beloved son. What was it?

What had she done?

Practicing birth control? No, everyone practiced contraception nowadays. Drinking vodka during the day? Maybe, she reasoned. That's been harmful to the family. Cursing out the priests and monsignor? Possibly, she thought, especially if they have the eternal power they claim to have. The trip with the Catholic Girls, she thought to herself.

"Maybe that's it," she murmured.

Marie knew she was somehow at fault for the death of her son. She should have refused to let him join the Marines, though she legally couldn't do that because he was over eighteen years of age. She should have taken out a second mortgage on the house to finance college. She should have threatened to divorce her husband if Jackie joined the military. She should have broken his goddamned legs while he slept.

She should have done *something*.

After a few more housekeeping chores, she was on her way.

She gassed up Mickey's car at the Power Test station on Route 6, paying 26.9 cents per gallon. She thought it might be a nice surprise to pick up her son Mike from summer school and take him out to lunch. They hadn't done that for quite a while.

Mike and Honey were sitting on the front steps of the school when Marie pulled the smoking '49 Ford buzz bomb to a halt.

"I know you like guys with cars, and that's going to be mine in a few more months," said Mike, pointing to the smoking wreck.

"For real!" said Honey.

Marie yelled out the window. "You kids want to go to lunch?"

"Sure!" they yelled, and they piled in.

"Oooh, shoot!" shrieked Honey as she took the poker in her shapely rear end.

"If it drew blood, you have to marry me," said Mike, as his mother popped the clutch and roared off in second gear.

Honey, who had been chauffeured around by boyfriends driving Corvettes, Thunderbirds and Chevy Impala Super Sports, just rubbed her can and laughed. She didn't mind at all.

Parking spots were at a minimum so Marie dropped the kids off at Tuller's luncheonette while she drove off to find a parking spot. It was about noon and parking was scarce in Peekskill during this time of day. She drove down Brown Street, South Street, then Main and Division Streets. No luck. She parked in the open church parking lot and that's when she saw the big Marine recruiter heading for the luncheonette. He was with his little Navy pal to get the blue plate special.

She remembered he took Jackie to lunch at Tuller's when he was recruiting him for the Marine Corps. When Jackie tried to pay, the recruiter pushed his hand back and said, "This one's on the Corps, Son." Then he added, "Next time, when you're a Marine, you pay."

Marie knew there was no next time. Just like there was no Quantico track team, or air wing mechanic, or radar technician, or administrative clerk or officer candidate school or Naval Academy or any of the 225 job descriptions in the USMC. It was all a hoax.

When Jackie had arrived at Parris Island and filled out his "assignment dream sheet," he wrote down as his first choice:

"Radar Technician, Quantico Air Station, Quantico, VA. His second choice, Officer Candidate School, Quantico, VA, and third choice, clerk-typist, Quantico, VA. He felt certain he would get one of his choices.

For an entire day, he took batteries of examinations that tested reading, mathematics and mechanical ability.

Jackie felt he did fine on the tests. He had been about a 3.0 student in high school. He had taken three years of math, three years of language, and all the required English, science and history courses.

He went to summer school a few times, but so what? He came out with better grades than many of his peers. Jackie was sure he would qualify for one of his choice assignments. Besides, the recruiter had said so.

One day while Carroll was on the rifle range, he was approached by a new brown-bar 2nd lieutenant wearing a Shirley Highway Ribbon (National Defense Ribbon). The lieutenant asked him what he wanted to do in "my Marine Corps."

Not forgetting to answer the question in the third person, Private Carroll said, "Sir, the private wants to run on the Quantico track team and be a radar technician."

"You wanna do what?" said the incredulous junior officer.

"Sir. The private wants to run on the Quantico…"

Cutting him off, the lieutenant said, "Son, there's a war going on and we have 95,000 openings in the infantry units and about two dozen in the radar tech field. If I were you, I'd get to know that rifle real well. I got a feeling you're going to be using it where you're going."

Pvt. Carroll now knew the "real skinny," as they said in the Corps.

Ninety-five thousand openings in the infantry. The grunts. The recruiter never said anything about that.

About a month after reporting to Parris Island, Private Jackie Carroll, serial number 223257, received his Military Occupational Specialty (MOS), which was the same as 95 percent of his platoon, 0311. Basic infantryman.

And two months after entering the Marine Corps, he – along with most of his platoon – got marching orders from Marine Corps headquarters.

Pvt. Carroll had told his mother that the platoon was washing its skivvies on cement washing tables outside the barracks one evening after having been put on report by the senior drill instructor for talking and "playing grabass."

The recruits washed their underwear using hand soap, scraping the dirty, shit-stained skivvies on the cement tables just like Marines in World War II probably did. It was still hot outside with the temperature in the 90s.

The senior drill instructor appeared at the top of the second floor barracks' landing holding what looked like sheet music in his hands. The DI, a short, redheaded firebrand, was laughing and dancing the Irish jig. He looked like he was drunk, which he may have been. The mid-shift DIs had a bad habit of spending the afternoons at a local slop shoot named Paula's, where they could drink cheap beer and get their fortunes told by Paula's sister – the one and only "Miss LaFontaine."

"Attention on deck!" he yelled. "No, at ease," he corrected himself. "For all of you who thought training was a big joke, I've got a joke for you. You're all going to Vietnam, except for the two queers who are going to Sea Service School. Please allow me to read:

From: Commandant, United States Marine Corps. To: Private Snuffy Smith – you can substitute you own names here, – after completing basic training at Parris Island Recruit Depot, you will report to Infantry Training Regiment, ITR, Camp John A. LeJeune, North Carolina for advanced infantry training.

Upon completion of training, and after appropriate leave, you will be assigned soonest to Ground Forces, Western Pacific. Congratulations on your new assignments and welcome into the United States Marine Corps. I am, Wallace M. Greene, General, Commandant.

The DI paused a moments to let the message sink in before issuing his next order: "Smoke 'em, if you got 'em."

Moving with a purposeful stride, Marie Carroll wanted to head off the DIs before they arrived at the luncheonette, thereby avoiding a scene that was likely to embarrass Mike and Honey. But just as Marie was about to enter the department store, she was cornered by that old blabbermouth Margo Miller, a former neighbor and drinking partner who had found salvation and sobriety at the foot of the cross.

"Hi Honey," said Margo, as she grabbed Marie in a big bear hug. "I'd love to sponsor you in one of our meetings."

Margo, who resembled a pudgy Patti Page, still had the alcohol bloat (her face was slightly swollen) but assured Marie that she was off the juice and loving life. She pressed Marie into her enormous bosom.

"And how's Mickey these days?" she asked. "Long time, no see."

There had been "talk" around town from time to time that Mickey was pounding Margo on the side, and Marie didn't trust her friend as far as she could throw her, which wasn't very far.

"Oh, Mickey's doing fine," said Marie, trying to break away. "I've really got to go Margo. I'm meeting some people for lunch."

In a condescending manner Margo said, "Sure you are. I'm sure you're meeting someone very important."

Marie had had about all she could take and was beginning to steam up when Margo said, "I'm sorry for your loss. We all are. How I loved to watch Jackie run."

Thanking her, Marie moved swiftly to the luncheonette counter where Mike and Honey were being shadowed by the big Marine recruiter.

Marie readied for her best volley, when Mike cut in: "Staff Sergeant Zimmer has orders to Vietnam. He's going to be in the same regiment that Jackie was in."

"That's right, Mrs. Carroll. I leave in a few weeks, and I'm proud to be serving with the 5th Marines, the same as your son," said the burley, flat-topped recruiter.

All at once, Marie could feel the hate and bitterness leaving her. She felt light on her feet. She felt a little childish. SSgt. Zimmer would have the same chance her son had – which was no chance – and that squared things with her.

"Good luck to you, Sergeant Zimmer," she said. "Who knows? They may need a radar technician or two in Vietnam. There's so many openings in a Marine Corps Division."

The two recruiters picked up coffee and sandwiches for takeout. The big Marine said, "We've got to meet some kids at the office."

Honey wanted to change the subject to something a little more lighthearted so she talked about French class and how Mademoiselle Plante was now a big fan of her son, Mike. Honey pressed Mike, asking him if he was ready to run some fast races.

"I'm still doing a lot of speed work," he said. "I haven't started training for cross country yet, so I'm ready to go."

He mentioned that *Track and Field News* and *The New York Times* were both doing articles on him for upcoming editions.

"I wanted to talk a lot about Jackie's death in Vietnam and raising money for the war memorial, but they only wanted to talk about track and field and what kind of workouts I do."

"What did you tell them?" asked Marie.

"I said I run mostly at Blue Mountain since this big softball game has taken up all of Depew Park. I run along the paths and hiking trails. I do repeat sprints up the side of Blue Mountain and along the upper lake. I figure I run at top speed for about 300 to 400 yards, and I keep repeating the distance until I'm too tired to run anymore."

"Were they impressed?" asked Honey.

"Don't know. They wanted me to do a lot more measurable stuff, workouts on the track and stuff like that. I told them I run quarters on the track once or twice a week after long runs. I can run six times four-forty (440) with a lap walk in fifty-two to fifty-three seconds without too much effort. I don't think they believed me. They kind of looked at each other in a funny way. 'Those times were way too fast,' they said.

"The *Track and Field News* reporter wanted pictures of me running at Depew Park on the track, but when we went over there, they were practicing softball and every inch of the place was taken up. So, they settled on a picture of me running along Route Nine with the Hudson River in the background."

Mayor Di Gregorio stopped by to chat with the Carrolls and Honey. He said hello to the kids but approached Marie very cautiously.

"I just want to let you know, Marie, that we're almost done with the architectural phase of the memorial, and we'd like input from you and some of the other Gold Star Mothers in town before we give final approval."

Marie was clearly pleased and thanked the mayor for his hard work.

"We've got six or seven more boys from the area still in Vietnam, and we pray each day for their safety. We'd rather not be building any memorials at all, if you know what I mean," said the mayor.

"Our family is grateful for the support you've shown us, but what do you think about our speedy little runner here?" she asked the mayor, as she pointed to her son Mike.

"I've gotten a dozen phone calls from newspapers and magazines asking about him," he said. "We're very proud of your family, Marie. All the work Mickey's done with the town's sports' teams, Jackie's great championships and now this new wonder." He put his arm around Mike.

Before the mayor left, he said, "Of all things, we received a call from the French Embassy in Washington, D.C. about our war memorial. Imagine that. They said their consulate in New York would be in contact with us with more details. I wonder what that's all about," he said, as he was leaving.

"Au revoir," said Honey.

Superior Court of
New York

The district attorney's office in White Plains had scheduled a preliminary hearing for early Tuesday morning in *State of New York v. Anthony Galer*.

Earlier, the DA had filed five felony counts against Galer for lewd and lascivious behavior, public indecency, corruption of a minor and two counts of battery on a police dog. The state was prepared to show that not only had Galer exposed himself to a group of girls playing volleyball at Drum Hill School in Peekskill, three of whom were minors, but he had also assaulted a working police dog by kicking it in the head and chest.

Information about police dog Sweetie biting off Galer's willie was nowhere to be found in the court documents. Everyone at the DA's office agreed that the act occurred "after the fact," and the perpetrator had only himself to blame.

The public defender's office had been directed to defend Galer in these early criminal proceedings but had all the usual problems with their client, who was surly on the phone. He cursed out the legal analyst who tried to gather information and even threatened her. After Galer twice failed to show up for scheduled meetings with their office, Mr. Marc Hinn, Esquire, the senior public defender (PD), decided to drive out to Lake Mathews to read his client the riot act. Nobody, especially someone they were directed to defend, was going to cuss out his staff and get away with it.

Hinn was a 40-year-old attorney and part-time civil rights activist who had made a few trips to Selma, Alabama with the freedom riders. He had been blasted with water hoses and given a few wood shampoos by baton-wielding Selma police officers. He was an excellent attorney, well-known and liked around the White

Plains courthouse.

Mostly disheveled in appearance, he had long hair, a bushy mustache and wore wrinkled poplin suits with loud ties that never seemed to match anything he had on. His shoes looked like he walked to Selma and back because they were worn down and practically falling off his feet. His appearance was in stark contrast to the other attorneys in the DA's office who wore dark, pinstriped suits, striped ties and neatly shined black wingtips. Most of those attorneys were putting in their time at the DA's office before they could join a big New York law firm and make serious moolah. That, or run for public office in Westchester County.

Senior Public Defender Marc Hinn wasn't going anywhere.

Hinn carried with him the standard accordion folders jammed with court records and witness statements that seemed ready to explode on the street as he hurried from his office to the courthouse numerous times a day.

A few days prior to the preliminary hearing, Hinn checked out a Dodge Fury and drove up the Westchester County parkway towards Peekskill. He figured the trip would take less than an hour. The Fury had a hot V-8 and was the fastest car in the motor pool. He punched the gas as he sped along the curvy road. The seasoned lawyer liked the powerful engine, and it felt good to get out of the office and away from the courthouse for a little while.

Hinn wasn't sure what he'd find when he arrived at Galer's residence, so he drove around Lake Mathews a couple of times formulating his questions. The public defender hated these sex cases more than anything else. He had little sympathy for sex fiends, but was sworn to defend them – and defend them he did. He was a bit angry with himself for not bringing a witness because if things went sideways during the Galer interview, he'd have to explain to the superior court judge exactly why his office was not representing this indigent felon.

The Galer's house was an old Victorian monstrosity with shingles falling off the roof, clear plastic covering many of the windows and a screen door that was somewhat off its hinges.

The place hadn't been painted in twenty-five years and in many areas the wood siding was rotting and splintering to the ground. The sidewalk leading up to the front door was cracked with dandelions growing in the crevices. Empty been cans littered the ground, along with some discarded milk containers.

Hinn identified Tony's lime green Dodge Dart from the Peekskill police reports. It had a flat front tire and sat in front of a rusted mailbox. A young girl about fifteen years old, who failed to introduce herself, met him at the door. She was rail thin, wearing a man's white T-shirt; her hair was in a ponytail and she had a severe case of teenage acne.

"I'm Westchester Public Defender Marc Hinn to see Mr. Tony Galer," he said, flashing his official credentials. "And you are?" the public defender asked the startled teenager.

"Don't tell him a fuckin' thing, you hear me!" screamed a growling voice from the interior of the house.

The young girl jumped back as if hit with a bolt of electricity. "Who the fuck is it? Answer me!" yelled the voice from within.

"It's the public defender's office. We need to talk about your case," said a startled Hinn.

Hinn began to get those same bad feelings he'd had while traveling down the Magnolia Highways of the South – surrounded and helpless.

He stepped back from the threshold of the door, where he instinctively knew shots would be aimed if violence erupted. The young girl had disappeared from view and Hinn now heard other voices inside the house – only these were of a different pitch. A soothing voice, a woman's voice.

And after what seemed like a long while, a woman appeared in the darkened hallway. She was hard to see at first. Tiny, little thing. Maybe fifty or so. She walked towards the public defender, who took a few steps back.

"I'm Tony's wife, Rose," she said, and motioned for Hinn to enter the house. "He's not going to bother you. You got my word."

"Rose Galer is a gypsy!" the public defender thought at first. Short, slight, big moon pie eyes and dressed in a macabre flowing outfit, she resembled gypsy women he had met while traipsing through Europe during his study abroad year in college.

Gypsies were everywhere in those days, begging on street corners, lifting wallets, and selling marijuana that was dried spinach. But this one seemed a little different. She extended her hand, and Marc Hinn shook it.

"He really done it now," she said to Hinn. "Probably do hard time, won't he?"

Before Hinn could answer, Rose chirped, "If he done what they said, he deserves whatever he gets. No one around here cares about him all that much."

Hinn walked into the living room as Rose led the way. What he saw shocked him.

A disheveled man lay sprawled on the couch. He resembled an aging Elvis impersonator. He was half-covered with a blanket and appeared to be sleeping.

Mucus was running out his nose, and one eye was partially open. The room was a mess with dried bloodied towels around his crotch area and ashtrays full of cigarette butts. A half dozen Kruger beer bottles lay empty on the floor next to horse and detective magazines.

"Is that your husband, Tony Galer?" asked Hinn.

"That's him. I told you he wouldn't be giving you any problems. His pain medicine was ready to kick in when you knocked on the door."

Visibly angry, Hinn began to pace back and forth in the living room, trying to avoid an angry outburst. God knows this family had had enough of them, he reasoned.

"Listen, Mrs. Galer. The public defender's office has been directed by a superior court judge to represent your husband at his preliminary hearing, which has been twice delayed. It is imperative that I speak with him. You know, interview him. How long will he be asleep?"

"Three or four hours," said his wife.

"This is just not going to do," said Hinn, murmuring to himself. "This is not going to do. Madam, the judge in this case is a very unforgiving type, and I'm making this last attempt to get information from Mr. Galer so I can properly defend him. Your husband has been rude and downright obscene in his dealings with people from our office.

"He refuses to give us a complete statement over the phone and skips his appointments. There's only so much more we can do. And the judge is going to lock him up if he doesn't cooperate," said the public defender. "I am duty bound to try my best for your husband, but there's only so much more I can do."

"What do you expect *me* to do?" a now animated Rose asked.

"You want to know why he's screaming one minute and sleeping the next, look at this," she said, and held up a bottle of pills and a few empty beer bottles. "He mixes his alcohol and pain medication. He's howling one minute, knocked out the next. Hell, that's the only time we get any peace around here."

Hinn's eyes scanned the room and he noticed the young girl who had earlier opened the door. She was standing in the corner.

"Who's this young lady?" he said.

In a genuine show of affection, Mrs. Galer walked over and hugged her daughter. "This pretty thing's name is Lilly," she said. "She was my change of life baby, and things haven't been too good for her. She has a learning disability so the school put her in an auto mechanics class. The kids made fun of her, so she quit school.

"I got two more kids, grown ones, Richard and Robert, but they're a lot like him," she said, pointing to her passed-out husband on the couch. "And they're over in Vermont hiding for something they done in town."

Hugging her daughter she continued, "Poppa's not mad at you, Honey. You know, he doesn't like you to answer the door and talk to nobody. It could be some of those people from the school looking for you."

Hinn walked out to the kitchen and pulled some papers from his accordion file.

"I'm leaving these with you, Mrs. Galer," he said. "Mr. Galer's preliminary hearing is next Tuesday at 9 a.m., at the Westchester County courthouse in White Plains. He needs to be there at 8 a.m. Someone from our office will meet with him for a short while to go over some things.

"If he's not at the courthouse, the judge will issue a warrant for his arrest and the sheriff or Peekskill police will come up here and arrest him. And you know what that means. Is there anything you want to tell me now, anything I should know about your husband, before the trial?"

"Mr. Hinn, I've been gone for almost two years because of his abuse," she said. "Living with my sister up in Cato, New York. It's mostly farm country, and I had a job working in the school cafeteria. It was good work and I liked seeing the little ones laugh and enjoy themselves. Worked at Wells College too with all those rich kids. And they was nice, too. But I come back because of my daughter Lilly and all she's been through.

"I kinda let my daughter down. I shoulda been there more for her, instead of running away like I did. Shoulda been there to protect her more."

Looking Rose straight in the eye, Hinn said, "Protect her from who?"

Mrs. Galer turned away from the questioner and slowly walked to the door, showing the public defender out.

A week later, Hinn and his two deputies were standing tall in Courtroom 6 as the clerk handed a file to Judge Steven C. Amidon, a gruff jurist about fifty years old, with a shock of gray hair perfectly combed in place.

"Are the people and defense ready to proceed with case number sixty-five dash two five eight one (65-2581), State vs. A. Galer?" he snapped.

The district attorney and Mr. Hinn stood to face the judge. The DA looked awkwardly at the public defender.

"Your Honor, because of Mr. Galer's medical condition we have been unable to properly represent him and…"

"That's not what I asked you, Mr. Hinn," the obviously annoyed judge interrupted. "Are you ready to proceed with this preliminary trial which is on its third try?"

Hinn shuffled in his shoes for a moment or two, thinking of the right things to say.

"Quite frankly, we don't know where the defendant is. He was advised of the date and time to be here and issued a stern warning about failure to appear before this court."

Then the prosecutor's office chimed in. "Your Honor, our office has had numerous problems with Mr. Galer in the past and…"

"The 'past' is not germane in this case, Sir, and I shouldn't have to remind the Prosecution of the rules of law," the judge interrupted again.

"Sorry, Your Honor."

As this prosecutorial transgression was being addressed, Rose

Galer – dressed like the gypsy lady of Bucharest – entered the courtroom and worked her way to the third row from the front, catching the eye of Judge Amidon.

"And Madam, who are you?" asked the judge.

Before the public defender could react, Rose Galer blurted out, "I'm Rose Galer, the defendant's wife, and he won't be here today."

Mr. Hinn moved towards her, yelling, "Wait!"

The judge cut him off. Looking directly at Mrs. Galer he thundered, "And why won't he be here today, Mrs. Galer?"

"I put the d-CON to him."

"Come again?" asked the startled judge.

"I put the d-CON rat poison to 'im. He's dead."

Someone shouted in the courtroom for her to be apprehended.

"He gave my beautiful daughter VD. The doctor told me so," said Rose, now crying. "So I put the d-CON to him in a peanut butter and jelly sandwich. I killed him for buggering my daughter."

The prosecution pointed at the deputies who pointed at the public defender, who pointed at Rose. The judge, who had fought as an infantry officer on the bloody island of Okinawa, banged his gravel again and again.

"Let's have some order and everyone please calm down."

The public defender rushed toward Rose, his offbeat tie fluttering behind him. His large accordion folder had slipped from his grasp and leaflets of paper fluttered to the ground, leaving a trail behind him.

He grabbed Rose around the shoulders, pulling her head towards his chest. Chaos reined in the courtroom, as the district attorney was trying to give orders to the deputies, who were now rushing toward the oddly-dressed little woman.

"Don't say another word," Hinn whispered in the woman's ear. "Don't say another word."

The Time
Trial

After losing to Mike Carroll in the Yonkers 880-yard spectacular, local West Point phenomenon Jimmy Wagner wanted a rematch at a longer distance, say three miles.

Although Wagner had finished fourth in the race, running an excellent time of 1:48.1 seconds, which was close to an Academy record, he felt he could do much better at a longer distance. With a few weeks to kill before fall semester began, he suggested a time trial to his coach.

Wagner had run against both of the Carroll boys in high school and knew them well. He had been the top distance runner in the state until Jackie came along. After that, Wagner was sandwiched in between the Carroll brothers in races all over New York. During his senior year in high school, he was selected for appointment to West Point, and with his excellent grades and athletic ability, his star shone as brightly as anyone in his class.

Unlike most skinny distance runners, Wagner was built like a football player, with legs like a linebacker. He could run all day and was fast as hell. In two years at West Point he was IC4A champion, Heptagonal champion and a genuine pain in the ass for the Naval Academy whose own elite runners lost to Wagner in every race from 880 to the 2-mile. They just couldn't beat him.

After Carroll's upset win in Yonkers, Wagner approached him after the race, first congratulating him on his great victory and then thanking him and his family for their supreme sacrifice. The Carroll boys always liked running against Jimmy Wagner in high school because he was such a great competitor. But, if the truth were known, they were envious of him. And because envy is a very big Catholic sin, they were ashamed of this shortcoming.

After all, Wagner got to go to West Point, not them. Certainly not Jackie who wound up as cannon fodder in a Marine rifle squad. Wagner got to march in Saturday parades at West Point in the most beautiful uniform imaginable with his family and friends watching. He got to run and win races in front of his proud parents.

Jackie got to march along fire ridges at Camp Pendleton and Okinawa, carrying a dilapidated World War II backpack. When he asked about running track for the Marines at Parris Island, he was practically called a coward by everyone from sergeant to lieutenant colonel.

And the famous dress blue uniform, the striking symbol of USMC tradition, the recruiters' best tool that "made women moist between their legs." Corporal Jackie Carroll was told he could buy one when he got back from Vietnam. The cost was about $180.00, two months pay at his current level.

So when word was relayed to Mike Carroll that Jimmy Wagner wanted a three-mile time trial to be run along West Point's rugged cross-country course, he said yes. It would be like old times, he thought, only his brother wouldn't be in the race.

Honey was the first to notice the Ford Galaxy 500 following her and Mike, as they strolled along downtown Peekskill. Honey and Mike finished their soda at the Big Embo malt shop shortly before he was to begin his four-hour shift at the Peekskill post office.

Like most people in town, she knew the Galer brothers from the movie theater as super creepy guys who supervised the long lines in front and took cash at the popcorn counter. The dates that took Honey to the movies had money and didn't need to use the back door like the Carrolls did. Hence, she was unaware of the violence exacted on freeloaders by Robert and Richard Galer.

"Don't look now, but I think a car is following us," said Honey. "It's been behind us for the past five minutes."

Mike Carroll never looked back. He didn't have to.

"Tell me, does the car have a foxtail tail on the antenna?"

"Sure does," said Honey.

"See you later, alligator," shrieked Mike as he bolted down the street towards the church parking lot.

In a flash, the fire engine red car roared by Honey, its motor racing and tires squealing. The two numnuts were hanging out of the windows. It took Division Street on two wheels.

Carroll had been careful to avoid strolling along Peekskill city streets since his last pizza guy attack on Robert and Richard, but this new love jones he developed temporarily clouded his thinking. He'd have to be more careful in the future he thought as he bolted along.

He knew the Galers were out to get him, but thought they were still on the lam after beaning Eddie Redlight. Carroll was told an arrest warrant was in the system for Robert and Richard and hoped this time they'd go away for a while. At least until he finished his senior year.

Cutting across the Assumption School parking lot, Carroll diverted from his usual lengthy running route to the Catholic rectory and asked to speak to Monsignor Healy. He thought this would kill a few minutes.

"What's the purpose of the visit?" asked the monsignor's secretary, a matronly woman in her early sixties.

"It's about attending the College of the Holy Cross," said Carroll.

The monsignor's very busy at the moment, but he always has time to talk about Holy Cross," she said. "He went there you know."

The secretary walked down a long hallway to the monsignor's private office, which was located in the rear of the building. The rectory was one of Peekskill's most handsome buildings – a very old, stone, multi-story structure with a meticulously kept front lawn and beautiful shrubbery. Behind the structure was a long garage that housed the church's fleet of black Chevrolet cars. The monsignor, due to his rank, drove a Buick.

The interior of the rectory was wood paneled throughout with expensive brass and crystal lamps located in the waiting area. A fine, deep red carpet covered the wooden floors. For some reason, it reminded Carroll of the blood of Jesus.

The priests lived on the upper floors. The ground floor contained the kitchen, dining room, a meeting room and the monsignor's private office. The place was quiet. Not a sound of any type could be heard in the building, as Mike Carroll thumbed through a Catholic magazine that featured Reverend Fulton Sheen in Africa discussing birth control with a group of pygmies.

This was a different setup from the St Joseph's Home where the sisters of the Franciscan order lived. Mike had played baseball and basketball out at the Home on one of his old man's Catholic Youth Organization (CYO) teams, and knew the place well. As punishment for his incessant chatter in class, Mike was assigned to working parties after school. He'd hop on the 4 p.m. bus that took the nuns back to the Home and then proceed with whatever chores Sister Agnes had for him – clearing brush, scrapping icy sidewalks, moving furniture, and even waxing the floor to the chapel.

Mike thought the nuns lived in a clean, but glorified barracks. He thought the priests lived in a four-star hotel.

After a while, the monsignor came into the waiting room.

"Your ears must be burning," said the monsignor. "I was just on the phone with track coach Ray Hillenbrand up in Worchester, Mass., and he's following all your progress very closely. He's tickled beyond belief about the possibility of you going to school there, and is already counting all his IC4A, Millrose, and NCAA relay titles he's going to win with you running the eight-eighty anchor. What do you think about that, lad?"

"I think it's great, Monsignor. I've got a three-mile, cross-country time trial up at West Point next week. I'm going to run against Jimmy Wagner, who was IC4A champion last year."

"Know him well, Son. Great, gutty runner. You might have your hands full in the three mile. After all, your race is 880," said the monsignor.

"Not exactly," said Carroll. "I've been running lots of distance since Jackie died. I just like doing it. Keeps my mind off that day at the train station, and I feel Jackie with me when I run. It's like there's two of us running inside the same person. Kind of like the Holy Ghost."

"There's only one Holy Ghost, Son, and HE belongs to the Church," said the monsignor in an officious manner.

"Well then, I don't know what it is, but my brother's here. I can feel him."

"How do you plan on running this three mile race? What's your strategy against Wagner?" asked the monsignor.

"Don't know. Haven't thought about it."

"Son, you have to have a plan," said the monsignor. "Now Jimmy Wagner is a great distance runner. Jackie was the only one who ever beat him in high school, and Wagner is much better now. And running in the hills at West Point, he's going to have an sharp advantage."

"What do you think I should do, Sir?"

The monsignor rose and walked around the large living room, stroking his chin. This is what the monsignor really liked— developing race strategies, like he had done when he was a high school runner and state champion in Massachusetts, and later, running two-mile relays legs for the Cross against the likes of Ireland's Olympian Ron Delaney, a Villanova University trackster. Those were the monsignor's glory days – before he got the calling. And now, he guided a big time parish, constantly searched for more money, and listened to people's woes when he should have been listening to ballgames on the radio.

Usually, Monsignor Healey's counseling sessions dealt with unhappy married couples. The monsignor knew if he could just get rid of alcohol and philandering, most of the marriages in town would have a decent chance of survival. And survive they must, since divorce was out of the question and the most mortal of all sins in the Catholic Church. If he could find a cure for these two ailments, many people could grow old together a little less miserably, he reasoned.

"This is what you do, Mike Carroll," opined the monsignor. "Stay with him as long as you can. Simple as that. He'll take it out fast, so stay right behind him and drag off his wake. When you two get to the hills, don't dare challenge him, or he'll crush you. Those big legs of his were made for hill running. He'll pound those hills for all he's worth. Because that's where the race is won or lost. And he's smart—that's how he got into West Point."

Now more animated in his delivery, the monsignor continued. "Let him pull a little ahead and think he's got the race won. You'll be at the two-mile mark by now with only one more mile to go. The final stretch is downhill. How do you handle running downhill?" said the monsignor.

"It's the best part of my race. If I'm near someone at the finish, and there's a downhill, I can run it like a sprinter."

"Excellent. Just excellent," said the monsignor, as he looked at his watch and excused himself for an evening mass. "We'll talk about Holy Cross next time."

Mike let himself out the sanctuary's back door, first scanning the area for trouble. The talk took longer than he thought. It was getting dark, and he walked the half-mile or so to the post office for his evening shift. He was late. Tomorrow, he'd explain to Honey about the ongoing feud with the Galer brothers. Hell, it wasn't a feud. It was a war.

In a few short days, it was time to run the hard, three-mile timed run.

Mickey loved the idea of Mike running cross-country but offered him no tactics or suggestions on the ride up to West Point. He knew Mike ran effortlessly, his feet hardly touching the ground. He'd just pitter-patter along using the least amount of energy possible.

Cookie Reams and Honey showed up along with Monsignor Healy. Reams had gotten to know Mike a little better since he'd begun his part-time job at the post office. Even though Cookie worked the day shift, he and Mike would sometimes cross paths at shift change. When he found out about the three-mile race, he had to be there.

Marie was absent, having been called upon to help a grieving Gold Star Mother who had plunged into a sudden, deep depression. Mickey thought it healthy for Marie to help others through their terrible ordeals.

A dozen or so runners showed up at the West Point cross country course for the race – a few Academy JV runners and some local club guys – none of them a threat to win. Unlike the Yonkers 880, there wasn't much tension, and actually it seemed like a fun training event. Nothing formal. Just a time trial. The athletes wore summer workout uniforms. Wagner wore an Army Ranger T-shirt, and Carroll wore a Holy Cross Basketball jersey that the monsignor had given him.

Before the race, Wagner spoke to Mike, telling him once again how sorry he was about his brother's death and letting him know that he often had written to Jackie in Vietnam.

"My Sunday school class sent him lots of drawings and

cartoons, and he appreciated it," said the West Point man.

Honey and Cookie walked over to Mitchie Stadium, where West Point's football team was beginning its fall workouts. There, ballplayers grunted and groaned as they pushed tackling sleds from one side of the field to the other, while another group ran through a seemingly endless series of tire drills. Quarterbacks threw passes to receivers, and everywhere head coaches, assistant coaches and student coaches were yelling at the tops of their lungs:

"Hustle, hustle, oskie, oskie." Oskie was slang for fumble.

There was no starters' pistol for the three-mile run. The West Point head track coach lined up the runners and told them to follow the course, which was marked at every turn with white lime chalk.

And they were off.

Some West Point JV runners bolted to the front of the pack as the group moved out across the flat, grass plain and headed to the first serious hill. Everyone was together at the half-mile mark, but this soon changed as the first hill came into play. Still, a couple of JV runners and even one of the local club guys from Highland Falls held the lead with Wagner, Carroll and a few others directly behind them.

Honey and Cookie were shouting encouragement while the monsignor issued strict orders to Carroll: "Short strides on the hills, Michael. Short strides! You hear me?"

Upon reaching the first incline, Jimmy Wagner began to dig in, leaning into the hill the way he always did, and he soon had a ten-yard lead on the pack. Near the mile mark, the steep hills began to flatten out a little. Wagner was still in front. The cheering from down below faded and was replaced by sounds of heavy breathing – downright panting, in some instances.

"Come on up with me," shouted Wagner to Carroll as they ran along. "Come on up with me, so we can chat."

In a moment, Mike Carroll was on Wagner's shoulder and they ran together along footpaths near Fort Putnam, high above the West Point Campus.

They were surrounded by history.

Fort Putnam was built during the American Revolutionary War. It was erected for the purpose of defending Fort Clinton, which was located down below at West Point. It was built to guard the Hudson River against marauding British warships, and was under the supervision of Rufus Putnam and his Massachusetts volunteers. The Fort offered spectacular views of the Hudson River Valley, and its restored, fifty-foot walls on the Western slope were almost impossible for an enemy to overcome. Both Wagner and Carroll had been to the fort many times, with Wagner studying the fortifications for his civil engineering classes and Carroll playing war games as a little kid with his older brother Jackie.

The lead runners were a little past the one-mile mark now, and Carroll felt himself falling behind.

"Stay with me. You can handle it," encouraged the lead runner.

Carroll made a big effort once again to catch up and run on Wagner's shoulder – and for a short while he did, but he couldn't sustain the pace and began to fade.

No matter how hard he pumped his legs, Carroll couldn't contain the gap that was widening between him and the great West Point hill runner. Soon, Wagner was a full twenty seconds ahead and almost out of sight as the runners plowed along the curving, leaf-lined paths of the Fort Putnam redoubt.

The woods were quiet here, Carroll thought, unlike Blue Mountain where there were always birds and squirrels chirping away. Carroll could hear his breathing and feel his legs pounding hard against the dirt path. He usually ran effortlessly, but he realized that he had never run steep hills at this sustained pace. This was a killer, Carroll thought.

After a while, the uphill climb ended with the hills gradually giving way to a beautiful plateau of late summer flowers. Someone had written "2 mile" on the path with white chalk.

Carroll couldn't see Wagner, who had to be 150 yards ahead by now. Running along the flat expanse gave Carroll a breather and brought some life back into his tired legs. One mile to go.

Up ahead, Carroll heard some cheering, and when he transitioned from the path to roadway, he saw MPs standing next to a jeep. They were there to block all vehicular traffic while the time trial was going on.

What a great place, he thought. At his own high school, the bus drivers actually tried to run him off the road and into a snow-filled ditch on Route 6. West Point – what a great place.

With less than a mile to go, Carroll could see Wagner now about 125 yards ahead, still a monumental distance to make up. But downhill running was his forté. Carroll reasoned that he ran downhill so fast because he was light on his feet. To him, it felt effortless to sprint down a hill. Whereas running uphill seemed like a form of torture, especially when the pace was too fast.

The MPs gave Carroll a big "atta-boy" when he raced by them.

"I'm going to catch your guy," he said to them, as he began his long downhill sprint.

"No way," they shouted back.

Carroll figured he was three-quarters of a mile from the finish – with a half-mile downhill before leveling off for a 400-yard sprint to the tape.

He was running by Michie Stadium, and he could hear the coaches shouting at the football players.

"Down, Up, Down, Up, Oskie, Oskie."

Carroll's legs were moving so fast that he felt he was in danger of falling forward and face down. He was simply bolting down the hills, running as fast as a sprinter. Carroll was certainly tired but not nearly as fatigued as on the way up.

Down below on the flats, one hundred or so coaches, athletes, and evening strollers stopped what they were doing to watch the sight unfolding before them. Wagner moved along with great purpose towards the finish line, but was being chased down by this wild-ass kid.

With two hundred meters to go in the race, Carroll had caught Wagner and moved up to his shoulder, even inching slightly ahead.

When he saw himself getting the better of Wagner, Carroll ratcheted back a notch and the two ran to the finish line together.

They finished in a dead heat.

The monsignor congratulated Mickey while Honey and Cookie were quick with the cups of water and sweat pants.

Wagner and Mike Carroll hugged after the race, and each walked away to join their friends.

The West Point coach had the race timed in thirteen minutes, twenty-five seconds, which obliterated the old course record by almost a minute. Carroll seemed uninterested in his time as he high-fived with Cookie while Honey rubbed down his sweating neck.

Jimmy Wagner's Timex showed him passing the two-mile mark in a little over nine minutes – about a twenty to twenty-five second lead on his opponent with the last mile remaining, and it was mostly downhill.

As a second-year engineering student, Wagner was unusually precise about his calculations, and he simply shuddered about what this all meant.

Mike Carroll had run his last mile in under four minutes.

The Catholic Girls

Mickey thought Marie's intervention with the troubled Gold Star Mother would help in her own healing process, but he was wrong. Five days after meeting with Mrs. Louise Alforni, a 39-year-old grieving mother from McKinley Street whose young boy, "Sonny," died of "multiple gunshots to the head and neck, near Nui Loc Son, South Vietnam," Marie was still in the tank, her behavior more bizarre than ever.

Mickey couldn't figure out what went wrong; Marie had seemed to be getting better. He pressed her for details.

"What happened at Mrs. Alforni's house?" he asked. "What did you two talk about? What is it? What's the matter, love?"

Marie was closed mouth on the issue, saying whatever transpired was between her and her new "Catholic" Gold Star friend.

Knowing Marie as well as he did, and that she had no use for the Church, Mickey sensed serious trouble. But the harder he pressed her for answers, the more withdrawn she became. It was no use. He couldn't get through to her on any level.

Marie had stopped getting up in the mornings to prepare sandwiches for the kids' long days at summer camp. The wash, although done by the children, remained unfolded, in a heap at the bottom of the cellar stairs.

Take-out pizza was on the menu night after night, which wasn't a bad thing as far as the kids were concerned, but was troubling for Mickey and Mike.

Around noon, Marie started with her daily routine of drinking vodka and playing the Zulu warrior "jungle music" at such a high decibel that it shook pictures off the walls. When Mickey and the kids returned home at night, Marie was passed out on the couch in a disheveled mess.

"What's wrong with Mom?" asked daughter Laura, shaking her unresponsive mother.

"She's got the blues," Mickey chimed in from the kitchen.

"Can she get a shot or something for it?" asked Laura.

"No, it's nothing like that. Mom's just tired, and sometimes when she thinks about Jackie, she gets sad," said Mickey. "Don't worry Honey, it'll go away."

"What will go away? Mom? Or the blues?"

"Why, the blues, of course."

Mike was the first to bring up the subject. He knew it would be confrontational, but there was no way around it. It was time.

"Mom might not be right in the head," he said to a startled Mickey, whose only response was to deny and defend.

"How could you say that about your mother? She's just stressed, that's all. You know what she's gone through with your brother's death."

"Dad, she needs help. Can we take some of Jackie's insurance money and send her to a psychiatrist?"

"No, no. We can't touch that money! It's for the little ones, for their future," said a defiant Mickey. "They all can't run as fast as you."

The Department of Defense had recently mailed a $10,000 death gratuity to the family. This, plus the $372.00 Jackie had in his pay account was all the family received for losing their young son in Vietnam. Many years earlier, Mickey had taken out a three thousand dollar whole-life insurance policy on each of the kids, but let the policies lapse when he could no longer afford the monthly premiums.

Mickey had made a Broadway production out of opening a special savings account with his son's Vietnam death gratuity. He marched down to the Peekskill Bank on Main Street and, in full view of tellers and customers, held the green government check for $10,000 high in the air while announcing that this money – Jackie's money – would be used to fund college and weddings for the other five children.

Most of the tellers who worked at the Peekskill Bank thought

Mickey's gesture was an outstanding one, but realized that the amount compounded at three-percent interest would do little to cover everyone's weddings and college expenses. Maybe it would provide enough money for a year's tuition, plus room and board, but that was for only one child.

"How can we get Mom in to see a psychiatrist?" demanded Mike.

"There you go again," said his father, growing more exasperated. "Psychiatrists are for Jews. Jews go to psychiatrists; Catholics see their priest."

Mike cut him off. "Mom hates the priests and she'll never talk to them."

"What's wrong with you people?" asked a visibly upset Mickey. "Look what the monsignor is doing for you. He's personally trying to get you into the best Catholic college in the country. Tuition free. Room and board free. Even this laundromat money. All free, care of the same church you and your mother always ridicule.

"This is just like the business with the orthodontist," said Mike. "Laura's teeth are so crooked the kids at school call her names, and she cries every day. And she's a beautiful girl. Absolutely beautiful. But you won't pay for her braces because only the 'vain' get braces."

"Don't blasphemy your sister!" screamed Mickey. "Leave her out of this."

"That's it, I'm going to call Dr. Sheldon's office and see how much a psychiatrist's visit will cost."

"You'll do no such thing!" Mickey shrieked. "You'll not take part in spreading any false rumors about this family. Word always gets around town when someone pokes their head in that Jew-boy's office. You want people saying your mother is a Lizzy Borden ax murderer or some such thing? Mom is tired and stressed out. That's all. She's just got the blues."

"Mom's a drunk, and you know it. And now she's crazy too."

"Never talk that way about your mother. I'll smack you, if you ever say anything like that again. And I don't care what a big track star you are."

"Mom's a drunk. People have been laughing at her for years. And your friends, your close, close singing friends at Sorentino's… Every time you and Mom came back from a night at the bar, me and Jackie would have to listen to the stories at school. Mom spilling drinks, Mom kissing men. Mom throwing fits."

"Stop, Stop!" yelled Mickey. "Your mother and I were great singers – Irish tenors, they called us. The tenor and soprano. We lit up the bar. Everyone wanted to come on Friday nights and listen to us sing 'Danny Boy.' They said I sounded like Bing Crosby and your mother like Gertrude Lawrence. How's that for compliments? You're not the only one around here who gets noticed. We'd have a nice dinner and Sal would invite us up to the bar for a few songs. Never paid for a drink."

Mickey was pacing back and forth now.

"We sang 'Danny Boy,' 'Stardust,' 'Ave Maria,' and, 'White Christmas' during the holidays. And we packed 'em in. They came up from Verplanck and Montrose and Croton… and even Angela Lansbury, the Broadway actress, listened to your mother sing one time and said, 'Marie, you belong on the stage.' Imagine that. A big time star saying that to your mother.

"I'm telling ya, they came up the Hudson River on the same New York Central train that brought your brother home. They didn't come in for a nightcap. They came to see her. That 'drunk' you refer to."

"Pop… oh Pop, you're taking this all wrong," said Mike.

"No, no! You had your say, now I'll have mine," Mickey stormed.

"She's had six kids, count 'em. SIX. You know how many kids the Protestant bitches on this street have? TWO. Just two kids. And you know why?" grumbled Mickey.

"You know why?" he screamed in Mike's face. "So they won't get cramped in their fancy cars driving to Sparkle Lake. Two in the front, two in the back, just like the commercials on television. Ain't that grand. Depriving a life, so you can drive comfortably in the country."

"You're not getting the point, Pop," said Mike. "This isn't about cars or kids. It's about Mom's sickness, or whatever you choose to call it."

Strutting his stuff, Mickey continued, "Who's got the biggest doughboy pool in the neighborhood? Answer me that, hot shot. Who's got the biggest, deepest, doughboy pool maybe in the whole city of Peekskill? Well, I can tell you now. It's us. Mickey Carroll's family. And you know why we have it? Because of that drunk in there. She's the one that made me buy it so you kids would have something to brag about. I wanted to buy the smaller pool, but she wouldn't hear of it. She used the money I gave her for her birthday to make up the difference," said Mickey, as he began to weep.

Marie appeared at the kitchen door and walked over to Mickey who was sitting, slumped down in a chair.

"What's all the commotion around here?" she asked. "I was just taking a little nap before dinner. I've got to get cooking now."

She looked lovingly at Mickey, and then pulling his head closely to her bosom, began to slowly rock him. Turning to their son Mike she said, "This has all been so hard on your father. He tries to be the Rock of Gibraltar, but you know, he's just an old accountant."

In her soprano voice with the pitch of an angel, Marie began to sing to Mickey:

Oh, Danny boy, the pipes, the pipes are calling
From glen to glen, and down the mountain side
The summer's gone, and all the flowers are dying
'Tis you, 'tis you must go and I must bide.
But come ye back when summer's in the meadow
Or when the valley's hushed and white with snow
'Tis I'll be here in sunshine or in shadow
Oh Danny boy, oh Danny boy, I love you so.

Mike walked out of the kitchen as Marie continued to sing and rock Mickey's head.

And I shall hear, tho' soft you tread above me
And all my dreams will warm and sweeter be
If you'll not fail to tell me that you love me
I'll simply sleep in peace until you come to me.

The French
Connection

At the French consulate in New York City, Monsieur Lambeau was busy drafting cables in his office – so busy in fact, that his hand hurt from writing. As a former paratrooper, Lambeau always penciled his messages. A trick he learned during years on the job when no typewriters were available in outposts such as Libya, Algeria, Chad and Vietnam.

Lambeau was writing to the French Council of Sport, the overall authority for amateur athletics in his country. The FCS controlled French participation in the Olympic games and national traveling teams that represented the country. Sometimes, the Council of Sport even put its nose in the final selection of the football (soccer) and rugby teams, which were professional but often bowed to the demands of the council.

The FCS was comprised of mostly old French aristocracy who served as unpaid directors. The real guts of the organization was centered in a Paris suburb, and it was there that decisions were made affecting athletes' lives.

It was at the FCS that Monsieur Lambeau ran into his first hurdle, and it wasn't the kind one sprints over. This was an archaic group of self-promoters who regarded Michel Jazy's world mile record as their own. And they guarded his great accomplishment as if it were a bottle of expensive Bordeaux wine. Lambeau read the FCS memo.

Translated, it read:

From: French Council of Sport, Paris

To: French Consulate, New York City, New York, USA

Via: French Embassy, Washington, DC, USA

Subject: Travel Schedule of Track Athlete Michel Jazy

On 1 August, this office received a cable from Claude Lambeau, French Consulate General's office, New York City. The cable asked for the council's permission to grant French-born world record holder Michel Jazy authority to run a race in the State of New York in the USA, as part of his return trip from California.

Further, Mr. Lambeau suggested that world record holder Jazy compete against a high school student along with some less notable club runners.

Because Michel Jazy represents the very best of French sporting tradition and his presence is requested all over the world in often large, televised track meets, the Council feels this race to be totally beneath his ability and stature as a world record holder and a great waste of his sporting time. Absent of comment from Mr. Jazy, this council rejects the request.

Lambeau was fuming when he received the reply from the Council of Sport.

How dare they, he thought. How dare they make light of a serious request from the field?

Lambeau knew that a diplomat's mission was never clearly defined and that he had to use his best judgment in most instances because there was no clear guidance in place. Protect France and promote its culture was foremost in all dealings, domestic and abroad. And this wasn't only about a track meet; it was about extending a helping hand to an important, friendly nation.

This disrespect was simply a case of battling back the French dogma that originated with some stuffed shirts along the Seine and infiltrated all areas of his great country's customs and culture.

France was not above reproach. Lambeau knew that. He had been around.

It was also suggested through the French diplomatic grapevine that former Parachute Colonel Lambeau was suffering from a reoccurring bout of river fever that he had picked up in Faya-Largeau during his posting to Chad.

"I've never even had river fever!" he shouted in the hallway, as he moved towards the radio room with great purpose. He was going to send a rebuttal cable.

Monsieur Lambeau had promised the Americans he'd make a best faith effort on the track meet, and he intended to keep his word. It's what the French did, he reasoned. It's what made them special. But there was more to this, he admitted to himself. Former Colonel Lambeau had friends who had been killed fighting in Vietnam. He had spent almost three years in that country and cut his teeth on guerilla tactics, covering thousands of miles of landscape on foot, in river dugouts and by airplane.

France had occupied Vietnam since 1884. Independence was proclaimed after World War II and the French continued to rule until they were defeated at Dien Bien Phu by the communist revolutionary leader Ho Chi Minh and his well-armed guerilla army.

Lambeau had missed the battle of his lifetime because he had transferred out of Vietnam six months before the communists attacked in force. He was far away from the fighting, reading message traffic from desperate French ground commanders who first asked, then begged for more paratroopers, artillery pieces, and ammunition. And later, whole blood, morphine, bandages, and finally, body bags.

From his posting in Algiers as military attaché, Colonel Lambeau had access to all the classified French military messages, and what he read day after day made him want to be "mort pour la France." The destruction of France's best fighting units: legionnaires, paratroopers, infantry, air assets, medical doctors and nurses, and civilian aid workers. All gone.

Next, came the systematic slaughter of thousands of French soldiers who surrendered because they were promised humane treatment by their captors. But what they got was a cup of worm-infested rice every other day and filthy river water to drink. They slept on the ground in rain and mud, in their own urine and feces. They were given no medicine for their festering wounds. And they died by the hundreds, deliberately killed by their guards at the direction of communist leaders.

When the end finally came for French forces in Vietnam and the high command ordered ground commanders to surrender to the Vietminh, Claude Lambeau walked to the roof of the his embassy overlooking the deep blue waters of the Mediterranean, took a long drag on his Gitanes cigarette and cried.

Now, Lambeau thought it was his turn to do something positive about Vietnam, and in a small way he was. Helping these Americans build a war memorial by having Michel Jazy run a track meet was no big deal.

The race would be covered by *The New York Times* and all the big East Coast newspapers. He would make sure of it. And Peekskill was close enough to New York City so that major television networks could film the race and play it on French national television.

Mais oui!

And then this young girl, Mademoiselle Sanders. How could she know about the fierce battles at Dien Bien Phu, he thought. Not much had been written about it at the time, a few books maybe, and certainly not much in America—or their leaders wouldn't have been stupid enough to commit ground troops to Vietnam. And how in God's name could she have known about the 5/7 Algerian Rifles and the fighting at Claudine and Dominique? Was she reading secret French message traffic? How could she know?

The New VIP

Nothing in the world could have made Sal Fraggo's day better than the letter he received from the superintendent of West Point – a three-star general officer – thanking him for "his generous contribution to the athletic program."

The letter came in the morning mail Marci was sorting. There were the usual bills, advertisements, and hand written letters requesting employment for some paisan right off the boat: "My cousin, he's from your home town in Napoli."

Bullshit. Fraggo knew his family were guinea bastards from Sicily, with half of them hailing from Catania and the remainder from Palermo.

"What a beautiful envelope," said Marci, as she rubbed the West Point letter between her fingertips. "And it looks so official."

"Let me see that!" yelled Sal from his inner office

Marci, looking every bit Annette Funicello with her beehive hairdo, white blouse, tight black skirt and stiletto heels, carried the letter into her boss's office. She wore some kind of ordinary perfume, that a lot of the kids wore, but on her it smelled as fine as the morning air. He studied the letter a long time before opening it. The letter felt important, and in Fraggo's mind, that made him important.

He held it out like a fine cigar, turning it around in his hand in order to examine every crease. And then with the utmost care, he opened it. A beautiful textured paper with an embossed engraving of West Point. At the very top of the page were three blue stars signifying the rank of the superintendent, a lieutenant general.

Dear Mr. Fraggo—

I am responding to your kind donation to the West Point athletic program, namely the varsity baseball team. It gives me great pleasure to associate our institution with fine people such as you.

At West Point, we strive for excellence both in the classroom as well as on the athletic field, hoping to develop excellent officers the country can be proud of. Our varsity teams compete against the finest collegiate schedule possible, including the biggest and best schools in football, basketball, track and field, baseball and many other sports.

We do not give athletic scholarships, and we seldom ask alumni for cash donations because most of our graduates are career military officers who have served their country first, and lastly themselves. Many do not have the means to send sums of money like they do at Ivy League Schools.

Our budget for sports continues to be tight as money first goes to fund academics, training and equipment, and lastly, sports. So when someone like you comes along and so graciously donates large sums of money for capital improvements to our baseball facility, we stand up, take notice and salute you.

Accordingly, I have put you on our list of VIPs. You will have complimentary season tickets to our football and basketball home games and sit in the 'reserved' section. You will be among Generals, Senators, Congressmen, Astronauts, Movie Stars and all others who have served their country and contributed to the health and welfare of West Point. You will receive in a short while, listings of all official functions at West Point for the academic year. You will be invited to many of these. I would personally enjoy your company in my private box for our opening home football game against Boston College.

Thanking you for your contributions to West Point athletics, I am

A.K. 'Archie' Bowers
Lieutenant General, U.S.A.

Marci was yelling from the outer office that Sal had important phone calls backed up, but he just waved her off. He didn't say a word as he continued to read and re-read the letter. Sal felt a rush of happiness that he hadn't experienced since the day he ran leadoff on Cardinal Spellman's 4 x 440 relay team. He had not only been exonerated from his bout of kleptomania at the commissary, but had in effect been "knighted" by the general in charge of West Point.

Very soon, Sal would be sitting next to astronaut Alan Shepard and maybe even Mamie Eisenhower. And he was going to bring Annette Funicello with him. Not bad for a kid the guidance counselor said would wind up working in a paper box factory in New Jersey.

"Sal! Sal!" yelled Marci. "Mr. Fraggo you have an important call from the mayor of Peekskill."

"Ah fangoule," said Sal, as he picked up the phone.

From her spot in the hallway she could see the expression changing on her boss's face. That happy and pleased look had given way to one of anguish. And, Sal wasn't saying much, which was never a good sign. For a long period he listened intently on the phone while doodling on his notepad.

"Can we give him more money?" Sal asked over the phone. "I can double his appearance fee. Double the fuckin' thing, and I'll throw in a few hookers from Manhattan. I know those guys are players. In other words, I'll do whatever it takes."

Sal was wiping his brow.

"OK, OK, I'll talk to you later," he said, hanging up the phone.

Fraggo picked up the West Point letter. "Hey Marci, come on in here. Let me read you this," said Sal. Nothing was going to ruin this morning for him.

"Was there a problem with the mayor's office?" asked Marci, who knew she was getting dangerously close to crossing the line into Fraggo's business.

Taken aback a bit by her question, Fraggo thought quickly about admonishing her, but gave way to her true feelings of concern.

"Nothing we can't work out," he said. "That flattop bastard King and His Court guy is carping about his appearance fee." Fraggo shook his head.

"Those idiots over in Danbury are offering him a lot more money to stay there and play in a doubleheader. If he does that, he'll have to cancel our Peekskill game with the All-Stars, and that can't happen."

"What are you going to do about it?" asked Marci.

"Nothing right now," he said. "Let me read you this letter."

Later that afternoon, Fraggo was at Indian Point power plant in Montrose, trying to settle a dispute with the general contractor. Seems company field accountants had as much trouble finding workers during the evening hours as Colonel Parrish did finding his mercenary army along the Ho Chi Minh trail. Beaucoup VC.

On any given night, two hundred or so workers should be on the grounds toiling in some capacity, but it was not always the case.

Company field agents wearing white hats (as opposed to red hats for laborers, green hats for carpenters and purple hats for operating engineers) couldn't find but a hundred or so workers. The grounds were huge, and there were a lot of places they could be. But no matter how hard the "white hats" looked for the men, they were nowhere to be found.

This had been a major problem on the job since construction began. As a matter of fact, it was a problem on all big, poorly-supervised construction projects in the New York and New Jersey areas.

Everyone on the job knew the routine. At 4 p.m., all laborers lined up at the accounting shack to pick up their "brass" for the mid-shift. And generally, they did. Two hundred, or two hundred and fifty, whatever the evening schedule called for.

Each individual was handed a brass cookie with a number on it identifying him or her. The workers carried these cookies with them throughout the shift and produced them whenever asked by company officials. Field accountants showed up unannounced a couple of times per month to run audits.

At the end of shift, workers lined up twenty minutes prior to quitting time and then returned the brass, throwing them back into the accounting shack's window in a conflagration of activity. Sometimes, a worker threw a boatload of brass cookies back in the window and beat it to the parking lot before the bean counters could get off their asses and give chase. It was a truly bad system made worse by union refusal to change procedures.

Fraggo now had to deal with a fifty percent no-show rate during an on-job inspection by the lead contractor. His guys checked in to work all right but left later on to practice softball for a few hours, then have a few beers, a little calzone, and a quick nap, or a quick poke to the girlfriend. Before long, it was time to turn in one's brass and go home after a good night's work.

Fraggo had concocted stories along the way about his men (who were also volunteer firemen) rushing to the firehouse to help with emergencies.

Another group of workers he said had to fish for eels near the warm water discharge area so they could give them to poor people in Spanish Harlem. Fraggo would make excuses for yet another cadre of his men who got caught napping under trees, saying, "Hey, my guys are not fighting gooks in Vietnam. They need their rest now and then."

When surprise inspections took place, Fraggo put on his thinking cap and went to work. He could plead his case the best way he knew how or bust balls and threaten a work stoppage, whatever the situation called for. Sal Fraggo was an old pro at dealing with the stiffs at the company. It's how he earned his stripes.

But this time was different. His home-run hitting transplant, Lil' Trenton Jackson, was caught pounding his licorice stick upside a prostitute's head on South Street in Peekskill. Her yelling summoned the cops who promptly arrested Jackson. When they searched him, they found fifty brass cookies that Lil' Trenton Jackson was to toss in the bucket with a perfect hand jive when he returned from his midnight pussy hunt.

Jackson even asked the cops to drive him back to Indian Point so he could give the cookies to a co-worker who could toss them in the bucket. Lil' Trenton Jackson was a stand-up guy.

The cops, of course, said no way and promptly reported all this to the operator of the plant. A police report was written detailing Jackson's sexual battery and his holding of fifty brass cookies; it was made to look as if he was trying to defraud his employer.

When confronted with this confusing situation of total job malfeasance, Fraggo, the newly knighted VIP of the West Point athletic department, thought he had the perfect answer: he'd call for a work stoppage.

But, first things first. Sal had to pop his long ball hitter out of the Peekskill hoosegow, and in doing so, had to put up a twenty-five thousand dollar bail bond. Not a big deal. Typically, a bond of this sort cost ten percent with the proper collateral. After a few calls to his mafia friends in the city, bail was arranged and Lil' Trenton Jackson was a free man, sitting back in Fraggo's stretch limo as it cruised along South Street.

"Stop here, man," Lil' Trenton Jackson yelled to the driver, as the car neared a string of seedy apartment buildings.

"What is it now?" asked Fraggo.

"I got to go in here and get my stuff," said Jackson, as he bolted from the car. "Be back in a few."

After fifteen minutes or so, Jackson emerged from the building carrying a bag of clothes and a few broken trophies.

"What's all this shit?" asked Sal.

"My woman put me out," said Jackson. "She said I got my last nut off a prostitute."

"Where are you going to stay?"

"In the reactor. We got a couple of cots in the tool shed, so for sure I won't miss any more work."

Oh Jesus, Sal thought. When's this going to end?

How did he ever get so involved with this softball team? He had as many as five hundred workers at any one time under his direct employ, and paid tribute to mob bosses in New York City and Brooklyn. From time to time, he found crude electronic listening devices in his lamps, door jam and phone. No telling what the feds knew about his business dealings. And now, the softball All-Star game was turning into a full-time job.

How in the fuck did I ever get involved in this softball tournament? Fraggo thought. He shook his head and wiped his brow.

Looking directly at Lil' Tenton Jackson, he said, "My man, I got to figure out a way to keep them from firing you. The shirts are on the warpath about your fuckin' up with the whores. We might have to put you on ice for a while. Let this thing blow over. They're going to want your ass."

"I'm sorry, Mr. Fraggo, it won't happen again. If you can do this for me, I'll hit more home runs for you than Mickey Mantle."

Sal smiled. That's all he needed to hear. He'd work it out with the company.

November
Company

Walking point twenty-five yards ahead of the main column, Sgt. Zoeller was the first to spot the tripwire – a thin vine, suspended about four inches above the ground. A miracle find.

In training back in the States, point men looked for trip wires until their eyes bugged out of their heads. From the swamps of North Carolina to the parched hills of Southern California, Marines and soldiers looked for the tiniest anomaly in the landscape in front of them – from a fresh mound of earth to fishing wire and camouflaged vines stretched along a trail.

In training, trip wires were hard to spot. In combat, they were next to impossible. Trying to slash one's way through an overgrown jungle path and finding one vine out of a million that was connected to an unexploded, American 500-pound bomb? An absolute miracle find.

"What the fuck is it now?" screamed Captain Oates over the PRC 25 radio, as the column came to an immediate halt.

Gunny Martin reached for the handset.

"Six, this is Two Actual. I'll check it out and get back with you. Over." With his heart nearly pounding out of his chest, Gunny Martin raced up along the column to Zoeller who was on his hands and knees. Gunny came to a complete stop. Using hand signals, Zoeller pointed to the trip wire then waved Gunny Martin back. No telling what the wire was attached to.

Zoeller was the best point man he ever had in the company, Gunny thought.

"What do I tell the captain?" Martin yelled.

"Tell him to take a real good shit," said Zoeller, as he meticulously followed the slightly discolored vine along the trail's edge.

"Easy for you to say."

"Do you think it's attached to anything?" asked Gunny.

"Don't know yet," answered the little point man, who was perspiring profusely as he half crawled along the trail. Zoeller had taken his helmet off and dropped it with his pack back along the trail. He was all alone out there now.

What balls, thought Gunny. What humongous balls this little half-pint squirt has. Someday when Zoeller is delivering mail in Ohio or Indiana or upstate New York and someone teases him about his five-point veterans advantage on the civil service test, I hope he remembers this day and then tells that civilian piece of shit where to go.

"Two Actual, this is November Six. Provide me an update. ASAP," screamed the captain over the radio.

"Six, this is Two Actual. Nothing yet. Our guy is checking it out," said Gunny. He handed the handset back to the radioman. "Everyone take five and rest for a few!" he yelled. "Face outboard, and don't go to sleep on me," he added for emphasis.

Scattered along the trail, Marines plopped down where they were. Many searched for spots of shade to shield them from the burning sun. Uniforms were drenched with sweat. Some Marines sat on their helmets, but most of them just dropped back on their heavy packs, trying to avoid getting goosed by a mortar or a rocket round they were carrying.

Along the trail they could hear the metallic sounds of M-60 machine guns, M-16 rifles, M-79 grenade launchers and 60 and 81 mm mortar tubes clanging and banging against each other. The column dropped first to their knees, and then to their asses. There was nothing quiet about a Marine rifle company "taking five" in the bush. November Company had already walked close to 12,000 meters up a steep mountain path in 110-degree heat, carrying enough ammunition to hold off half the North Vietnamese Army.

Corporal Jackie Carroll leaned back on his pack, thankful for the break. His pants were completely ripped through in the crotch and with no skivvies on (underwear was seldom worn in the jungle), his wiener lay on the dirt trail like a tired little reptile.

He drank water from his canteen and massaged his hands and knees, which were severely bruised and cut from his near death fall.

In a few days, these cuts will be infected, he thought. Everything got infected in the jungle.

Jackie Carroll reached into his pants' cargo pocket and pulled out some letters from home. While out in the bush, Carroll would read and re-read his favorite letters. It made him feel closer to the ones he loved. He found a manila envelope with a dozen or so Easter drawings that his good friend and running partner Jimmy Wagner from West Point had sent him. Wagner taught a Sunday school class and always remembered his friend in Vietnam.

Carroll looked at the drawings, which were done with crayons on yellowed drawing paper. He held one of them up and studied it. This one was his favorite because it reminded him so much of home. It was a drawing of Fort Putnam near West Point where he had played as a young kid with his brother, Mike. It showed the high walls, old gun emplacements, barracks, and the Hudson River below. In the center of the drawing, the little boy had written CP for command post.

What a smart little kid, Corporal Carroll thought. He probably had a father who was a major or colonel teaching at West Point.

Corporal Carroll carefully folded his favorite drawing and put it in his right breast pocket so he could look at it again later. He put the remaining drawings back inside the manila envelope and stuffed it inside his cargo pants' pocket.

Just then, a mighty pissed off Captain Oates and his radio man passed by with purposeful stride, moving towards the front of the column.

"Stay alert, Marines!" Oates shouted, as he moved along the column. "Stay alert."

Up ahead, Captain Oates stopped to quiz Larry the retarded Polack Pulaski.

"How many extra barrels do you have for your gun?" asked Oates.

"Two, Captain," answered the machine gunner.

"I've got one, and the second platoon is humping the other," said the corporal.

"Get all the barrels up with you. Might not be time when we hit the gooks."

The big machine gunner passed word back in the column for

the extra machine gun barrel to be passed forward. The M-60 machine gun fired at a cyclic rate of about 500 to 550 rounds per minute. It was, of course an absurd amount of rounds because the gun would never be fired that fast. It just wouldn't work. The rounds would begin to jam or alternatively "cook off" due to high heat. Barrels on the machine gun would actually turn bright red from overuse, and when that happened, the 7.62 caliber rounds might begin to "cook off" with the gun firing itself whether the trigger was pulled or not. The heat would be so intense in the chamber that rounds would fire before the firing pin even hit them. That's why troops carried interchangeable barrels.

And never lose the asbestos glove. Without it, the hot barrel would burn a Marine's hand through to the bone. It had happened before, but never to the retarded Polack. He had the asbestos glove tied to his belt.

Up on point, Sgt. Zoeller traced the trip wire to a camouflaged mound of brush on the side of the trail. Ever so methodically, he put his hand in the pile until it came upon something hard and cylindrical. There were no "bomb techs" that traveled with the rifle companies. If a booby trap or land mine was found, it was either blown in place or marked for an air strike. Usually, the person who found it had to deal with it. And at this hour, it was Sgt. Zoeller.

Zoeller was a sweating mess now. He brushed back the leaves and vines to reveal a dull green, American-made MK-82, 500-pound bomb. He slowly crawled back to meet the remainder of November Company, which had moved one hundred yards from the device.

"It's a five-hundred pounder, Gunny," said the skinny point man. "It would have wiped out an entire platoon."

Captain Oates, who was listening to this dialogue, walked up to Zoeller and shook his hand.

"When we get back, I'm putting you in for a Silver Star medal," said the captain. "What should we do, Gunny?"

Gunny Martin lit a cigarette and scratched his noggin and then his balls.

"This is bad juju, Captain. Real bad juju. Means the Gooks are up ahead and waiting for us. This bomb was to slow us down so they could continue to dig in. We got 'em on the run, but I think they're going to dig in and fight. Charlie knows we'd take casualties and have to call in a med-evac helicopter. This bomb would give him another hour or so to get ready, and fuck us up at the same time."

At that moment, the captain's radioman was shouting that Red Rock Six (the battalion commander) was on the net.

"Oh, shit!" said Oates.

Turing to his radio man, he said, "Tell Redrock, I'm inspecting an explosive device and I'll get back with him in a few."

Captain Oates knew the battalion commander wasn't going to like that response, but he had other things on his mind and keeping some rear area pogue happy wasn't one of them.

The captain and company gunny came up with a plan. After the bomb was neutralized by removing the trip wire from the trail, the column at rout step would move up the path towards the objective. If the enemy was setting up ahead, November Company might catch them flatfooted while still digging in and waiting for the 500-pounder to go off.

It wasn't a great plan, thought the Gunny, but it was a plan and better than anything the fuck-ups in the rear could offer.

"Saddle up," came the command, as the column of Marines moved out at a rapid pace.

Corporal Jackie Carroll felt a jolt of adrenalin as he marched with the column. Along with thousands of rounds of ammunition, the big machine gunner had all his extra barrels close by. Captain Oates told Red Rock Six that his Marines had successfully avoided a dreaded 500-pound bomb that would have caused enormous casualties, to which the battalion commander actually gave the captain an "atta-boy."

Gunny Martin continued to shout at the troops: "Move out and keep your interval."

The little emaciated point man lead the column.

Ahead on the trail, elements of the 324th and 351st North Vietnamese Divisions continued to dig in, as their overall commander waited for his prize booby trap to go off. After all, they had hauled the bomb for miles, suspended from skinny bamboo poles, waiting for a chance like this. The booby trap had to go off. When it did, it would pinpoint the Marines' position, slow their advance, and inflict heavy casualties.

The NVA troops had followed their orders precisely and were dug in forty to fifty meters above the trail, which ran about a quarter of a mile. To the front, where the ambush would stop the Marines, hundreds of heavily-camouflaged soldiers waited in their fighting positions. They had a total of fifteen light machine guns and hundreds of mortar rounds.

The overall NVA commander was looking at his watch while studying his map. By his own very precise calculations, the Marine infantry unit should have already passed the 500-pound bomb. They couldn't have found it, he thought, as his best men had placed it and no one ever discovered their booby traps.

Had the Marines changed plans? he wondered. Had they moved off the trail?

Could an air strike be coming in that would wipe out his forces before they could engage the enemy in close-in fighting?

"Danh o dau?" (Why no bang-bang?), asked the senior NVA commander to his operations officer. He was growing exasperated. *"Danh o dau?"*

The NVA commander blinked first. He decided to send a small reconnaissance platoon down the trail to determine where exactly the enemy was. His 25-man platoon could melt into the jungle if they spotted the Americans coming up the trail. If Marines were digging in, waiting for reinforcements, the reconnaissance platoon would pick that up and relay the information back to headquarters. The NVA commander could then change his plans accordingly.

Eighteen-year-old Lin Duc Pham was selected to be part of the NVA recon platoon. During the long march down south, he had shown himself to be a capable soldier, and now he would be in the lead element of this prized and historic communist NVA division. But all Pham wanted to do was go home to his family's house along the Red River in North Vietnam and finish his pharmacy degree.

The First Marine Division's biggest battle since the Korean War began with, of all things, a little white chicken running across the footpath. Most Marines would have thought nothing of it. But most Marines were not like Sergeant Don Zoeller.

He saw the chicken up ahead and temporarily froze in place. A little chicken caused him as much worry as a 500-pound bomb. But this was every bit as lethal, thought Zoeller.

First, there were no villes (villages) around. No people. Chickens couldn't last a day in the jungle with so many predators around.

The NVA loved to eat them and stole as many as they could find from local villagers. They carried live chickens on their cartridge belts and popped them in boiling water at night for a good meal. Whenever Zoeller had found NVA campsites in the past, he found chicken feathers and bones and every now and then, a lucky chicken that got away. Like maybe this one.

The NVA were close, he thought. Real close.

The point man gave the word for Marines to get off the trail and move a few meters into the jungle.

"Get off the trail, and do it now!" he yelled. "And everyone quiet, not a damn word."

From the captain (who now regarded Zoeller as the reincarnation of legendary Marine Chesty Puller) to the newest private, the column melted into the surrounding jungle and was absolutely still.

Moving down the path with stern resolve, twenty-five heavily armed and camouflaged NVA soldiers walked right into the gun sites of the 2nd platoon of November Company. Before the captain could squawk on his radio, intense gunfire erupted from the front of the column.

All hell was breaking loose.

Ten to fifteen NVA were killed right off and the remaining soldiers ran back up the hill toward their lines. Spooked NVA soldiers on the other end of the path then accidentally gunned down their own returning troops.

The great ambushers had ambushed themselves.

The fight was on.

Corporal Jackie Carroll's heart was pounding as rifle rounds exploded in the dirt around him and cracked in his ear. This was nothing like Peekskill, nothing like the punishment inflicted on him by the hated Galers, nothing like the state finals. Nothing like it.

The communist forces were no more than three hundred yards

away, and they were there by the boatload – between seven and nine hundred men. Captain Oates rushed up to meet the lead elements of his column. He and the Gunny stood by while an interpreter questioned a wounded NVA soldier.

"*Doi ho o dau va boa nhieu ngoi?*" (Where are your forces, and how many are there?) he screamed at the dying man. "*De ho o quan doi nao?*" (What unit are you with?)

Before the soldier could answer, the dull thud of mortar rounds shooting out of their tubes could be heard in the distance. And there were many dull thuds.

"Incoming!"

Thoop, thoop, thoop, thoop, thoop, thoop, thoop, thoop.

Corporal Jackie Carroll looked up to see what looked like a swarm of bees descending on their positions.

The explosions were deafening. Marines were torn to ribbons as mortar rounds fell from the sky with deadly accuracy. As enemy 82mm mortar rounds found their marks, a mist of fine blood settled on the path.

Shrapnel hit Carroll in the first volley, cutting off his left ear as well as an index finger.

"Wrong hand!" Carroll screamed in pain. "You dinks hit me in the wrong hand. I can still shoot!" he yelled, as he rolled around in pain on the ground.

"Oh shit. Oh God. Oh Christ."

Gunny Martin took shrapnel in the back, buttocks and legs, but he was still around as if nothing happened.

November Company's 60 and 81 mm mortar sections flew into action, assembling their tubes and base plates in record time and lobbing their own shells up the hill. Lt. Behring, who began his career as an artillery officer, had the Marine mortar sections well trained and ready for action. And it sounded great.

Outgoing. Thoop…thoop…thoop…thoop…thoop…thoop… thoop….

Captain Oates and Gunny Martin radioed for immediate artillery strikes on positions directly in front of them. Gunny Martin knew the company was in a bad way – strung out on the trail like it was – but he also realized that they had saved themselves by not walking into an ambush site.

"Copycat, copycat (artillery support unit), this is November Six (Captain Oates). Request immediate fire support on target Rita as follows: From Gunslinger up three point five, right four point six. Repeat. From Gunslinger up three point five, right four point six. Fire for effect. No spotter rounds. The Gooks are all over us."

At the direction of the corpsman on the scene, Jackie Carroll was helping wounded men off the trail. About eight to ten Marines had been killed in the initial volley with another ten or so wounded. Some very badly.

His squad leader – Sgt. Don Zoeller, the bravest person he'd ever seen – was lying in a heap along side of the trail, practically decapitated.

Carroll's own wounds were now being treated. The corpsman put a large tape bandage where Carroll's ear had been; it didn't bleed much and surprisingly, it didn't hurt either. And now, he had only nine fingers.

"I'm all fucked up. What a freak show I am!" Carroll yelled to the retarded Polack.

The command group made a calculated decision to send half of November Company climbing straight up the hill to protect their right flank. The left flank provided little worry because it was a steep cliff and no forces could maneuver in that terrain.

"Carroll, get up there with the retarded Polack. Get all the ammunition you guys can carry and do it now!" screamed the Gunny. "They're going to flank us as soon as they figure out we're not waltzing into their fuckin' trap."

Captain Oates was on the PRC-25 talking to the battalion.

"Red Rock Six, this is November Six. Have encountered heavy enemy contact at target Rita. Friendly casualties at this point about ten KIA, and ten WIA. Request immediate Med Evac for seriously wounded. Have Med Evac land south of our position by three hundred yards. We will transport our wounded to that area. Request double ammunition re-supply and extra water for the troops. Unknown enemy size, estimate about five hundred to seven hundred; cut off by Red Rock Six.

"November Six, I correct your last. Enemy size now estimated to be in the range of two thousand, based on Viking flyover. Two large NVA forces have joined together in your vicinity. Intelligence

151

believes units from the 351st and 324th divisions and possibly a local Viet Cong battalion, maybe the 30th Vietcong battalion.

"Repeat. Enemy forces now estimated to be two thousand. Break... remainder of Red Rock battalion heavily engaged on Hill Papa. All friendly forces are now totally engaged with enemy activity in your AOR (area of responsibility)."

Turning to the Gunny, Captain Oates said, "We're fucked, and we're on our own. There's two thousand NVA up there and a hundred of us down here. Let's spread out, dig in and give 'em all we got."

"Captain, that reminds me of my old girlfriend."

"What?" Captain was amazed.

"My old girlfriend!" yelled the Gunny, "We'd be screwing and she'd say, 'Flattop, gimme all you got.' And I'd say, 'I already have.'"

The men cracked up as explosions, bullets and static from the radio filled the air.

"You're funny as hell, Gunny. If we make it back, I'll buy you a beer."

"At the officers' club, or the enlisted swine club?" asked the Gunny.

"Whatever club you want," answered the Citadel graduate before he bolted towards the lead squad's position.

Humping a couple hundred meters straight uphill with enough ammunition to hold off an army, Larry "the retarded Polack" Pulaski, Jackie Carroll, two full machine gun teams and four ammo humpers set up their guns to control all high ground above November Company. They brought with them two 3.5 rocket launchers, twenty rockets and pockets full of hand grenades.

The retarded Polack knew the gooks would rain down mortars on their machine gun positions. It was the calculus of combat: machine guns killed infantry forces with direct fire and mortars killed machine gunners with indirect fire. It's the way it worked. Pulaski knew that if he were to die today, it would be from a mortar round.

With machetes in hand, sixteen Marines began cutting apart all the logs and trees they could to fasten them into an overhang that might absorb everything but a direct hit. They also had a PRC-25 radio with them to warn the company if the bad guys were attacking from the flanks.

A temporary lull had settled over the battlefield.

Directly in front of the Marines' position, a young NVA soldier was crying out in pain, bleeding from a gunshot wound to the neck. He was shouting for someone to help him.

"Lam on cuu toi." (Please help me, I'm wounded.)

The enemy soldier stared up through the trees at the blue sky above. No one was coming to save him, and he knew it.

"Lam on noi voi cha me toi thoung ho." (Tell my father and mother I love them, and I'm sorry.)

It was decision time for the North Vietnamese forces. The commander called his senior officers together and told them of his decision.

"We will use our great strength to overwhelm the Marines. We have ten companies of men against their one or two companies," he said, although he wasn't sure of the American numbers.

"Before dusk, we will launch a continuous series of attacks. Four companies will flank the Americans from the high ground, and four companies will attack down the trail. Two will be held in reserve. We have set up eight, 12.7 mm heavy machine guns around our perimeter to deal with their bombers and helicopters. We have with us the best anti-aircraft gunners in the People's Army. We will let their air cover get complacent, and when they come in low, we'll blast them out of the sky.

"Our forces will fight into the night, if necessary. Take all enemy radios, charts, maps and other intelligence items. We need to provide this material to our division intelligence officers. This time, a green flare means to break contact completely and move back to base camp tiger. Begin the flanking movements immediately."

Corporal Carroll and Pulaski were scanning the horizon when they saw the strangest thing. The entire side of a hill moved. They stole a glance at each other before Pulaski turned his focus back on the hill – that's when he saw something shine from within the greenery. Without saying a word, he began firing his M-60 machine gun directly into the area. A moment later, the other M-60 joined in, pouring sustained fire three hundred yards directly in front of them. They kept shooting hundreds of rounds into the moving mountain. And then… the mountain began to fire back.

The onslaught began.

NVA forces by the hundreds stormed the Marines, firing their weapons while slipping and sliding on the high ground. Much of their fire initially went over the heads of the two American machine gun crews.

Carroll picked up the radio to the company commander.

"November Six, this is Tinker Bell. We got enemy troops in the open. Three hundred yards to our front. Fire for effect, with whatever mortars you have left."

"Say again your last, Tinker Bell," responded the captain. But it was no use. Carroll couldn't hear. He had only one workable ear and that was ringing with the blasts of the machine gun.

"This is Tinker Bell. Out."

Captain Oates sent mortar rounds to pound enemy positions to the front, but it seemed to be having little effect on the advancing communists. Jackie Carroll was feeding belts of shinny new 7.62 ammunition into Pulaski's machine gun as it raked the battlefield.

The bad guys spotted their position and began directing their own grazing fire in the American's direction. The rounds were coming close.

Using his asbestos glove, Pulaski changed the red-hot barrel and inserted a new one.

"Let's… let's… give it a rest for a while. The gooks are probably zeroing in their, their… mortars on us. Get more belts ready," said Pulaski.

Down near the footpath, Lt. Behring and Gunny Martin were giving the enemy hell on the front line, throwing back human waves of assaulting soldiers.

"They keep coming, how many fuckin' men do they have?" asked the lieutenant.

"Six didn't tell you?" asked Gunny Martin.

"Six didn't tell me shit," answered the lieutenant.

"Two thousand," said the Gunny.

"Two thousand what?"

"Two thousand NVA soldiers. Viking spotted them joining forces up ahead."

"Mother of Mercy," said the lieutenant

Lt. Behring's mortar men had run out of ammo and began serving as riflemen on the front lines, doing what all Marines were trained to do. And doing it well. Behring had friends back in the artillery battalions –guys he went to artillery school with. Wasting no time trying to reach battalion headquarters, Lt. Behring put out a Mayday to all Marine artillery units in the AOR. Something that was sure to get him in trouble with his CO and battalion commander.

"Copycat, copycat, this is November two Alpha. We need everything you got from all guns on target Rita. Gimme a smoke round, then I'll guide you in."

"Shouldn't you check with the captain?" asked the Gunny.

"Fuck the captain. This is my show."

In short order, a 155mm smoke round landed about three hundred yards west of the enemy positions.

"Copycat, adjust your fire three hundred meters to the east, and let her rip! This is Jim Behring, 'the Fort Sill lonesome boy' and I need your help. We're in danger of being overrun." Behring knew when he used his real name over the radio net, his Marine career was over.

Sixteen hundred NVA soldiers moved to within two hundred meters of the Marine positions, as the most God-awful artillery barrage in the history of the Vietnam War was unleashed on the 351st and 324th communist divisions. The ground shook as hundreds of artillery rounds slammed home from 105mm, 155mm and self-propelled 8-inch guns.

The noise was deafening. When Jim Behring was a college student, he would make trips to the Antietam battlefield in Maryland and walk through the "cornfield" where Union forces had charged headlong into Rebel cannons and muskets. It was the greatest slaughter of the American Civil War – and now it was happening again, right in front of his eyes.

Up on the flanks, Corporal Carroll, the retarded Polack and the machine gun crews cheered as the massive artillery barrage stopped the NVA cold. After about thirty minutes of firing, the big guns went silent – but not before a lone enemy machine gunner found his mark and riddled the Americans with a hundred rounds or so.

Carroll felt a savage blast slam into his upper legs. Blood began to fill the bottom of the machine gun pit. The legs that had carried him through the trails of Blue Mountain convulsed and cramped.

The retarded Polack was shot through the face, knocking out some of his teeth, and two of the ammo humpers were dead, both shot through their heads.

"Where did he come from?" asked Pulaski of the enemy gunner, while spitting out blood and teeth.

"Dunno," said Carroll, withering in pain.

It was dusk, and a brief lull had fallen over the battlefield. Hundreds of NVA soldiers lay dead and dying. The Marine forces were down to forty men and not much ammunition. Relief helicopters had been unable to pick up the wounded and deliver more ammo because of the heavy enemy rifle fire.

Air strikes were coming in to support the Americans, led by Huey helicopter gun ships that were firing their mini guns and Zuni rockets at enemy forces.

Right behind them were medical evacuation helicopters, and others filled to the brim with much-needed small arms ammunition.

As the CH-34s attempted to land, enemy heavy machine guns tore them to ribbons. One helo dropped right on top of seriously wounded Marines, burning many to death. Two other helicopters took numerous small arms hits while maneuvering in the area, with one of them belching fire from the engine. They tried mightily to land but couldn't.

When heavily-armed Hueys attempted to strafe the gun positions, other enemy anti-air sites nearby shot one more American helicopter out of the sky. In less than ten minutes, the U.S. lost three helicopters and their entire crews.

But the big guys high above would have none of it. From ten thousand feet came the call from a strike group of F-4 Phantom jets.

"November Six, this is Charles Gonads and Company. We're going after those anti aircraft sites. After that, we'll give you whatever ordinance we have left. Gonads out."

With that, the F-4s dropped down and began plastering the anti aircraft sites. Huge fireballs lit up the sky. After a few more runs, the heavy machine guns quit firing.

As Charles Gonads and Company made a low pass over the battlefield to deliver its promised ordinance, two communist 12.7 machine guns opened up to cut a wing in half.

The plane made a quarter turn and crashed immediately into the side of a hill in a huge fireball explosion. Another Phantom roared onto the battlefield, and this time six 12.7s fired point blank, causing the pilot to bank so steeply that he lost control of the jet and it too crashed into the side of the hill with-another humongous explosion.

The tide had quickly turned.

Seriously wounded men were now dying from lack of medical attention; the remaining Marines were getting dangerously low on ammo and drinking water.

After a few "higher" battlefield passes, what was left of Charles Gonads and Company made their way back to Danang.

"November Six, this is Charles Gonads. It's dark and you're too close to the NVA for us to continue bombing. We'll be back in the morning with every plane we've got. Hang on and Semper Fi. Gonads, out."

There was only one other aircraft in the American inventory that could be of help, but it wasn't worth the risk as far as Capt. Oates was concerned. That plane was "Spooky," the C-47 fixed wing aircraft with a 7.62 mm Gatling gun. It could fire thousands of rounds per minute and put a bullet hole in every square foot of a football field. It was feared as much as a two-headed dragon by the NVA.

The Americans feared it as well. Spooky had a bad habit of firing into Marine positions when they were engaged with Charlie. If the enemy was far off and isolated, the plane and its mini-guns were a piece of artwork. If it was closer in, the plane was a piece of shit. November Company had been riddled by Spooky on two occasions in the past, and in both instances, the Marine Company had not even requested air support.

Rumors circulated around I Corps about battlefields full of NVA and Americans with bullet holes drilled directly in the tops of their heads. And there was absolutely no defense against this type of fire from the sky.

And whether it was trigger-happy air force gunners or the bobbing and weaving of the aircraft in flight, the plane was not to be trusted near one's front lines. Experience had taught the commander this lesson.

Spooky would not be requested to help the desperate men of November Company. No fixed wing aircraft or helicopters would be coming either.

It was dark, and the Americans were on their own.

The NVA commander was on the field phone to his division headquarters in Laos. Division HQ had been communicating directly with Hanoi via Secure High Frequency, HF links. Old Russian communications gear, but it worked.

The NVA had been ordered to wipe out the Marine unit, whatever the cost.

Up in their machine gun positions, things couldn't have been worse. Corporal Carroll was working to patch himself up as best he could; all the medical corpsman were dead. The PRC-25 radio was full of holes and off to the side. The 3.5-inch rocket crewmen were badly wounded and moaning. One of the rocket men tried desperately to crawl back to the main body to get ammo and bandages, but was shot dead by a sniper.

Carroll bandaged up one leg with the extra field dressings he carried; for the other leg, he improvised a dressing by placing his soft green Marine Corps utility cap over the entrance wound. Reaching into his cargo pants' pocket, he pulled out the manila envelope containing the West Point Sunday school drawings and held them against the exit wound. He fastened his web belt tightly around the leg. The bleeding began to slow.

Jackie Carroll and Pulaski talked about what the night might hold for them. They bantered back and forth about another attack.

Pulaski, who had been with November Company twice as long as Carroll, thought the NVA had had enough. In past battles – although none of them as deadly as this one – the NVA either quit after a few frontal attacks or when the price became too steep in terms of lives lost.

"It's my guess that maybe one more smaller attack is coming," Pulaski said to Carroll. "It'll be to cover their main forces withdrawing from the area. All of these motherfuckers will be out of here by midnight."

Pulaski looked a mess. To stop the bleeding from his cheek wounds, he had twisted together white shit paper he was carrying, inserting it into the bullet holes. One hole in each cheek.

Carroll looked at him and began to laugh.

"You know the old saying?"

"What saying?" asked Pulaski.

"You never have a pussy plug when you need one."

Both men were now laughing and holding each other's hands.

Meanwhile, one full company of NVA was in a serious crouch, crawling towards the American machine gunners. Much of the enemy was too close to the American lines for Lt. Behring's artillery to be effective. If he called in another major barrage, he'd kill Marines this time. That much he knew for sure.

Wounded, but still functioning, Pulaski devised a plan to hold off one last attack. He knew he had only enough ammo for one more sustained effort, and he'd have to make the best of it.

The final NVA attack he thought would come from the front and right flank. He positioned one of his machine guns to cover the area to the right front above them and locked the barrel in place with two heavy logs.

He then belted seven bandoleers of ammunition together into one long, 700-round belt. He stretched the belt out flat on the ground so nothing would stop them from properly feeding into the machine gun. After sustained fire, the gun would cook off rounds and, in effect, fire itself. Pulaski used the best Kentucky windage he could to level the machine gun barrel so it covered the field of fire.

This, he thought, would keep the gooks' heads down.

The other gun would be manned by himself and Jackie Carroll to cover their direct front. Pulaski also knew that the NVA mortar teams would continue to blast his positions, but with both of them wounded and Carroll unable to walk, changing their physical location was out of the question.

At about 9 p.m., a thunderous explosion went off about four hundred meters down the trail from the November Company command group. An NVA sapper team had spent hours navigating the rugged cliffs moving around the trapped Marine unit and finally detonated their 500-pound booby trap bomb. It blew the trail to smithereens. Now it would be almost impossible for reinforcements to reach the stranded Marines without having to climb up a sheer cliff.

If the Americans decided to helo in reinforcements, NVA anti-aircraft gunners would shoot them down.

Lt. Behring ordered artillery flares fired over the heads of November Company. In a short while, the battlefield was illuminated as 155 mm rounds burst open to light up the night sky. Marines looked out to see hundreds of NVA moving towards them at a low crawl, totally camouflaged. Enemy mortars immediately began to rain down on their positions.

After a volley of about fifty rounds, NVA soldiers raced directly at the American front lines. Marines opened up with a withering defense as enemy soldiers moved to within forty yards of their positions. For thirty minutes, the assault continued. The Americans finally pushed them back, but it came at a steep price.

Gunny Martin and Lt. Behring were badly wounded. Captain Oates, shot in the leg, crawled to where the men lay dying. They were both gasping for air and their faces were turning the sickening blue color of death. The captain was still giving orders, organizing the remaining troops. He rubbed their heads and poured water on their lips. He kissed the gunny and the lieutenant and yelled to his nearby troops.

"Whoever makes it back, I want the gunny and Lt. Behring recommended for the Medal of Honor!" he yelled. "And that's an order from your captain."

Pulaski had it figured right. It would be one more attack, but it wouldn't be a small covering maneuver. Two full companies charged the machine gun positions. Pulaski and Jackie Carroll fired hundreds of rounds at the charging NVA. Jumping over to his second machine gun, Pulaski continued to shoot until the barrel turned red and the gun began firing itself, almost all of it perfectly aimed.

Not bad, he thought, for a retarded Polack.

A direct hit from an 82 mm mortar pounded the machine gunners, pulverizing skin and bone. Pulaski was blown clear out of the pit while Jackie Carroll crashed backward. Carroll found himself starring straight up at the night sky, his eyes fixating on the bright light of a parachute flare. Neither man moved; the overhead flare went out.

By midnight, the battle was over.

NVA commanders fired green flares and their troops melted back in the jungle, some beginning a perilous climb over the mountains, back to their base camp.

Thirty-one wounded Marines were still alive and holding their positions along the trail. The NVA had lost almost five hundred men.

A few days later at combined division headquarters, NVA intelligence officers were studying captured American maps, charts and radio call signs.

There was one document in particular that they thought was of great importance – a tactical drawing of a fortification located high on a hill overlooking a river. It revealed steep walls, gun positions, barracks locations and an area described as the CP (command post). It was crudely drawn and had a coded name: Fort Putnam.

What's New,
Pussycat?

Honey Sanders met Mike Carroll after he finished a long afternoon run and immediately began carping about how she'd like to see the movie, *What's New Pussycat?* It was playing at the Verplanck Movie Theater. The song by the same name had been an immense hit all summer long, and everyone was singing it. Ordinarily, Carroll would have no problem fulfilling any request by the beautiful and talented blonde bombshell, but this request bordered on insane.

Carroll knew that the Galer brothers would be working taking tickets, selling popcorn, breaking arms, and doing whatever they needed to do to maintain order and create profit for the owners – half of which went in their own pockets. Walking in with Honey Sanders would surely draw a lot of attention, but not the kind Mike Carroll wanted.

Even if he managed to get into the theater unnoticed, the brothers would lock onto Honey's bright blonde hair and check her out sometime during the flick. They'd also check out her date to see if it was someone they could mess with and humiliate. So, in spite of the risk, he gave in to save face with his lady.

Promptly at 6 p.m., Carroll pulled into the driveway of the Sanders home driving Mickey's rusted buzz bomb. He yanked the silver-colored hand break all the way back so the car wouldn't roll down the hill while he went to the door. He also cut the wheels toward the curb, like he'd learned in driver's education.

He was wearing a bright madras shirt, white chinos, and penny loafers, and he was covered from head to toe with English Leather cologne, a gift from Honey after his West Point time trial.

He had just gotten a haircut from Fat Al the provolone down

the street and looked all of twelve years old. Fat Al was a retired New York City barber who still didn't "speaka the language" too good. He had sold his business, but kept his prized barber chair that he had set up in his in-laws basement. The only things Fat Al ever said to the kids whose hair he was cutting was: "You wanna short?" After the haircut, as he was getting ready to slap some heavy-scented green goo on one's gourd, he'd say, "you wanna wet?" And "that'sa all," he'd ever say.

The Sanders house was big, but not ostentatious. Honey lived in an upscale part of Peekskill, a neighborhood of beautiful brick, split-level homes with wide expansive lawns. Most of the residents were professionals, worked for IBM or were executives at Fleischmann's Yeast in Verplanck. The tract of houses where the Carrolls lived was nice, but sort of cramped and plain.

He rang the bell, and Mr. Sanders answered the door and invited him in. Walking through a marble foyer into the living room, Mike noticed lots of family pictures on the walls. Photos taken at ski resorts, beach clubs, Christmas, Thanksgiving, and in the backyard around a beautiful, in-ground swimming pool – not a collapsible metal doughboy with a slapped-together douche bag for a filter.

Mike was directed to sit in the living room by her father, who introduced himself as Steve. A very manly name, Mike thought. Honey would be down in a few moments, he was told.

"You know these women," said Mr. Sanders, who was trying for a laugh. "Your car doesn't leak oil, does it?"

"A little, maybe," said Mike, as he began to move towards the door. "I'll move it from the driveway."

"Don't be silly. Stay put. Honey will be down in a few."

Steve Sanders was a big guy – about six-feet three-inches tall and two hundred pounds—and not an ounce of fat on him. He wore dark-rimmed glasses – stylish for the time – and nice clothes with logos on the shirtsleeves. He, too, had on penny loafers and was wearing English Leather cologne. He was in his late 30s or early 40s and, according to Honey, was an engineer of some type at IBM in Poughkeepsie.

Steve Sanders excused himself.

"I've got something cooking on the grill. Too bad you kids

aren't staying for dinner," he said. "Big steaks, and plenty of them, if you change your mind."

Tonight's fare at the Carroll house was macaroni and cheese with cut up wieners. It was Mickey's favorite and that of his brothers and sisters. And it was Jackie's favorite dish so now, of course, it was also Mike's. But still not as good as a steak. Mike thought that his family should eat more steaks, roasts and chops, and maybe now with Jackie's death gratuity they would.

After a few moments, Mrs. Sanders – a 40-year-old Donna Reed look alike – walked into the living room holding a Manhattan. She looked just like Honey and had an even more beautiful set of cans hidden under some type of V-neck sweater.

Mrs. Susan Sanders was wearing a tight (but not obscenely tight) dark skirt and mini heels. Her blonde hair was in a stylish cut. She wore light-colored red lipstick that matched her nails; she appeared ready to go out on a date.

But how could that be? thought Mike. Her husband was fixing big steaks on the grill.

"Meat's almost done!" he yelled from the backyard.

Mrs. Sanders offered Mike a soda and then said, "We're sorry for your family's loss. All of us mourn your brother's death in Vietnam." They were true words of sympathy.

"A bunch of women from our golf club have been meaning to get over and see your mother. How is she doing?"

"Mom has her good days, and some not-so-good days," he answered.

"I couldn't even imagine losing a…" She caught herself. "Well, we're going to get over and see your mother as soon as we can. I'll make sure it happens."

"Mom would really appreciate that," said Mike.

In a few moments, Honey came down the stairs and into the living room. She went over and put her arm around her mother.

"Has Mom been talking your ear off?" she asked as she hugged her mother.

"Nothing of the sort," answered Mike. "We've been catching up on the latest town news."

"Did she tell you about her hole-in-one?"

"Oh Honey, not now," said Mrs. Sanders.

"OK, then," said Honey. "I'll let him see for himself."

Honey walked over to a table containing magazines and books and picked up a copy of the *Peekskill Evening Star.*

Turning to the sports section, Honey showed Mike the article and then began reading aloud:

MRS. SANDERS ACES SEVENTH DURING LEAGUE PLAY

Susan Sanders of Peekskill recorded her first hole-in-one last Thursday, when she aced the hundred and forty-five yard seventh hole during league play. Sanders, who led her team with an eighty-four, used a five-iron to complete the shot.

Witnessing her great accomplishment were teammates, Madge Henderson, Judy Tramponi and Helen Nalons.

Honey then turned the page to finish reading the article.

"No, no!" her mother shrieked, as she tried to grab the newspaper.

"Oh, Mom, you're just too modest," Honey said, and continued to read. "I want to show him your picture."

Honey approached Mike and, as she flipped the page, stopped dead in her tracks.

MEMORIAL SERVICE SET FOR SLAIN TRACKMAN

Mrs. Sanders grabbed the paper from her daughter. "We're so sorry," she said.

Mike began consoling them. "It's OK. I have the article. We've seen it, and it's in a scrapbook my mother is keeping. I never made the connection, Mrs. Sanders. I didn't know you were Honey's mother. Funny, I can't even imagine my mother playing golf. Congratulations to you. You're a great champion, Mrs. Sanders."

A little beagle then ran into the living room and sniffed at Mike's shoes.

"This is Dobie," said Honey, as she picked up the dog and kissed his nose.

After a moment, the last household member came into the

room, chasing the dog.

"Mike, this is my sister, Mitzi," she said, introducing the twelve-year-old.

Mitzi had dark hair and wore glasses, much like their father.

"You better hurry up and get the dog out before your father sees it," said Mrs. Sanders.

"We love Dobie, but he pissed on Dad's loafers the other day, and now he's banned from the house," Honey explained.

Honey offered to give Mike a quick tour of the place. The spacious master bedroom had walk-in closets and high ceilings. The kids each had their own room with different furniture and color schemes. Honey's room had mirrors on two walls.

"I wanted to be a ballerina when I was little," she said.

"Oh, I thought it's because you liked looking at yourself," joked Mike.

In one hallway were the kids' school pictures from kindergarten on up. There was also a family tree with Steve, Susan, Honey and Mitzi, and of course, little Dobie. Funny, Mike thought.

In his house, everyone was named after a saint. All the names in his immediate or extended family sounded alike. There were John, Michael, Mary, Peter, Joseph and a few variants like Marie or Megan – but essentially, all the same saintly names.

Downstairs in a finished basement, was a small bar with six barstools and large mirror with "Steve's Bar" written across the top. The bar area had recessed lighting, knotty pine paneling, and an assortment of beer signs and clocks. It even had a refrigerator and icemaker.

There were more family photos of camping trips, cruises and Yankee games. One picture was of the family sitting in a beautiful Chevrolet Super Sport convertible, with Steve and Susan sitting in the front bucket seats and Honey and Mitzi sitting in the back. Just like in the commercials.

"When my parents are gone, we can come down here and get a few brews," said Honey.

"I wouldn't mind one now," answered Mike.

"Not a good time," said Honey. "My old boyfriend put a pretty big hit on Dad's alcohol, and he's been on the warpath ever since. Another time."

Honey then put a monumental kiss on Mike who was sitting on a barstool. She rubbed her breasts into his chest and slid her hand into his crotch, setting off an immediate boner.

"Maybe after the movie, we'll go someplace," she said.

Honey opened a sliding glass door leading to the backyard. Mike was still sporting a tent in the front of his pants when she pulled him through the door; he came face-to-face with her father, who was putting barbecue sauce on his New York cuts.

"Too bad you kids aren't going to eat here," he said again, looking at Mike, whose hands were buried in his pockets. "And Darling, don't let that little piece of shit in the house anymore."

Mike jumped back, as if caught by the old man.

"Not you, Son. That damn dog. It pisses all over my shoes and sneakers."

"Daddy, come on. Dobie's just going through a stage," said his daughter.

Ignoring the conversation, Honey continued the tour. The Sanders backyard had a screened-in porch, with beautiful lawn chairs and accessories. The porch contained more family pictures – Honey and her sister on horseback, water-skiing, cheerleading, and Steve and Susan in various states of embrace.

Why so many pictures? he thought. His family had pictures too. How about a photo them stuck on the toll road with Mickey fixing a flat tire? Or one of his mother grabbing on for life as her car door flew open and almost tossed her out on the pavement? Or one of nuns getting the razor sharp poker in their ass when they sat in the back seat? How about some backyard scenes of everyone cursing and fighting when they tried to assemble the above-ground pool? Or a picture of a thousand gallons of water cascading through the back yard when the metal brace gave way in the doughboy pool. And the grill catching fire and burning the shit out of the hotdogs after gasoline was poured on the charcoals? How about a photo of family members running out to the street to scoop up whiskey bottles after the raccoons knocked over the garbage cans? And the school bus coming for a pickup?

Lots of family photos, Mike thought.

Honey then showed Mike Carroll something that he truly did like: A 20-foot by 60 foot in-ground pool with a diving board. The water on this balmy evening was bright blue, but a little darker in the deep end. Carroll studied the depths – from three feet in the shallow end to eight feet at the deep end. What a beautiful pool, he thought.

"Dad hooked up lights so we can swim at night," she said. She leaned in to Mike and whispered, "I caught Mom and Dad out here skinny dipping last week. Dad moved the light switch after that."

"Will you invite me over to swim one day?" he asked.

"Sure. We have lots of pool parties, and we can even invite your parents if you like."

"That would be great. Maybe next year with my parents. My mother's still not right, you know. This has all been so hard on her."

Mrs. Sanders called out to Honey from the kitchen window. "Darling, you have a phone call."

"Be right back," she said to Mike, as she bolted to the house.

Mike watched her jog off. God, he'd love to have her as a training partner. One he could never, under any circumstance beat. Because to beat her meant he had to get in front where he could no longer see her, and that would be worse than anything else. Tonight, she wore what she called her modified cheerleading outfit – collarless white blouse, short skirt and sneakers with Bobbie socks. Her hair was in a ponytail the way she wore it when she led cheers for the varsity football team.

Failing French class was the best thing he'd ever done. Up until that time, Honey was strictly a football player's girl. She actually hated him and his track friends.

At awards banquets, the cheerleaders would laugh and giggle when awards were given out for "best runner," "most dedicated" or "most improved." Once, a cheerleader yelled: "Biggest homo!" when Coach Phil gave out an award. This caused everyone in the audience to crack up; it pushed the track team members further down the athletic ladder.

Honey was a completely different person than the one he envisioned. Had she changed, or was it he? Why in the world would the best-looking girl in the school go out with him and drive around in Mickey's piece of shit car? It couldn't be the running, because she always scoffed at that.

Like they said in the Catholic Church, it had to be one of the mysteries.

Out of the blue, big Steve Sanders yelled over, "Mike, what religion are you?"

"I'm Jewish," he answered in all seriousness. "We worship at Temple Beth Shalom over by the Beach shopping center."

Old man Sanders was flipping his steaks and practically flipped one over the house. "Isn't Carroll an Irish-Catholic name?"

"I'm only kidding, Mr. Sanders. We're Catholic through and through. Most of us have gone to Catholic schools, and I may be going to Holy Cross College in Massachusetts."

"Oh, that's nice," he said. "We're Episcopalian, which is a lot like the Catholic church. In fact, once mass starts, most people can't tell the difference. Our religions are fairly identical, except we don't take orders from Rome."

"Neither does my Mother," said Mike laughing.

Steve Sanders also mentioned that the big news around town was that the softball game between the firemen and The King and His Court was cancelled because the King and his boys were staying put in Danbury for a double-header.

"A lot of disappointed people for sure," he added.

Honey was now yelling to Mike that it was time to go.

"We gotta gotta leave now. Bye, Dad," she said.

The two teenagers walked through the house, saying goodbye to Mrs. Sanders, who was sipping another Manhattan.

"I think Mom drinks too much," said Honey. "Does your mother drink?" she asked Mike.

"From time to time," he answered.

Mike backed up the car, revealing a big oil and grease stain in the Sanders' driveway.

"Is your father going to be pissed?"

"He's pissed at everything, but he'll get over it. Dad's an engineer, you know, and they're a little different from most people."

One of the few things that worked in Mickey's car was the radio, and it was playing – of all songs – "What's New Pussycat?"

Honey knew the words by heart and, like most women on the planet, loved singer Tom Jones.

"He's really sexy," said Honey. "You're sexy too, especially in the last two hundred meters of a race when those 'motha-fuckin' sparks be flying.'"

Honey tried to roll up her window to keep her hair from blowing. When she got the window halfway up, it fell out of the track and down into the door.

"Sorry 'bout that," he said. "I can pull over and help you get the window back in the track."

Honey waved him off and began to sing her favorite song. Her hair blew in the evening breeze as Mickey's buzz bomb moved along Route 6.

What's new Pussycat?
Whoa, whoa, whoa, whoa,
What's new Pussycat?
Whoa, whoa, whoa, whoa,

Pussycat, Pussycat,
I've got flowers
and lot of hours
to spend with you.
So go and powder your cute little pussycat nose,
Pussycat, Pussycat
I love you,
Yes, I do...

Honey rubbed Mike's leg as they cruised down the street.

"I'd rub something else, but I'm afraid you'd run us off the road," she said. "Does this car have seat belts?"

Mike laughed. "We got it all – seat belts, padded dash, collapsible steering wheel and three bald tires with no jack in the truck. We got it all, Pussycat."

The Galers spotted Mike Carroll and Honey about a block from the Verplanck Theater. Richard was out in front, sweeping cigarette butts and candy wrappers off the sidewalk when the two hand-holding lovebirds strolled up to the ticket window.

If the need arose, Mike had gathered the courage to fight one or both or them, even though he knew he'd get his ass kicked. But it would look good in front of Honey, he thought.

All those years of running away from these two pricks had

made him fast. In fact, Mike thought, they had made him the runner he was today.

"Two tickets with a student discount," he boldly said to Robert through the ticket window.

Honey knew of the animosity between them and was ready to deliver any blows necessary to help her man. But she didn't need to, not on this night.

Earlier in the afternoon, after Mike had agreed to take her to the theater, Honey had called the Peekskill police department and talked with her cousin, Detective Ritchie Gannon. Her cousin then waltzed over to the theater to inform the Galers that if there was any trouble at all, they would be arrested for violation of probation and both of them would be looking at two to three years at Sing Sing or Attica. Neither one of them wanted any part of that.

Honey had another reason for keeping Mike healthy. When he was out talking to Steve in her backyard, she had received a phone call from Monsieur Claude Lambeau, the French consular general in New York. He informed her that the French Council of Sport had approved world record holder Michel Jazy to run a race in Peekskill, New York.

Lambeau had convinced the French government that Peekskill was indeed a famous town because General George Washington crossed the Hudson River at the location with French General Rochambeau. From there, they fought on until the last major battle of the American Revolution and defeated British forces at Yorktown. Michel Jazy had also read about Mike Carroll's 880-yard race and his spectacular time, and his brother's death in Vietnam. Jazy wanted to run the race.

Peekskill was indeed a famous town and now would become the scene of one the greatest track races ever run.

The Good
Shepherd

With Rose Galer in Westchester County lockup for the murder of her husband, Public Defender Marc Hinn made it his business to rescue daughter Lilly from the squalor of her rural home.

Hinn was defending Rose Galer and had interviewed the young girl about the incest she experienced. The little girl told stories that curled the hair of seasoned defenders. The interviews with Lilly left the men in the office physically sick and the females crying.

Getting this young thing to a safe environment was priority number one for the public defender. Defending Rose Galer was number two.

"Take care of my little angel, Mr. Hinn. And don't worry too much about me," said Rose. "I should spend some time in hell for what I didn't do to help her."

Hinn was conflicted about the case. On one hand, he was perfectly happy to be defending Rose her for killing the no good son-of-a-bitch she was married to. On the other hand, Hinn was angry as hell with Rose for leaving her daughter behind to be terrorized.

Because her lone surviving parent could no longer care for her, Hinn went to Westchester County Children's Services and obtained an order to remove Lilly Galer from her home of record. Hinn told the children's court that Lilly's older brothers were in and out of jail and unable to provide a stable or safe environment.

On a warm summer morning, Marc Hinn and two burly New York state troopers showed up at the Galer residence to remove Lilly from the home.

Armed with a court order, Hinn knocked on the front door and waited. There was no movement inside. Hinn knocked again and again, but there was still no answer.

Becoming alarmed, the troopers took action; using only hand signals, they moved to the rear of the house to cover the back exit. As they got halfway around the house, the back door flew open and Richard and Robert Galer bolted out and sped towards the woods like their asses were on fire. They were half dressed and neither had on shoes. The troopers yelled for the pair to stop, but the Galers kept on running.

A moment later, Lilly came to the front door, half asleep, to meet Mr. Hinn.

"What's happening?" asked the startled public defender. "Have those two hurt you?"

"Oh no," said Lilly. "I've been sleeping."

The state troopers had joined Hinn at the front of the house and also questioned Lilly. She told them that her brothers Richard and Robert were always in trouble with the law and when a policeman shows up unannounced, it was standard practice for them to bolt out the back door and hide in the woods.

"They'll be back in an hour or so," she said. "When they see your cars leave, they'll come back down."

Hinn asked the troopers to go through the house and make sure it was secure while he sat on the front porch and gabbed with Lilly.

"I want to tell you that your mother is doing fine, and she asks for you all the time," said Hinn. "She's doing the best she can in jail, and misses you very much."

"What's going to happen to her? Will she be able to come home soon?" asked her daughter.

Hinn then explained the gravity of the situation and told Lilly that her mother was charged with a count of murder in the first degree and there would be no bail for this crime. He told her that he hoped to have the charges changed to manslaughter and would do everything in his power to have them dropped all together.

"She was protecting me," said Lilly. "Momma killed Daddy because of what he done to me."

"Exactly. That's what we've told the judge. And Honey, that's how we're going to defend your mother."

"Does this mean she's coming home soon?"

"Afraid not," said Hinn. "Your mother is in serious trouble, and she's going to be in jail for some time. That's why we've come here today, Lilly. Everyone's concerned about your welfare, and we can't leave you here any longer. The court has decided that you'd be better living somewhere else, and we're going to take you there."

Lilly looked around, first at Hinn, then at the big state troopers who had come back to the porch. "Are you taking me to jail?"

"No Lilly," said Hinn, hugging the little girl. "We're taking you to St. Joseph's Home in Peekskill until your mother's case is decided. It's a beautiful place overlooking the Hudson River and the good Sisters will help with your schoolwork. They're very kind and will…"

Lilly interrupted: "Can I bring my cat?"

"Well, um," Hinn muttered.

"If the cat doesn't go, I don't go."

"Sure," said the public defender, shrugging his shoulders. "We'll work it out on the other end. What's your cat's name, Honey?"

"It's Leroy," she said. "Leroy the cat, and he's one bad mothafucker."

The troopers began to laugh and tried to look away.

"You can't talk like that 'round the nuns," said Hinn. "They're religious people, and they don't curse or say things like that."

"I won't curse anymore. Just try to get my mother outta jail, and tell her one other thing."

"What's that, Lilly?"

"Tell her, I forgive her."

In short order, Lilly had packed some of her belongings in a small, brown suitcase. She filled three pillow cases with her personal effects: combs and brushes, pictures from school, ribbons from the county fair (she and her mother had won awards for best grape jam and chili), comic books, – and a large manila envelope containing $46,000. A small fortune.

"Mr. Hinn, momma gave me this money a long time ago and I've had it hid ever since. Daddy tried to get it, so did my brothers, but I hid it good."

"Where did she get this money?" he asked.

"Grandma left it for Momma after she died, and Momma left it for me. For years, Daddy tried to find it, but I told him I didn't know anything about it."

"How long have you had this cash?" asked Hinn.

"Long time. 'Bout seven, maybe eight years. Daddy used to beat Momma all over the place trying to find out where the money was. But all she'd say was, 'There's no money. What are you talking about?' Daddy never believed her. That's when he started spying on me, thinking I had it. He'd search my room and out where I played …everywhere," she said.

Astounded, the public defender asked, "Where did you hide it?"

"Out back in the hootch, under Leroy's litter box. Daddy hated cats and would never go there."

Hinn didn't know what exactly to do with this large a sum of money. He could probably confiscate it to be used by the public defenders' office in Rose Galer's defense or he could turn it over to County Children's Services. After all, he had declared Lilly Galer indigent in order to get her into St. Joseph's.

Or, he could march down to the Peekskill Bank and open up an account for her, which is what he did. He made himself a co-signer. Lilly deserved a break in life and maybe this small amount of money might help, he thought.

Sisters Agnes and Imelda were the first to greet Lilly when she arrived at St. Joseph's Home. The troopers had stayed on to help with the child's move. While Lilly carried a meowing Leroy in a Campbell's soup box, the big troopers hauled Lilly's suitcase and stuffed pillowcases up the walkway to the front door to meet the nuns.

Hinn feared their reaction because he hadn't had time to discuss Leroy the cat with the nuns beforehand.

"What do we have here?" asked Sr. Agnes, looking inside the box.

"It's my cat, Leroy. I've had him since he was a kitten."

The two nuns looked at each other. Using a half-century of experience in dealing with abandoned and abused children, Sister Agnes said, "We can't have animals in the dormitory young lady, but we have a nice place for your kitty out in the shed. You can visit him whenever you like. Animals are God's creatures, too."

Sister Agnes next led Marc Hinn to her office, where they

signed custodial agreements and other legal documents. As Sister Imelda showed Lilly Leroy's new home, the two troopers walked back to their car, backed it out of the driveway and headed off.

Changing The
Game

The Carroll phone was ringing off the wall when a half-dazed Marie decided to answer it.

"This is Mayor DiGregorio. I'm trying to reach Michael," he said in a huff. "Is he around?"

"No Mayor, he's out for a run. Can I help you with something?" she asked.

The mayor told Marie that the French consulate had called to inform him that Olympian and world record holder Michel Jazy would run a race in Peekskill against her son. The race would take place in a few weeks and already ABC and CBS sports had left messages at his office.

"Mike's in great shape," she said. "But I don't know how he'll do against a world record holder."

"It really doesn't matter, Marie. No one expects the boy to win. But what a great day this is for your family and our town. This is going to put us on the map. It'll be the biggest thing happening to Peekskill since... ah, since... the end of World War II."

The mayor went on to say that the softball game between the firemen and King and His Court had been cancelled.

"We're going to replace the softball game with a one-mile track race at Depew Park. We already put the lights up for the softball game, and now we're going to run the race instead. The French want the track meet run as late as possible so it can be broadcast live in Europe. So we're going to run it at midnight.

"Marie, we're going to build the finest war memorial you've ever seen with the money we make. We're going to honor your fallen son, Jackie. And it will be his younger brother Mike doing it. What a great day. Once again, this town thanks you."

Marie hung up the phone, changed out of her pajamas, and jumped into Mickey's '49 Ford buzz bomb. She headed to Blue Mountain State Park where she hoped to catch her son on his morning run.

She drove up to where the high school cross country races started and finished. She got out of the car and lit up a cigarette.

What nice things the mayor said about the family, she thought. It made her feel really good.

But what if Mike does poorly in the race? Would the mayor then think less of the family? She knew everyone in town thought she was nuts; it was a foregone conclusion.

Would the family be ridiculed and laughed at if the world record holder made Mike look like a fool? God, I'm sounding just like Mickey the pessimist now. But it could happen, and then what?

Marie reasoned that she was walking a thin line of late with her drinking and melancholy, but she also knew that her sons – both of them – were the fastest things on two legs. First Jackie, and now Mike.

She knew a little about track herself. Anyone who could run five hard miles and then ten minutes later, run a 49-second quarter was no one to be messed with – and that's just what Mike had done a few days ago.

Marie hoped that the Frenchman, Michel Jazy, would run at a strong pace. Her son would run the race of his life. She was sure of it.

Mike spotted his mother right away, leaning against the side of the car smoking a cigarette. She seemed content. His radar picked up no troubling signals, as he rounded a turn and ran up to the car. "What are you doing here, Mom?" he asked. "I was planning on running home."

She smiled and said, "The last thing I want to do is disrupt your training, but I have big news for you."

Mike immediately thought about the Monsignor Healy and the College of the Holy Cross.

"Is it about college?" he said.

"Nope, guess again."

"The pool collapsed!"

Marie laughed. "You're going to run against world record

holder Michel Jazy in Depew Park! He's agreed to run a mile race against you. Somehow, the French sports people worked it all out."

"That's great," he said. "You know, Mom, Honey set that whole thing up. She went down to the French consulate in New York and talked to all the important people. She practically did it by herself."

"You've got great friends," his mother said. "And pretty ones, too."

"Yeah, she's beautiful. But Mom, she's not as pretty as you."

Marie hugged her son for a long time.

"You know Mom, this is the first time you've really hugged me since Jackie's death," he said as she buried her head in his shoulder.

"I'm sorry, Son," Marie answered. "I'm just so sorry for everything."

Marie took off in second gear with the RPMs roaring uncontrollably. Before she realized it, she was navigating down Washington Street to the A&P on Main Street. When she pulled into the parking lot, she saw big Ruben sitting on the curb in front of the store.

"Hi Ruben," she said.

"Hello, Mrs.… ah… Mrs.… You know, how are you doing?"

"I'm doing fine. Going inside to buy honey and steaks for my son. He's going to run a race at Depew Park against the world record holder," she said proudly.

"That's wonderful. The boy a yours sho is fast. I'll come down and watch," he said.

Marie stocked up on jars of honey and Swiss steaks, and even a few New York cuts. Mike loved all kinds of steaks, and because they were so expensive this made him fast, she reasoned. Marie wasn't sure how much money she had in her checking account because she never bothered to balance it. That was one of Mickey's chores, and as an accountant, one he seemed to enjoy.

She also picked up some potato chips, soft drinks and candy for the kids —something she seldom did. Today, we *all* celebrate, she thought.

On the way home, she stopped to visit Mrs. Louise Alforni, the Gold Star Mother whom she told Mickey was her new "Catholic friend." Driving up the street on this humid New York morning, she spotted Mrs. Alforni sitting on her front porch in her pajamas with her hair undone, smoking a cigarette. A total mess.

She was holding up some old T-shirts and pants and rocking back and forth in a metallic lawn chair. She was talking to herself. Marie was already sorry she made the turn onto McKinley Street.

"These just came back," Mrs. Alforni said, as Marie walked up to the porch.

"From where? What are you taking about?" asked Marie.

"The Army sent 'em. They were in Sonny's duffel bag that came back from Vietnam. And you know what else – what else the Army sent back?"

"You're torturing yourself, Louise. Let your husband go through Sonny's things," said Marie.

"These were in his pockets." Mrs. Alforni held up a handful of rubbers. "That means he had sex with whores and he probably didn't go to confession. It's a mortal sin!" she screamed. "It's a mortal sin! Sonny can't go to heaven now, and I'll never see him again. Never, ever!"

Mrs. Alforni was up on her feet now now, beside herself with grief. She was moaning and carrying on so much that the mailman yelled over to offer assistance.

"Need help?"

Marie waved him off. "It's OK, George. She's having a bad day."

Mrs. Alforni said she had tried talking to her husband about the rubbers, but he told her to shut up.

"Oh, Marie, look what's happened to us. We both lost children. Don't you see, Marie, confession didn't work for us. I'll never see Sonny again. Never touch his hair or his beautiful face. Revenge is mine, sayeth the Lord," she screamed out to the street. "Revenge is mine…"

"Shut up now. Shut the hell up!" Marie interrupted as she shook her.

Neighbors were coming out of their houses and kids stopped riding their bicycles to look at the distraught lady.

Marie reared her hand back and was on the verge of smacking Mrs. Alforni when George the mailman hurried onto the porch.

"I delivered the military box yesterday," he said, referring to Sonny Alforni's personal effects from Vietnam. "I feel terrible. I knew what it was. I've done this before, and it's always the same reaction."

"The Army should just throw this stuff in the China Sea or whatever ocean is near Vietnam," he said, while holding onto a kicking Mrs. Alforni. She continued to swing her arms and kick her legs. "Why do they do this to these parents?"

Mrs. Alforni made a break for the street, running up to the kids in front of her house and scaring them.

"Don't use these. Don't ever use these, ever," she screamed, holding out the rubbers to show the little kids. "If you do, you'll never see your parents. You'll go to hell and never see your mother and father in heaven."

Marie and George the mailman pulled her out of the street and wrestled her to the front lawn. The mailman still had his big mailbag strapped to his shoulder and struggled to keep his balance. Mrs. Alforni rolled around on the wet grass, crying and cursing. Marie had her hair tightly in her grasp.

"Pull yourself together," said Marie, taking charge. "For Christ's sake, pull yourself together!"

While the mailman held down Mrs. Alforni, Marie bee-lined into the house and called John McCracken, the town MD. His office was only a short distance from the Alforni's house, but she found out that the local doctor was out on a call in the countryside and wouldn't be back for an hour or so.

Marie was alone with her Gold Star friend after George begged off to finish his morning mail delivery. She walked her friend back into the house and fixed a pot of coffee. Mrs. Alforni's other kids, an eight-year-old boy and a twelve-year-old girl, sat silently in the living room watching cartoons. They seemed to pay no attention to their mother.

"Where does your father work?" Marie asked.

The older girl answered that he worked in Tarrytown for General Motors and wouldn't be home until end of shift at 4:30 that afternoon.

"Can we call him?"

"No," said the girl. "Mom's been calling him every day, and now he won't take any more of her calls. If Mom calls him one more time, he'll be fired."

Compassionate workplace, thought Marie.

Mrs. Alforni had calmed down and was sitting on the floor folding Sonny's clothes, reading his letters, playing with his dog tags, and examining a little Kodak camera.

Marie was walking back and forth from room to room, checking on both Mrs. Alforni and her kids when the younger boy without a trace of emotion asked, "Does it hurt to get shot in the head? Can you feel it, or is it just like passing out?"

Marie tried to think of a suitable answer to the question. She could tell there wasn't a lot of dialogue in this house with the mother hysterical and the father hiding at work. Then came a knock at the door.

Thank God, she thought The doctor is here.

Dr. McCracken was one of the town's newest MDs. He was a local kid who went to college and medical school and then came back to Peekskill, an unusual career move at the time.

He knew about Mrs. Alforni and had sedated her when the Army delivered the telegram about her dead son.

Speaking first to Marie, the doctor asked, "How's she doing?"

"Not good, Doctor. She received her son's personal effects from 'Nam yesterday. She's been pretty much out of it since that time, according to the kids. When I got here she was screaming and running out in the street. I'm surprised nobody called the cops."

Quickly, the doctor examined the distraught lady and gave her a sedative. In a few moments, she was sleeping in her unmade bed.

"Is anyone taking care of the kids?" asked the doctor.

"The husband's at work. Apparently, he's also out of his mind with grief and can't put up with her behavior any longer," said Marie.

"Only two more weeks until school," said Dr. McCracken. "If the kids can make it that long, they'll be fine." Marie tucked Mrs. Alforni in for a long sleep and then made the kids some breakfast. She told them to have their father call her when he came home from work, but Marie knew she'd never hear from him.

After a while, Marie was on her way home and reflecting on the day's events.

Killing these American kids in Vietnam made little sense to anyone, and the grief it brought to families was far greater then ever anticipated. It was as if the entire family was wiped out, and the pain each person felt was measured by their individual displays of grief. In Mrs. Alforni's case, the entire family was sick with sadness – barely able to sustain themselves – but because of her hysterical nature and acting out, she got all the sympathy.

Her husband, whose grief was more contained, could just as likely have thrown himself off the Bear Mountain Bridge and, to that end, everyone would be surprised. "Tony was holding up fine. What happened?" his neighbors would say.

Or the kids – one or both of them – could hang themselves in the closet and the neighbors would say, "What happened? They were adjusting so well."

It was impossible to measure pain and hurt from one person to another. It was a personal thing. Marie was beginning to figure this out. The grief part. She had made a big show at the train station when Jackie came home from Vietnam, attacking her husband.

Didn't Mickey feel just as bad? Who was she to garner all the sympathy, notoriety and applause? Am I just selfish? she thought. So selfish that even in death it has to be about me, the poor, grieving mother? Always about me?

Stopping at Mrs. Alforni's had been a handful, but it began to shake Marie from her nightmare to see what these other families went through – what *all* family members went through.

Upon arriving home, Marie decided that despite the day's events, she needed a drink – and in the worst way. She had scratch marks on her face and a sore right shin where Mrs. Alforni clawed and kicked her. Her blouse was ripped.

Marie took the vodka bottle from the refrigerator and filled an eight-ounce jelly glass halfway to the top. She got a couple of olives from the vegetable bin and dropped them into the clear, cold drink and stirred it with her finger. The house was hot, well over 80 degrees and she was still sweating from the wrestling match with her Catholic friend. Her mouth watered in anticipation of this perfectly prepared drink. This was her time now.

Marie hadn't eaten breakfast; she had had only coffee when the mayor called to tell her about the upcoming track race. If she drank now on an empty stomach, she could be a mess when the kids come home from summer camp. And if Mike and Honey showed up after class, she would be an embarrassment. Again.

The kitchen window was open, and outside a beautiful bluebird chirped away. She watched the bird for the longest time before touching her drink. She remembered how son Jackie loved these brightly colored birds and tried to feed them whenever he could with bread, potato chips, and corn flakes. What a kind, gentle child. What a good kid.

Then, the bird flew away. She stared for a while at the vacant tree branch.

Marie then walked to the kitchen sink and turned on the faucet. She poured her glass of vodka down the drain. She went to every hiding place in the house – the laundry room, closets, tool shed, attic and even behind the doughboy pool, where she kept a bottle stashed for a nighttime belt. She emptied them all out and threw the bottles in the trash.

There was no soul searching on her part. She just did it.

But Marie knew there would be a price to pay – a terrible price. In a few weeks' time, her son would be running in the race of his life and she would be sober to see it. Detoxing would be hard; she had tried it before, and always failed. This time, she would succeed.

She called Mickey at work to tell him about the upcoming mile race and to apologize for her poor behavior and her long, long slide into oblivion. At first, Mickey was elated by the call and hoped Marie was indeed feeling better. She sounded so content. So at ease with herself, he thought.

And then Mickey began to panic. He shook uncontrollably. Suicide. She was planning to kill herself.

Mickey bolted through the door of his building, almost wiping out a security guard on the way to the parking lot. The shotgun. It was in the house, and Marie knew where the shells were hidden. The 12-gauge shells were hidden from the kids, but she knew where to look and find them. He drove as fast as he could; rounding the curvy Route 6 on two wheels half of the time. He ran red lights. He failed to yield to pedestrians. Mickey was sweating and his heart was beating hard.

What would he tell the kids? What would happen to the family? Who would sing "Danny Boy" with him?

The car flew up the driveway and screeched to a halt, inches from the garage door. Mickey bolted from the car, screaming: "Darling, Darling, I'm home now, and we're going out tonight. Let's hurry to Penney's and get you a new dress."

Mickey fumbled with the front door keys. His sweating hands dropped them to the ground.

"I'm home now!" he continued to yell. "And Mike's with me, and all his friends are here, too."

He opened the door and rushed in. It was totally silent. He looked in all directions then, sniffed for gunpowder. Mickey was near the breaking point.

And then, there she was – sitting in the living room reading a *Look* magazine. Marie was eating a grilled cheese sandwich and drinking a glass of milk.

With his shirttails hanging out, sweat pouring down his face and glasses cockeyed on his face, Mickey collapsed into a chair.

"Are you strong, Darling?" she asked Mickey.

"What?" He was confused.

"Are you strong?"

"Sure," he answered, temporarily relieved from his nightmare.

"For the next four to five days, I need the strongest man I've ever seen."

"Why's that?" asked Mickey.

"I've quit drinking, and the detox will probably kill me," she said. "I'm going to sweat it out, and I need your help."

"What's happened to you?" asked her husband.

"I'm going to be sober for my son's big race, and then… for the rest of my life."

Leroy

"That cat's got quite a set of balls on him, wouldn't you say, Sister?"

Eddie Redlight was talking to himself again. This time about Leroy's humongous nuts, that bounced to and fro when he walked. Since his bump on the head, the sisters noticed Mr. Redlight was a bit more animated and continually jabbering to himself about this or that. It was 2 a.m., and he was standing in his favorite spot out where he could see across the Hudson River and track the progress of nightly freight trains. He could see their little lights far off in the distance. Sometimes, he walked down to the tracks so he could feel the speed and power of passing trains. It was in his blood. Only tonight, he wasn't alone. His new best friend, Leroy – the big tabby cat – was rubbing against Eddie's legs and purring like a diesel locomotive.

Leroy's owner, Lilly, had no problems adjusting to the routine of St. Joseph's Home. The nuns were kind and helped her with schoolwork, even though she was about four years behind kids her own age.

At some point, the sisters would have Lilly tested for aptitudes but that would take a while. The Catholic schools had to wait until all the public schools were tested before it was their turn. That's just the way it was.

Lilly helped Sister Russell cook in the kitchen and serve food in the Sisters' private dining room. She loved the job, and could eat as much as she wanted.

Except for being yelled at a few times for cursing and smoking cigarettes with Eddie Redlight, little Lilly from Lake Mathews was doing about as well as any of the kids at the orphanage. And a lot better then some. Lilly's craving for cigarettes was something the nuns knew they'd have to deal with, but slow as she goes. Bad habits didn't develop overnight, and they weren't cured overnight.

Eddie Redlight and the big tabby became inseparable. Where Eddie went, Leroy followed – all over the grounds, down to the train station and into town. When Eddie took to painting the dormitory eves, Leroy was there prancing on the roof and gently rubbing against Eddie's arms as they swung back and forth with a paint brush.

When Eddie was out raking leaves, Leroy was close behind, ready to pounce on any creature stirred up by the commotion. When Eddie puffed on his smokes late at night, his nocturnal, purring friend was right there to keep him company.

Lilly introduced herself to Redlight as Leroy's owner. Lilly knew a lot about cats and talked a blue streak about them.

She also bummed cigarettes from Redlight and asked him about his life.

"Why's a person so old still living in an orphanage?"

She asked him about the long, jagged scar that ran across the length of his forehead. Eddie told Lilly that he'd been hospitalized from a head injury and the nuns had brought him back to St. Joseph's Home to recuperate. He explained that he was then hired full-time as a maintenance man.

"Basically, I work for my room and board," said Eddie.

"That makes two of us," Lilly responded. "My mother's in jail for killing my father, and the court put me here until the trial's over."

"Why did she kill him?" said Redlight.

"Something bad he done," she answered, and offered no further explanation.

Being the big churchgoer that he was, Sal Fraggo visited St. Joseph's Home bringing toys and games for the kids. Fraggo also gave them substantial amounts of cash to help with facility repairs. The place was one hundred years old so the electrical and plumbing were constantly on the fritz. And everything cost money – lots of money.

The Sisters loved Sal because he paid his own workers to repair the brick walls and stone sarcophagus of St. Joseph's little cemetery where one day they would be interred. Sal helped to pay for the beautiful statues of St. Joseph and the Blessed Virgin that overlooked the hallowed grounds. Sister Agnes, the head nun, thought Sal Fraggo was on a fast track to heaven.

What Sister Agnes didn't know was that Fraggo was filling up the cemetery with murdered gangsters from Brooklyn and the Bronx. They were piled up one on top of the other, wrapped in raincoats and tarpaulins. Some had been shot in the head, others garroted. A few who like to talk to the FBI had had their manhood shoved down their throats.

Yes, the good Sisters loved Sal Fraggo, and he surely loved the good Sisters.

When Sal's big limo pulled up in front of St. Joseph's Home, he was met by Sister Agnes and Sister Imelda, who always served as his official greeting party. Sister Agnes was especially thrilled that Fraggo gave most of his money to the Home and not to the monsignor in town. A sore spot with Monsignor Healy.

"What are you doing to get his money?" the monsignor once asked Sister Agnes.

"We say lots of prayers for him and thank St. Joseph," the Sister responded.

"I pray over at Assumption, and I don't get anything," he grumbled.

Sister Agnes loved one-upping the monsignor, who cruised around town in a brand new black Buick, while she and her nuns traveled around town in a dilapidated school bus.

As he approached the front door, Fraggo spotted Eddie Redlight high up on a ladder swatting bees as he tried to get the best of a hornet's nest.

"I know him from somewhere," said Fraggo, pointing in his direction.

"That's Eddie Redlight. You probably know him from town," said the Sister.

"Isn't he the village idiot who stands on the street corner?"

"Yes, he well may be. We hired him to take care of the grounds and do some painting around here," she said.

"Just remember, Sister. We take care of the cemetery. So keep him out of there. My workers are proud Italians, and don't want anyone messing with their gardening," said an alarmed Fraggo.

"You have my word, Mr. Fraggo."

Once inside, Sal Fraggo got down to business. He presented Sister Agnes with an envelope containing $5,000 in cash.

"We took up a collection for your heating oil costs this winter," he said. "Buy your oil from Danny's Fuel in Peekskill. He'll give you a break on the price and this money should cover it all. Pay him in cash. I guarantee the service."

"Thank you, Mr. Fraggo. We'll say extra prayers for the safety of your construction workers," she said.

"And another thing: Our big softball game has been cancelled so I spoke to the mayor, and we're having some kind of track meet between the kid who's brother was killed in Vietnam and some world record holder from France. This thing might be on television, if you can believe that, and we want a good showing so the entire orphanage is invited. I'll pay for your tickets."

"We know the boy running the race, Mr. Fraggo. Our Sisters taught him at Assumption School."

"Oh, yeah?" asked Fraggo.

"He worked off detention here at the home. A lot of detention."

Sal Fraggo liked Mike Carroll already.

"I've got to get back to Indian Point, Sister. See you at the track meet."

Sal walked out to his limo along with Sister Agnes.

"And Sister..."

"Yes, Mr. Fraggo?"

"Be sure to keep your new handyman out of the cemetery."

It didn't take long for word to get around town that little Lilly Galer had a bank account of almost fifty thousand smackers. Tellers always talked too much and those working at the local bank talked the most.

Little Lilly may have had the largest non-business account in the whole city, and when her two brothers found out, they were determined to get their hands on some or all of it.

After all, they were in hock for the old man's funeral; that set them back over a thousand dollars. Not one single person, outside of the two brothers, showed up for Tony Galer's funeral, which was a one evening, two-hour event. Then, it was onto Potter's Field for the man who did far more bad then good in his life.

Richard and Robert sat drinking at their local watering hole, planning and scheming to get their whack of the loot. They hadn't even known Lilly was at St. Joseph's Home until a popcorn vendor spilled the beans while making a delivery at the Verplanck movie house. And they hadn't cared. For weeks, the brothers made no attempt to find their sister.

"It's kinda nice not having that little pain in the ass around," said Richard.

"Yeah," answered his brother. "But we have to do the cooking now."

Leroy the cat was out making his rounds at dusk when the black hairs on his tabby back suddenly stood up. Leroy stopped dead in his tracks, his nose scanning the area like a radar antenna. Tonight, Leroy smelled trouble, not poon tang. He moved immediately into cover, then jumped up on the wall and looked in all directions.

Leroy heard familiar voices coming from a parking area behind the brick wall.

Robert and Richard Galer, with a snoot full of beer, decided they'd pay a visit to St. Joseph's Home and talk to the good nuns about their sister. In short order, they were sitting in Sister Agnes's office, demanding to see their next of kin. The nun knew Lilly had brothers – the public defender had told her so – but she also knew they were abusive toward the little girl and in no way out for her best interests.

"We just want to see if she has everything she needs," said Robert.

In a short while, Lilly was brought into the room. She showed no elation, no fear, and no emotion. Nothing.

Sister Agnes had never seen anything like it among family members.

"It's okay, Sister. You can leave us alone," said Lilly.

The head nun departed and the brothers got right down to business.

"So you had the money all along," said Richard.

"Yeah," piped Robert. "Half of that is ours. We had to go into hock to bury Daddy. We need that money."

Lilly looked at both of them for a long time before answering. She tapped her feet and then began tapping her fingers on a small wooden table. Except for her movement, the room was totally quiet.

"Have you fed my canary?"

"What the hell are you talking about?" asked Richard.

"Have you fed my canary?"

"Hell no," laughed Richard. "After you left, we let the damn thing go."

Lilly stood up to go, but Richard reached across the table, grabbed hold of her arm and squeezed it hard. He pulled her face next to his. She could smell the beer on his breath.

"Let go or I'll call the Sisters! Those troopers who chased you two up in the woods are still after you, and I'll call 'em. Swear to God."

Reluctantly, Richard let her go. She eyed them both with contempt.

"We want the money, and we're going to get the money," demanded Robert.

"Momma left it to me. It's mine, and I want you both to stay the fuck away from me," said Lilly.

"Listen to that mouth. What do the Sisters think about your nasty cursing?" asked Robert.

"Have you seen Momma?"

"No," said Richard. "And, we don't intend to. She poisoned Daddy."

"Yeah, that's right," said Lilly. "She poisoned Daddy, for what he done to me. If I'd a known what Momma was going to do, I'd a killed him myself."

"I got news for you, Lilly. When Daddy got drunk, he'd say you weren't his kid. He swore Momma screwed some sailor and along came Lilly."

"That's a lie!" she screamed.

"We don't know where you came from, but we want our money. Give us half, and we'll go away," said Robert.

"That money's for my education," said Lilly.

Both brothers began to laugh.

"What education?" asked Richard.

"I'm going to college, when I get out of here. I love animals, and I'm going to be a veterinarian," said Lilly.

"You're retarded, Lilly. You ain't going to no college. You couldn't even finish grammar school. We were just hoping that you could someday count change," Richard said, continuing,

"We figured in a year or two to get you a job in the laundry mat in Peekskill—cleaning the machines and making small change."

"You figured wrong," answered Lilly. "I'm going to Cornell University. Momma worked up near there and said they had programs for me."

"They got programs. Retarded programs for people like you," said Robert.

"Momma was just shitting you. A big joke, that's all," he said.

"She killed Daddy and lied to you," Robert yelled. "Momma left us all. Momma was no good."

Lilly felt like throwing up. She walked to the door.

"How's your cat, Lilly?"

She froze in her tracks.

"We saw Leroy sitting on the wall when we drove up," said Richard. "That's our cat too. Maybe we'll keep the cat, and you can keep the money. We love animals too."

Lilly turned her back on her idiot brothers and walked out the door. Before going to her room, she stopped at the chapel to pray. It was empty except for old Sister Ann Marie who was sleeping in the front pew.

Lilly got down on her knees.

Bless my mother and bless my cat,
and bless my bird and bless the Sisters,
and bless my friend Eddie Redlight.
And please send to hell my brothers,
So they can join my father.

Lilly bowed her head, made the sign of the cross, and then walked back to her dormitory.

The French
Record Holder

Oslo, Norway, (Associated Press) — France's Michel Jazy set his second world record tonight with a come-from-behind victory in the two-mile run. Trailing Australia's Ron Clarke with only 300 meters to go, Jazy turned on the speed to pass his rival and set the new mark of eight minutes, five seconds (8:05). Clarke finished three seconds behind, shattering the old record.

Jazy already holds the world mile mark in three minutes and fifty-three seconds (3:53), besting that of Olympic champion Peter Snell.

Jazy, who was slowed earlier in the season with an injured foot, regained his form of late and is now poised to set records in any distance race he enters. His next meet will be in two weeks in Los Angeles, California, where he will enter the ten thousand meter run.

In the Oslo race, promoters were quick to point out that tonight's meet was attended by 22,000 spectators – more than had ever seen a track meet at National Stadium.

Season bests were also recorded in the javelin, shot put, and 800-meter run.

Honey cut the track article out of *The New York Times* and brought it to French class. Mike Carroll read it over with quiet detachment, before putting it down without saying a word.

"Well, what do you think?" she asked, trying to gauge his reaction. When none was forthcoming she asked, "Like, are you going to answer me?"

Carroll was in a daze, and it showed. He picked up the newspaper story and glanced over it again without saying a word. He scratched his forehead and rubbed his hand through his short crew cut. His mind was a million miles away.

"My workouts aren't going that good," he volunteered. "The last couple of days have been a struggle. I'm missing my marks in the 220 and 440s and even feeling tired running distance."

Concerned, Honey leaned forward and whispered, "Maybe we need that skinny dip sooner than later."

Honey looked at his face, but there was no smile, no reaction. Under usual circumstances, he'd be a little pudgy down under. Something was definitely wrong.

"What's the matter?" she insisted.

"I'll tell you after class."

It was the longest forty-five minutes Honey could remember. What was it? she thought. Is he getting cold feet? Maybe he's not the athlete everyone thinks he is. Does he have another girlfriend? No, Honey dismissed that idea as foolish. After all, who in town is better looking than me? Was it family problems?

After class, they sat on the steps in front of school, Mike Carroll not saying much.

"OK, what the hell is the matter?" asked a now angry Honey. "We need to figure this out before your mother comes to pick you up."

"She's not coming to pick me up. I'm thumbing home today."

Honey smiled and said, "We can thumb home together."

"You can't come to my house now," said Carroll, as he walked away from Honey towards the road.

"And why not?" she asked.

"Because my mother's detoxing from all the alcohol she's had," he blurted out. "She quit drinking the other day and is going cold turkey up in Jackie's room." His voice was quivering. "She's outta her mind. She's in real pain, and there's nothing anyone can do for her. Momma's sweating and vomiting and rolling off the bed and onto the floor. It's awful. She's smacked her head, and has dried blood in her hair. She looks a terrible mess.

"She's ranting and raving. No one knows what she's talking about. Last night, she was packing her things so she could meet up with the 'Catholic Girls.' She tried to jump out the window when we held the door shut. It's another nightmare, and it's killing the family."

Honey put her arms around Mike and hugged him as hard as she could.

"You shouldn't have to go through this with your big race coming up. Nobody should have to go through this shit."

"Momma's doing it for me," he said. "She told Dad she wanted to show us all she's not a loser," he said as he began to tear up. "Mom's doing it so I can win."

Honey suggested Marie see her mother's psychiatrist.

"When my mother gets depressed or drinks too much, Dr. Sheldon gives her a shot and calms her right down," said Honey. "After a few days of rest, Susan Sanders is fine and ready to start drinking and playing golf again. My father says it's the best money he spends."

"Well, my father won't send her to a psychiatrist. And besides that, she won't go."

"How long do the DTs last?" asked Honey

"Four or five days," answered Mike. "Dad says she's halfway through."

Mike walked toward Route 6. He turned back towards Honey, and said, "I can't run when Mom's in such pain. I just can't. When she's better, I'll start up again."

Against Marie's wishes, Mickey decided to contact Monsignor Healy to find out if anything could be done for his suffering bride. Mickey thought maybe a special prayer could be said for Marie or that the monsignor might agree to come over to the house and hold her hand.

"A bad idea, a very bad idea," said a red-faced Monsignor Healy to Mickey's suggestion. "Marie will surely attack me, and then where would we be?"

The monsignor then turned on Mickey: "You were the one who brought liquor into your own house, and you continued to feed her needs until she lost all will to resist. I see the Maries of this town every day, and it's always the same scenario – a compliant husband or wife and a boatload of gin. I pray for them and their families because they really need the prayers, but I also pray that people like you wake up to what you're doing to the family."

Mickey, the long-suffering father, was now taking his licks.

"A lot of these mothers are prone to hitting the John Barleycorn when they can no longer have children. Probably in the genes. Can't you see that, Mickey? When menopause comes upon them, they feel useless in life, totally useless. They don't work outside the house so they have nothing. And the alcohol is a way out for them. I'm sure you've heard this all before.

"And most never come out of it. Some try, but fail. The alcohol is the problem. It's the devil. No doubt about it. And because there's no divorce in the Catholic Church, there's no way out for the family either. Except for the kids. They take off as fast as they can. You see, Mickey, that's the only way the kids can survive. They have to get away from that terribly destructive behavior.

"They pick colleges as far away as the trains will take them. They join the Army and Navy and never come back if they're smart. And they wind up in Vietnam…" his voice trailed off in the realization of Jackie's death. "I'm sorry Mickey. I'm very sorry for your great loss."

With his big jowly face propped up on his hands, Mickey was sitting on the couch in the large, wood-paneled rectory room listening intently. The monsignor's voice changed from demanding and accusatory to soothing.

"You have a fine family Mickey. A boy that was a hero in Vietnam and another who is going to be the greatest runner this country ever had. You have a lot to be thankful for," said the monsignor. "I don't have all the answers, Mickey. The Lord works in strange and mysterious ways."

Mickey said nothing during the monsignor's tirade, and sat silently for the longest time after he finished speaking. In the background, the only thing that could be heard was the sound of dishes being stacked in the dining room. Not even noise from the street penetrated the inner sanctum of the rectory.

"What do you know about the 'Catholic Girls'?" asked Mickey.

The monsignor sat upright in his chair.

Mickey continued, "Marie keeps telling me about the 'Catholic Girls.' What does that mean?"

The monsignor's demeanor changed. His hand tapped on his knee, and his face turned ashen. "I have no information to provide on that subject. Mostly gossip and Protestant rumors anyway."

Mickey now demanded, "My wife is half outta her mind with craziness and she's screaming about the 'Catholic Girls.' Monsignor, you're a man of the cloth. Please answer me."

Monsignor Healy rose and walked to the door, with Mickey close on his heels.

"I am a man of the cloth, and I've taken important vows which I intend to keep. We'll say extra prayers for your wife for as long as you wish and continue to support Michael's admission to the College of the Holy Cross."

After Mickey left, Monsignor Healy knelt down in his small private chapel. He said a few prayers for Mickey, his family, and his suffering wife.

Pressing
On

It was if the softball game never existed. The King and His Court were old news by September. The town of Peekskill became so engrossed in the upcoming track meet that all other matters of state ceased to exist. The superintendent of schools asked for, and received, permission from Albany to begin the school year a few days late. An early season football game was rescheduled. Nothing was to interfere with this great event. The city's entire work crew was detailed to Depew Park and the War Memorial site on Division Street. The mayor liked to say it was like a scene from the Chinese Cultural Revolution.

Bleachers were imported from all over Westchester County, and a new scoreboard was quickly put up with a giant clock that showed minutes and seconds, but unfortunately, not the tenths-of-a-second which were necessary for a track meet. The football boosters had been trying for years to get a new scoreboard, and never could. Hand-held stopwatches would be used by the officials.

Of course, the little Italian man with the aviator sunglasses was right in the middle of the action, volunteering his union workers for every type of project. The services he would later bill to another "paying" job. Sal Fraggo forked over $15,000 for event expenses such as renting bleachers, erecting bathrooms, and building new corrals for the peacocks. Fraggo got between five and ten thousand dollars from the crime syndicate for every stiff he buried at St. Joseph's Cemetery. Fraggo prayed for a lot of murders in Brooklyn and the Bronx.

CBS television contacted Mayor DiGregorio and decided to go along with the French request and broadcast the meet at midnight so the Europeans could get up early and watch the race.

Failure to follow this request could be a deal breaker for CBS.

The race would be advertised as "The Midnight Mile." The network began erecting the additional lighting needed for the broadcast. Huge cranes began arriving at Depew Park to hold the high intensity lights. It was really a big show in itself.

And money? CBS sports said it would underwrite the cost of the war memorial up to $100,000, a sum unimaginable to city officers.

Officials from the Amateur Athletic Association (AAU) visited Peekskill to measure the track. They laid out sophisticated devices all over the oval and then announced their findings: The Depew Park's track was short by close to two feet in the quarter mile. That translated to a total of eight feet in a four-lap mile run, or about one or two seconds.

Not to worry, said the officials. The inside lane could be adjusted to meet the requirements. And soon, that was done. The Peekskill oval was exactly 440 yards around so if a world record was set, it could be counted.

Extra officials would be brought in with additional stopwatches. Seven watches alone would time the first place finisher just in case it was a world record, which no one was really counting on. Most thought Michel Jazy would toy with the local boy runner until the last lap and then turn on the gas and leave him in the dust. New York City newspapers and television broadcasters were just hoping for a mile under four minutes.

If Jazy could just break four minutes, it would be considered a great race because to do so without any serious competition was difficult, at best.

Breaking five minutes would be hard for Mike Carroll on this third day of his mother's painful withdrawals. He and Mickey labored night and day to keep her from jumping out of the upstairs' windows. They force fed her and cleaned her up when she needed it. They also took turns feeding and driving the little ones to day camp and the movies.

"What's the matter with Mom?" the kids constantly asked.

"It'll be all right. Your mother's on her way to a full recovery," Mickey would boldly answer.

"Recovery from what?" asked Laura.

Mickey told the kids that Mom had been real sick since Jackie was killed in Vietnam – a combination of a stubborn flu, summer fever and the blues. Mom was sad and sick, and that made for a difficult combination.

"Why don't you send her to the hospital?" Laura persisted.

"Your mother doesn't like hospitals. Grandma went into the hospital with the flu and the next thing we knew, she had pneumonia and died. We don't want that happening to your mother, so we'll take care of her," said their father.

Mike Carroll looked a wreck; he failed to return Honey's phone calls. Alarmed, she drove over to the house along with her mother. But Mickey, who was on duty at the time, refused to let them visit with his sick wife.

"Marie will be taking visitors next week, and we all thank you very much for bringing over this food and good will."

"Where's Mike?" asked Honey.

"He's at camp with the kids."

"Has Mike been training? He has a big race in two weeks," said an exasperated Honey.

"Mike's taking a few days off. He's helping with his mother's fever – and besides that, he said his legs hurt. That's it!" said Mickey with a nod. "He's resting his legs."

Honey and her mother left the Carroll home and drove straight out to Mohegan Lake summer camp where the kids were swimming and playing. As they walked from the parking lot along a tree-lined path, they saw Mike lying across a picnic table, fast asleep.

Honey approached and kissed him on the cheek. His eyes opened and he kissed her back. Then he saw Mrs. Sanders standing nearby.

Embarrassed, he said, "Sorry, Mrs. Sanders."

"No problem here. You kids spend some time together, and I'll walk down to the lake and put my feet in the water."

Honey studied Carroll. He looked like hell. He had bags under his eyes and appeared thinner than usual. He looked sickly.

"Have you been eating?" she asked.

"Yeah. Mickey's macaroni and cheese. As much as I want," he answered.

Honey rubbed his head and shoulders. She hugged him like a

child and spoke to him softly. Mike softly moaned.

"You need to regain your strength and start running again. You're a great champion Michael. Your mother, if she was better, would want you to do this."

The two embraced for a long time.

"Dammit! You can beat that Frenchman. I just know it," said Honey.

"That's the same thing Mom said before she got so sick."

Later that day as Mike pulled up to the house with a carload of hungry little kids, he noticed Mickey smoking a cigarette and raking cut grass from the lawn.

Alarmed, he shouted, "Where's Mom?"

"She's in the back, Son."

Mike ran to the back yard, leaping over the lilac bushes. There, he saw Marie Carroll sitting in a wooden Adirondack chair reading a newspaper; a cup of Lipton's soup rested on her lap. She had on a clean yellow dress and her hair was neat and combed. She even had on a light shade of lipstick.

"The papers are saying big things about you," she said. "How do you feel?"

"How do *you* feel?" asked Mike.

"I'm fine. Just a little hungry, that's all. I may even jump in the pool if it doesn't cool down."

The kids ran in the backyard and hugged their mother, amid laughs and tears.

"You're better, you're better! What happened to the summer fever?" they asked.

"It went away," said their mother. "Your father and brother nursed me back to health."

Mike Carroll ran upstairs and changed into his running shorts, as his younger brothers and sisters gathered around his mother, tugging at her, rubbing her arms, and running their hands through her hair.

"Go for it, Mike," said Marie as he readied to high jump into the pool. Doing a perfect Western Roll, he cleared the side of the biggest doughboy in the neighborhood, sending an avalanche of water over the sides and knocking over the misplaced water filter. Everyone began to clap hands and cheer.

Looking Out For A Friend

"Have you seen Lilly?" Sister Imelda asked Eddie Redlight, as he pushed a wheelbarrow loaded with broken rock across the common area. "She wasn't at mass this morning, and missed all her classes as well."

Eddie hadn't seen Lilly for a couple of days and hadn't seen her big-balled cat Leroy either. He told the Sister that and then began searching the school grounds. Eddie Redlight looked high and low throughout the dormitories. He knew of secret places in the attic where kids hid out from the nuns or smoked, but she wasn't in any of those.

Redlight searched the chapel and cemetery, the Sisters' dining room and the main cafeteria. He checked the storage and tool sheds and even the dilapidated school bus. But no joy. Lilly wasn't around, and some of her personal belongings were missing as well.

Lilly was AWOL, and Eddie Redlight knew it because Leroy's bag of cat food and dish were gone. But where had she gone?

Eddie reported his findings to Sister Agnes, who told him that Lilly and her brothers had had a contentious meeting a week earlier. After the family get-together, Lilly simply was not herself. She began missing classes and skipping cafeteria assignments with Sister Russell. Lilly had also been caught a couple of time sneaking Leroy into the dormitory and hiding the cat in her day locker, which was strictly against the rules.

Sister Agnes said new kids sometimes ran off for a few days or so, but came back when they found they had no place to go. But, she confided in Eddie, she was worried about this little girl.

"She was getting along so well," said the Sister. "Usually, when kids are unhappy it shows in their daily lives, but we never saw a down day for Lilly until her brothers came along."

"Sister, I believe her brothers were the ones who hit me in the head with the pumpkin. I didn't want to say anything to her because I know how fragile she is. But I know it was her brothers who did this to me," said Eddie, pointing to the scar on his head. Sister Agnes knew the truth as well.

"Those two Galer brothers are mean as snakes. Maybe they took her somewhere or she's hiding from them," he said.

Sister Agnes told Eddie she'd wait a few days before contacting the police, as runaways from St. Joseph's were old news to them.

Eddie felt lightheaded this particular day. He was supposed to lead a work party of older kids to clean out drainpipes around the chapel, but he begged off the assignment. Since his beaning on Division Street, Eddie had suffered bad headaches that alternated with an alarming dizziness – probably residuals from the concussion. Today, starting when he got up for breakfast, he had felt these spells coming on so he decided to mop and shine floors in the cafeteria and maybe do some light landscaping. He would stay off roofs and ladders altogether.

Eddie sure missed his little friend, Lilly, and her bad-ass cat Leroy. They liked to talk about the movies and who was playing what roles. Because of Eddie's work schedule during his railroad years, he'd catch a lot of afternoon matinees. And during that time of day, he was often alone in the theater. Just him, a few other pensioners, and that big screen. Eddie liked movie theater popcorn and movie theater soda. He loved Western flicks. Any kind of Western. Randolph Scott, John Wayne, Crash Corrigan, Ward Bond and Walter Brennan were all his heroes.

Lilly, on the other hand, liked comedies. She loved Jerry Lewis and (like most people in America) was genuinely saddened when Lewis and Martin broke up as a team. How could they do that to us? she thought.

She loved the Little Rascals, and Laurel and Hardy. Phil Silvers, Peter Sellers, Buddy Hacket, and Jonathan Winters were all favorites. Lilly could watch Pink Panther movies all day long and recite punch lines after the show. And besides that, it got her out of the house and away from her old man, which became especially important after her mother took a powder to upstate New York and left her alone.

Lilly loved the movies and so did Eddie Redlight. And they both loved God's simplest of creatures, especially dead-end tabby cats.

So it was around 2 a.m. when Eddie Redlight pulled on his pants, slipped on sneakers and walked out to the ballfield for a smoke. It was a clear night, the end of a long hot day. August days in New York could be miserable with high humidity; without air conditioning, the big dormitories stayed hot until early in the morning. The kids complained and complained, but not much could be done to resolve their discomfort. Sometimes, the nuns would borrow the big fans that were used in church on Sundays to circulate the air and bring some relief. But no fans were coming to the home lately.

Eddie took long drags on his cigarette and mumbled to himself (as was his custom) when he spotted a big cat walking on the wall toward the stairway. It was too dark to tell if it was Leroy, but nonetheless, Eddie followed it off the convent grounds and down the long walkway to the railroad tracks – a distance of about two hundred yards.

The moon was bright, and Eddie was about twenty-five paces behind the cat, which was walking away at a good clip.

"Leroy. It's me, Eddie," he yelled to the feline. "Pssst, pssst, pssst ..."

The cat turned to look at the little man following him, but continued on to the railroad tracks.

With the moonlight reflecting off the Hudson River, he got a good glimpse at the kitty. It was Leroy. Eddie was sure.

"Pssst, pssst... Leroy, it's me. Come here, kitty."

It was no use. The cat wasn't coming to Eddie, not on this night. Redlight decided to stay back and follow Leroy as far as he could.

The cat jumped over a small iron fence and onto the railroad tracks, walking down one of the rails for a good while. There were three sets of rail lines running through Peekskill. Some of the tracks supported long freight trains that maneuvered up and down the Hudson River day and night. Other rails supported passenger and commuter trains.

The New York Central Railroad opened up commerce along the Hudson River Valley, and these big trains loaded with timber, coal, iron ore, and gypsum sped through Peekskill all hours of the night blowing their horns as they rocked by at fifty miles per hour.

The cat felt the rumbling of the train long before Eddie did. He jumped off the rail and walked alongside, pacing himself on the edge of the wooden ties. The train was within a quarter mile now and Eddie moved off the tracks completely and stood ten yards to the side. Eddie knew from years of working on the railroad that one could be sucked onto the tracks by the fierce movement of air between cars. He wanted no part of that.

Two hundred yards ahead, the big diesel locomotive churned and burned as it gunned its way down the track toward him and Leroy.

"Get off the track you stupid cat."

Made no difference. This cat, Leroy, did have had big nuts because he wasn't giving the train the respect it deserved, thought Eddie. The locomotive sped by, stinging Redlight's face with blowing dust, gravel and ash.

At the last instant, the cat jumped into the weeds as the train roared by.

How could he do that? thought Eddie. Let the train come that close, before bailing out? He admired the little feline more then ever.

Eddie watched the red caboose lights disappear in the distance, as the train rumbled southward towards New York City, blowing its horn. And after his eyes readjusted to the darkness again, Eddie was back on the trail of the big tomcat.

But the cat was nowhere to be seen. Eddie continued walking; the moon shinning brightly off the steel rails.

And then, he thought he heard something. There was a human voice. Someone was out there.

Eddie Redlight spotted a small hooch surrounded by brush and sticker bushes maybe twenty yards off the tracks. Carefully, he approached the little hut. Then, he heard a voice he recognized.

"Bad kitty," came the voice from within the hooch. "Where have you been, bad kitty? You had me worried sick."

Eddie stuck his head in the door to see Lilly sitting by a candle petting her cat.

"So, this is where you went!" said Redlight.

Startled, the girl jumped back into the corner. "Stay back! I've got a knife, and I know how to use it!" she yelled.

"It's me, Eddie Redlight. Are you going to cut up your friend?"

Lilly ran to Eddie and gave him a big hug.

"I wanted to tell you, but was scared you'd tell the Sisters," she said softly, rubbing the scar on his forehead.

"I'd never tell the Sisters. We're friends, remember?"

"My brothers were coming after me, and I had to get away. They found out I had some money in the Peekskill bank, and they want it. They've come back a couple of times and tried to get Leroy. They said they'd kill him if I didn't give 'em the money."

Eddie hugged her. "Poor girl. You should have said something. The Sisters would call the cops."

"Wouldn't do any good. My brothers always get away from the cops. One or both of 'em would get out and find me and kill Leroy."

Eddie sat down in the hooch with the little girl as Leroy stood boldly at the front door. His silhouette reflected in the candle glow like a Halloween scene. The hooch was about ten by fifteen square feet and four feet high. It was made of old wood boards, tree branches and cardboard. Vines also crisscrossed the walls and big green leaves covered the planks. Lilly had made a bed of flattened cardboard boxes to cover the dirt floor. Eddie, who had slept in his share of lean-tos over the years, thought this was a pretty cool hiding place.

Eddie didn't know what to do. He was the adult and she was the child, but having been on the receiving end of tormentors much of his adult life, he knew about cruelty.

Another big train was fast approaching. Rounding the turn its million-watt candlepower spotlight shone through the walls of the hooch like a prism. It was as if the train was coming right into them.

The engineer blasted his whistle in long, loud blasts as it neared. Then, a rush of air whipped through swirling dust and gravel in all directions as it rocketed by the little hooch. The noise was deafening.

The train moved on past and disappeared down the track, and all was quiet once again.

Eddie knew he had to do something. But what? She couldn't stay here. The location was on the edge of a hobo jungle and sometimes frequented by criminals and lunatics. If she went back to St. Joseph's, she'd run off again, and the next time he might not find her.

Lilly showed Eddie her poke of food, which she had hauled away from the home upon her departure. She had filled a pillowcase with bread, peanut butter and jelly, and salami. She had also packed in cans of tuna fish, iced tea mix, boxes of corn flakes and Cheerios. She still had a fair amount of food left, and got her drinking water from a nearby stream. But she missed having a cigarette at night.

Eddie and Lilly promptly lit one up.

"What am I going to do with you, Lilly?"

Before she could answer, a loud hissing and spitting was heard. Her brothers Richard and Robert suddenly appeared at the doorway, their faces flickering in the candlelight like two prehistoric monsters. They had hold of Leroy.

"All the retards are here together," said Richard.

"Yup," answered his brother. "First, we followed the cat, then we followed Eddie, the Retard, then we found Lilly, the Retard. What do you say Richard? How about let's tie Leroy down on the tracks."

As Robert pulled a burlap bag from his back pocket, the big tomcat took a hard swipe at Richard's pockmarked face, drawing blood that dripped down into his eye.

"God damn!" he yelled.

Richard pulled a buck knife from his waistband, "I'm going to kill this thing right now."

"No!" his brother intervened.

The cat then scratched Richard's right forearm, bloodying his faded Navy tattoo.

"Gimme the damn thing," said Robert, as he grabbed for Leroy.

Leroy fought and scratched and twisted and turned until the brothers lost control of the crazed feline. After bouncing off the walls a couple of times, Leroy found the front door and scooted out into the night.

The Galer brothers charged after their feline ransom, giving Lilly and Eddie Redlight a chance to get away. The pair bolted out the back of the hooch. Lilly knew the woods real well by now, as they raced along the dark, twisting path. Eddie struggled to stay up.

"Come on!" she yelled to her lumbering friend.

Lilly went back after Eddie who was huffing, puffing and losing ground.

In the distance, she could hear her brothers cursing and moving along the path behind them.

"A couple of hundred yards to the wall. That's all," she pleaded.

Eddie Redlight made one last effort to catch up with Lilly, and then they were at the high brick wall. Her brothers were fast approaching.

Skinny little Lilly gave Eddie a boost over the top, where he tumbled onto the ball field on the other side. Lilly pulled herself up with the agility of a cat as Richard's knife sliced the underside of her sneaker. She fell to the ground on top of Eddie, now safely on convent grounds. The brothers halted their chase.

"We'll be back, Lilly!" Robert shouted from the woods, as the pair hobbled towards the dormitory. "We want the money."

Skinny
Dipping

Mike Carroll's workouts took a dramatic shift to the upside after his mother's self-imposed alcoholic nightmare ended. Pangs of sadness still filled parts of Marie's day as she recounted her beloved son. For the most part, she seemed to be on the road to recovery – so much so that son Mike was out on the trails of Blue Mountain churning and burning the cross-country miles.

Carroll reasoned that he had lost maybe a week and a half of training because of his mother's illness. His weight was the same, but his endurance was a bit below normal. He could feel it. If he got in ten good days of training and rested a few days before the race, he'd be fine.

Prior to his stand down, Mike was running repeat quarter miles faster than ever. One of his favorite workouts was eight quarter-mile sprints with a quarter-mile jog in between.

In mid July, he recorded his workout in his notebook. "One mile jog and stretches to loosen up, followed by 8 times 440—times were: 55.2, 56.1, 56.0, 54.7, 54.6, 52.3, 52.9, 52.0. This was followed by an eight-mile run through Blue Mountain to home at five-minute mile pace."

Another workout Mike recorded was: "Six-mile run at five minutes per mile. At four-mile mark, ran timed mile in 4:19."

On a Sunday distance run, he wrote down: "Ten miles in 51 minutes. Never felt tired." But, Mike Carroll was tired now. Dog tired. Doing the same workouts took a great deal more out of him, and to be honest with himself, he couldn't sustain his earlier pace. But not to panic, he reasoned. Move up a notch each day in training. Run and drink lots of water and soak in the doughboy at the end of each workout.

"Are you ready for a skinny dip?" Honey asked Mike over the phone one evening.

"Um... Um... Yeah... Sure I am," said the startled teenager.

"I was going to make you wait until after your big race, but what the hell. Come on over tomorrow night," said Honey. "My parents are going to an IBM picnic, and they're spending the night in Poughkeepsie."

Mike Carroll put down the phone and imagined that in twenty-four hours, he and the most beautiful girl in Peekskill would be doing the big nasty. He would float on his back in her pool while she made love to him in every manner possible. After all, she had the experience. And then, when she was craving the Big Embo, he'd slide it in ever so professionally, and she'd scream with such sensation that neighbors would take notice and be jealous of her mysterious lover.

Nice story, Carroll thought, but he was still a virgin. Besides a primal lusting for sex and reading skin magazines regularly, he knew nothing about the subject, and Honey would surely pick up on it. She had already asked him if he was a virgin to which he repeated an emphatic, "No."

But Honey prodded: "I don't believe you. With who? Where? Nobody fucks you track guys."

"Oh yeah," said Mike. "We have our own groupies. You're not the only one who frenches on the bus."

Honey, threw her gorgeous head of blonde hair back, looked Carroll straight in the eye and said, "You're full of shit. Unless you're screwing some prostitutes in Ossining, you guys are all virgins. Period. And especially you, mon ami."

Carroll knew Honey couldn't be fooled so easily. He was a virgin, just like all the guys on the track team – with the exception of maybe one or two lucky ones.

Mike Carroll was the typical late-developing kid, like so many others he palled around with. A pimply face and a pretty stiff boner in class is about all he had to offer the fine ladies of his high school. Going into his senior year he was still a virgin and not fooling anyone.

Mike learned to deal with the verbal abuse from the lucky guys who were "getting some," and give it back on occasion, like the time at the Penn Relays when he was jiving with some black runners from New Rochelle High School before a mile relay race.

"Hey, Peckerwood," said one of the black dudes. "Ya got a lady?"

"Uh-huh. A nice one too," said Mike.

"She got big white titties?"

"The biggest, Bro."

"You having sex with her?"

"Man, what do you think?"

"Does she like brothers?"

"Light-skinned ones, maybe."

The black guys all broke up and laughed their asses off. "You a jive turkey," one of them said. "See you at the finish line."

Mike Carroll knew in his heart that he wasn't going to fool the beautiful Honey Sanders.

After a track workout, which was comprised of a hard five-mile run and a series of medium sprints all run at top speed, Mike Carroll cashed his post office paycheck for $25.30 and walked to Circle Men's Shop in Peekskill to buy a new Jantzen swimsuit. He thought it was kind of funny to be buying a swimsuit when the whole purpose of the night was to go swimming without one, but he guessed he'd have to wear a bathing suit at some point.

Mike hadn't owned a bathing suit in years. Mickey had the kids swimming in their underwear for the longest time, and now he wore track shorts whenever he went in the water. A new bathing suit was in order. The one he bought was blue with large white stripes on the side, like one he saw in a Beach Boys commercial. And he paid a princely sum of $16.50 for it, more than half his paycheck.

Mickey Carroll's rusted '49 Ford buzz bomb pulled up to Honey Sanders's house at six o'clock in the evening. Per earlier instructions, he let himself into the house. He walked through the hallway of beautiful family pictures and into the backyard, where he found Honey grilling some of her father's big steaks.

Mike had his new bathing suit rolled up inside a towel. "I bought a bathing suit today," he said

"I don't know why. You're not going to need it," she answered. "Help yourself to a brew. You know where they are," said Honey, as she turned the steaks. In a moment, Mike was back with a cold Piel's beer in his hand.

"You seem a little nervous," said Honey.

"Not at all."

Honey was wearing short shorts and a white blouse with no bra. Her hair was in a large ponytail, just like when she cheered.

"My sister's spending the night at her friend's house," she said. "We have to be careful. Sometimes she sneaks home."

"You make it sound like we're robbing a bank," said Mike.

"I know my sister."

Honey and Mike sat down to a wonderful dinner of steaks, corn on the cob and fresh green salad with tomato slices. They drank beer and even had a shot of Steve's peppermint schnapps.

The backyard was shielded from the neighbors' view by large bushes on the perimeter. The pool sat in the middle of the backyard and the water appeared as blue and inviting as anything he'd ever seen. Honey and Mike picked up the dirty dishes and carried them into the house.

"Go dive in. I'll be right out," she said. "And take a couple of brews with you."

In a flash, Carroll was swimming naked in the pool, with a half-dozen cold beers lined up on the side. He swam from side to side with his little stiff monster creating a wake of its own.

Honey walked out wrapped in a huge beach towel, which she discarded at the side of the pool. She faced Mike totally naked, the moonlight reflecting off her perfect body. Her breasts sticking straight out like he always imagined. His heart pounded; he thought he was having a heart attack.

The most beautiful woman in Peekskill, surely since the American Revolution, stood before him.

She dove into the water and swam between Mike's legs. She surfaced and they hugged, her large breasts floating on the water. She reached down and stroked him.

"Ooooh, what do we have here," she said. "A live torpedo?"

"Yeah, and it's ready to explode," he said.

The two kissed and fondled each other for a long time. He slid his hand down between her gorgeous legs and felt her all over. She moaned and groaned. They were standing in four feet of water when Honey bent over to hug the wall.

"Take me from behind," she said.

Mike Carroll was on his way to obliging, rubbing her beautiful rear and nuzzling up to her when a full-blown ruckus erupted inside her house. In a split second, lights were turned on and "You did this" and "You said that" boomed through the house, courtesy of her parents, who were locked in a hell of a fight.

"Holy shit. They're home!" said the wet and feverish Honey Sanders.

Honey moved with the speed of sprinter as she bolted from the pool grabbling hers and Mike's bathing suits, which were hanging near the porch. She jumped back into the water putting on her suit while he did the same.

In a moment, the back pool lights came on, illuminating the place like Stalag 17.

"Are you kids back there?" Susan Sanders yelled.

"Yeah, Mom. We're swimming in the pool."

"I'll be down in a minute," she said.

Oh, Christ, what is it now? thought Honey.

"What's going on?" asked Mike.

"They must have gotten into a fight. Happens sometimes. Then they come home to really battle it out."

"Your house isn't much different than mine," said Carroll with a laugh.

In a short time, an obviously drunk Susan Sanders was poolside, holding a Manhattan in one hand and a beer in the other.

"I'm leaving that man," she said to Honey. Her anger was clearly visible. "I'm sorry you have to hear this Mike, but you'll find out soon enough. Your father's been fucking some young engineer from RPI. I found out tonight and I'm leaving him."

Honey was taken back. "Oh Mom, you're exaggerating."

"I am, huh? Well you didn't see what I saw. This pretty little thing on his 'team' was all over him at the party. After a few drinks, she's all over him! 'Steve's such a good boss.' 'Steve's so funny.' 'Steve's the best dresser in the office.' This tart has a few drinks and she's slobbering all over that two-timing bastard up there," she said, pointing to the house.

"And they've taken trips together," said her mother swilling down her drink. "This Karen has accompanied him to Allentown and Philadelphia. I've known for a while. Flowers delivered to the wrong address. Midnight phone calls. Matchbooks from nightclubs. No passion in his lovemaking ..."

"We don't need to know all that, Mom," Honey interrupted.

"They play tennis together in mixed doubles. I was a great tennis player in high school and your father has never asked me to play. Not once. 'You're such a good golfer,' he tells me. 'Go play golf with your friends. I'll find someone to play tennis with,' he says like a goddamn martyr."

Mrs. Sanders began to cry.

Honey hugged her mother and rocked her head as Mike picked up his towel and headed for the car. He waved to Honey as he walked across the lawn, alongside the beautiful in-ground swimming pool – the biggest and deepest in town. He had wisely parked in the street so he wouldn't leave any tell-tale oil stains in the Sanders' driveway.

Mike Carroll sat in his car thinking about the night. Technically, he was still a virgin, but only by the slightest of margins. But he felt really good for some strange reason. Running is what he felt like doing now – over Blue Mountain, across Ft. Putnam, along the Hudson River, around the track – wherever.

Steve Sanders walked out the front door with his hands full. He was still dressed in his picnic clothes — white tennis shorts, sneakers, and a dark blue Jantzen V-necked shirt. He was smoking a cigarette and carrying a large suitcase in one hand and a beer in the other. Compared to his hysterical wife in the backyard, he seemed not to have a care in the world.

He opened the trunk of his car and placed the suitcase inside. He backed his car out of the driveway and sped off into the night without ever looking back.

Lights, Camera...
Action

The countdown to the great track race was on. In Peekskill, the mayor's office set up a special liaison officer to handle media inquiries. Requests for press passes were coming in from all over the country as well as from Europe, South America, Japan and Australia.

Reporters from *The New York Times, The Herald Tribune, The New York Daily News, The Bronx Irish News, The Los Angeles Times, The Miami Herald, The Knoxville News-Sentinel,* and *The Winchester (Tennessee) Herald Chronicle,* as well as *Track and Field News* were arriving in Peekskill in need of interesting background stories. So, too, were overseas reporters from Italy, France and Spain.

Most reporters jumped on the slain brother angle, describing an emotionally fragile teenager running a race to honor his older brother. Scribes fanned out around Peekskill, talking to teachers, priests and neighbors.

"Has Mike Carroll ever been in trouble with the law?" asked one reporter to Peekskill's chief of police, Joe Bongiorno.

"No, he's a great kid," came the response, even though the chief knew Mike and brother Jackie had gotten picked up a few times for juvenile pranks – such as taking a crap on someone's front step and spray-painting a police horse's nuts bright orange. Kids' pranks.

A reporter from *Paris Match* magazine visited Mademoiselle Plante and asked many questions about Mike Carroll and his good friend, Honey Sanders.

What made them contact the French consulate? Did they really think Michel Jazy would race a high school kid? What did Mike Carroll think about the war in Vietnam?

Questions, questions, questions.

Media people descended on the Carroll residence, taking pictures of Marie and Mickey in son Jackie's room reading his last letters from Vietnam and looking at photos of him in uniform.

Mickey and Marie played it straight with reporters, telling them that son Jackie had been promised a spot on the Marine Corps track team, but instead had been shipped off to Vietnam immediately. The parents said they were skeptical of the Marine Corps recruiters' sales pitches and should have asked more questions at the time.

A reporter asked Marie if she thought her son should be spared Vietnam service because he was a good athlete.

"Twelve months ago, I didn't even know where Vietnam was," she answered. "How important of a place could it be?"

And the above ground pool. The press took stills and shot video not only of the Carroll kids swimming in the biggest doughboy in the neighborhood, but of Mike doing a perfect Western Roll as he high-jumped into the pool like Valeri Brumel, the Russian Olympic Champion.

Camera crews took pictures of Mike running along the paths of Blue Mountain State Park – running at such a fast pace that leaves and dust were trailing in his wake. They made for great shots and were featured on the evening news.

The chargé d'affaires, Monsieur Claude Lambeau, showed up in Peekskill to give the mayor a plaque from France. Monsieur Lambeau also gave the mayor a check for $10,000 towards the war memorial.

Lambeau posed for pictures with Mike and Honey. When he found out that Honey was a student and not a teacher he said only, "Mais oui!" He was such a good sport about everything, Honey thought.

Lambeau insisted on seeing Jackie Carroll's grave in Assumption cemetery and knelt by his tombstone and said a long prayer for his infantry soul mate. "Mort pour l'amerique."

Le chargé d'affaires also offered Honey a job in the consulate should she ever need one.

"You speak better French than I do," he offered.

Honey responded that she was going to college, but after that, "Who knows?"

Giving out more interviews than anyone in the city was Sal Fraggo and his lovely assistant, Marci. Fraggo would park his giant stretch limo out in front the mayor's office and invite scribes into his vehicle for a cappuccino.

According to Fraggo, he was responsible for the entire race. As he explained: "You see, we undertook a big project to expand our town's war memorial for the boys killed in Vietnam. We were supposed to have this softball game between our brave firefighters and the legendary King and His Court softball team.

"At the last minute, the softball game was cancelled because of a bunch of pricks, I mean town officials, from Danbury, Connecticut. This leaves us in the lurch," says a pontificating Fraggo. "So, I go see the good Sisters of St. Joseph and after much prayers at the foot of the cross, we come up with a race between our lad, Mike Carroll and the flying Frenchman, Michel Jazy."

The press liked Fraggo's cappuccino, but didn't believe a thing he said. The race was the work of the dedicated French consulate in New York, and they all knew it.

Actually, the press people were more interested in interviewing Marci than Fraggo. During the lead-up to the big race, Marci was offered a half-dozen jobs by various media outlets.

Fraggo *was* an important fixture at "The Midnight Mile." His men supplied thousands of dollars of free labor. They erected bleachers, built bathrooms and laid cement curbs for the track; they helped on additional lighting and with the installation of the new scoreboard.

After a half-hearted attempt to get his money back from the West Point athletic association, Fraggo let the matter go.

They're brave soldiers, what the hell, he said to himself.

Even Cookie Reams made the tabloids. Reams, who had become an unofficial coach to Carroll, was photographed at the track timing his runner's workouts.

Media folks dug up Reams's athletic history and, once again, brought up the fact that he was Peekskill's top all-around athlete. He starred in basketball, track and football and was now helping his protégé train for the race of his life.

They printed photos of Mike and Cookie jogging along Depew Park's cross-country course.

Pictures appeared of Mike, Cookie and Honey discussing race strategy while sitting on Fraggo's new bleachers. Fraggo was also photographed timing Mike Carroll as he ran along the track during workouts.

"Hey, kid… Let me ask you one thing…" Fraggo said to Mike one day during workouts. "…Do you think you can beat this Frenchman?"

"I'm going to try, Mr. Fraggo," said Mike.

"We all try," said Fraggo. "But it's about winning. Do you think you can win?"

"Yes I do. I think I can beat anyone I run against."

"That's what I like to hear, Kid. That's what the doctor likes to hear. Big betting odds are on the Frenchman, and if you win, we all win… if you get my point," said Fraggo.

"I get your point, Mr. Fraggo. And we're all going to win."

A week before the meet, CBS threw a curve ball at the entire operation.

Since they were televising the meet and had sponsors lined up, the network of course, wanted the best ratings possible.

Network executives wanted the race format changed. Instead of Peekskill's Mike Carroll taking on world record holder Michel Jazy in a sentimental mile race, the network wanted top U.S. milers to be entered.

This would make for a better race and increase advertising revenue, they figured.

The French adamantly objected. Michel Jazy was coming off a big race only two nights earlier in Los Angeles where he hoped to set a new world record in a distance event. He would be in no shape to face speedy American milers two nights later. The French sports people didn't want their number one runner put at such a disadvantage, running a race in an exhausted state against rested athletes.

The French cried foul. This race was supposed to be a lightweight event to raise money for a war memorial and all participants understood that. To change the rules at this late date was wrong.

The French said no. CBS balked as well. And Sal Fraggo went berserk.

Second athletic event, still no joy. Fraggo cussed a blue streak, and more. He threatened to put every CBS executive face down in St. Joseph's cemetery next to his gumbahs from Brooklyn.

Screaming at Marci, he said, "There's plenty of room for those fucks at St. Joseph's. I'll have my crews out there on Sundays digging holes if I have to.

Fraggo called the network. Fraggo called the FCC.

CBS told Fraggo to go to hell, and the FCC didn't call back.

"The nerve of those cocksuckers!"

Fraggo had lined up Joey Dee and the Starlighters as the entertainment, and Marci was going to make her debut lip-syncing a few of Annette Funicello's hit songs.

"It was all set. How could those pricks do this to me?" he screamed to Marci.

Fraggo dug his heals in. He wasn't a Capo in the crime family for nothing.

"Get me my rolodex," he shouted to Marci. "I'll fix their wagons."

Sal Fraggo then began calling every steward in the unionized entertainment business – unions that controlled camera operators, sound technicians, and electricians.

If CBS fucked up this track meet, their executives would be operating cameras and painting sets because there wouldn't be any organized labor on the job.

Mickey was in Sorentino's Italian restaurant across from the train station picking up some pizza pies for the kids' dinner. It was a busy night for takeout, and the kitchen was backlogged. He was sitting at the bar drinking a Jenny cream ale and bullshitting with the bartender – but mostly, Mickey's thoughts turned to his own life.

He wished Marie were with him tonight in this place where they had sung such beautiful music. Mickey wished things had turned out differently– that his son Jackie was with him at the bar right now, old enough to drink and gulping down a cold beer after a long run. Jackie would be a sophomore in college, maybe NCAA champion, but surely IC4A champion. Surely.

Towards the end of the bar, Vince, the nighttime bartender, was cleaning and stacking glasses. In an hour or so, things would pick up after the locals had digested their dinners and come back down to the bar for a bump and a beer.

Vince was chatting with Gus the conductor. Sixty-three years old, gray hair and very much overweight, wearing coke bottle barney goggles, Gus had worked for the New York Central Railroad for thirty-plus years and was now retired. Mickey waved to him on the way in. Gus was a good guy and everyone in town knew him. During the summers when his bosses weren't looking, he let the local kids ride free down to Yankee games and kept a dozen or so seats reserved for the card players on their way home from the city. Gus always let the sisters from St. Joseph's Home ride for free, and he stayed on the lookout for their little runaways searching for parents who no longer cared about them.

In his retirement, Gus was a lost soul. He wandered around Peekskill with nothing to do. He had no interests or hobbies, and his wife didn't want his brooding ass hanging around the house. On his retirement date, Gus was given a lifetime rail pass, which he used two to three times a week riding the train some forty miles away to New York City just to pick up the *Daily News* and *Daily Mirror* newspapers.

Gus finally got to sit in a train seat after all those years of standing and yelling, "Next stop, Croton Harmon... Croton Harmon will be the next stop... Please watch your step!"

Gus liked looking out the train windows at the Hudson River. Its strength and power never failed to impress him. The railroad was a great job, he told everyone. Never paid much, but a great job.

And like many of the old railroad guys, Gus the conductor was drinking too much these days and telling stories. Lots of stories.

"Hey Vince, did I ever tell you the one about the 'Catholic Girls'? These girls they get on the train at Grand Central Station and they're going to Canada to become Novices, you know, Sisters in the Church. Maybe fifteen or twenty or so. Every week it seems. A dozen or two going on to become Novices – to Canada to study for their calling. Most, real young..."

"Why do they have to go to Canada to become nuns?" the bartender interrupted.

Gus continued. "And some well-dressed man gives me their tickets and asks me to keep an eye on them. To make sure they don't get off before Montreal. The man never explains anything.

Just gives me their tickets and a hundred dollars for me to keep an eye on them. He refers to them as the 'Catholic Girls.' Strange, right?

"These girls are never any bother on the trip. They mostly sit and read. No one seems real happy about giving up their lives for Jesus, I'll tell you that. I've seen trainloads of soldiers going to Vietnam that were a lot happier than these 'Catholic Girls.' They seemed pretty sad, if you ask me," said Gus, drawing long on his cigarette.

"One day up in Hudson, New York, two of the 'Catholic Girls' bolt off the train. It's raining and sleeting, worst possible day. They're running down the street screaming that no one is going to hurt them. We catch up to the kids and now the cops are there, and the girls are crying hysterically. The cops don't know what to do. We don't know what to do. Nobody knows what they're talking about."

"What happened?" the bartender interrupted.

"They got back on the train and continued with the trip, but come to find out that these 'Catholic Girls' aren't going to be become sisters – they're going to Canada to get abortions because they can't get 'em in New York."

The bartender asked, "How many girls are we talking about?"

"Over the years," said the conductor thinking out loud, "Hundreds, yeah, hundreds and hundreds."

Mickey's pizza pies were ready for pickup. He finished his beer and put a bunch of quarters in the jukebox. He played "Stardust" and "Bluebirds Over the White Cliffs of Dover." He scrolled down to "Danny Boy," his hands tightly clutching the jukebox. His eyes fixated on that song title for a long while, but he didn't play it. His knees shook like the day his son's body came home from Vietnam.

"Are you OK, Mickey?" asked the bartender.

"Fine, just fine," he answered.

Turning to Gus he said, "There's plenty more songs, play whatever you like."

Mickey paid for the food and said goodnight to Gus. He also thanked him for letting his kids ride the train for free to Yankee games.

"Buy Gus whatever he wants," he said as he threw a ten spot on the bar. Mickey put the pizza pies in the front seat of his car and drove away from the restaurant.

BOLO
(Be On The Lookout)

The Peekskill Police Department issued a BOLO alert for Robert and Richard Galer. It was immediately fed into the New England crime reporting system, which notified every law enforcement jurisdiction from Pennsylvania to Maine.

RICHARD GALER

DOB: 5/14/40
HT: 6' 2"
WT: 175 lbs.
HAIR: Black
EYES: Brown
IDENTIFYING MARKS: tattoo, right forearm

LAST KNOWN ADDRESS: 14 Maple Ave., Lake Mathews, NY
WEAPONS REGISTERED: .38 S&W, .22 Winchester

WANTED FOR KIDNAPPING, EXTORTION AND GRAND THEFT

ROBERT GALER

DOB: 8/19/41
HT: 6' 0"
WT: 170 lbs.
HAIR: Brown
EYES: Brown
IDENTIFYING MARKS: 3" scar on forehead

LAST KNOWN ADDRESS: 14 Maple Ave. Lake Mathews, NY
WEAPONS REGISTERED: none noted

WANTED FOR KIDNAPPING, EXTORTION AND GRAND THEFT

The New York State Police staked out the Galer residence in Lake Mathews, detailing four undercover vehicles to watch the house. The troopers also spied on the house from a boat anchored across the lake.

Lilly Galer had told the troopers earlier that the brothers used the surrounding woods as escape routes, so with most of the routes roadblocked, the police sat back and waited.

Eddie Redlight had prevailed upon Lilly to talk with Sister Agnes about the threats coming from her family. Lilly was reluctant to do so for fear of retribution from her two brothers. She would also have to reveal the large sum of money she had deposited in the Peekskill Bank, but she decided to tell the head nun, anyway.

"Not to worry," said Sister Agnes. "We have a lot of good friends in the police department and FBI." She looked directly at Lilly, with a sudden seriousness.

"Don't fear. We can protect you, young lady… and maybe bend the rules so Leroy can sleep in the dormitory. We wouldn't want your brothers snatching him up in the middle of the night."

"How about my money?" asked Lilly.

"That money is yours, and we wish you only the best," said Sister Agnes.

Authorities filed felony/kidnapping charges against the Galer brothers, based on statements made by Eddie Redlight and Lilly Galer. The brothers had held them against their will in the little railroad hooch at knifepoint, which constituted kidnapping in the state of New York. It was also a federal crime. To compound their problems, the brothers had stolen bags of money (including lots of change) from the Verplanck Theater and a nearby laundromat.

The Galer brothers were on the lam, and Lilly knew that's when they were most dangerous and unpredictable. They had friends and distant relatives over in Rutland, Vermont. When Lilly was a child, her mother had taken her there to see her cousins. She loved Vermont – the lakes, horseback riding, and picnics. She was just a child but remembered Robert and Richard shooting squirrels with their .22 rifles. When there were no more squirrels around, they shot her cousins' cats. Pretty soon, her family was asked not to come back to Vermont. Her life was always like that, she thought.

Robert and Richard knew a lot of people in town, and had many acquaintances in the rummy bars they frequented.

But the car – a beat up red Ford Galaxy 500 with a foxtail tail on the antenna – was a dead giveaway, thought Lilly. How could anyone miss a car like that? It had drunk bumps all over it. Everyone in town knew the Galers' car on sight. If they continued to drive that ride around Peekskill, they'd be hammered for sure.

One afternoon, Lilly asked Eddie Redlight to walk into town with her so she could do some shopping; she didn't want to go alone. After getting permission from the Sisters to leave the property, the pair headed downtown. Eddie need a few things, too – some smokes, toiletries, socks, and salt-water taffy, which he loved to eat while cutting the grass and sweeping the sidewalks.

But first, Lilly had to go to the bank and get some cash. She filled out a withdrawal slip like Marc Hinn had showed her and got in line to see a teller. All eyes in the bank turned in her direction. Everyone knew who she was, and bank employees knew how much money she had in her account. There weren't too many secrets in a small town.

Lilly wanted to take out $600 in cash. This was quite a large sum, the teller confided to Lilly. The teller asked her to wait so she could confer with the manager. After a while, the manager – a scholarly-looking man about fifty years old – came over.

"Hello, Miss Galer. I see you want to withdraw some money."

"Yes, I'm living up at St. Joseph's Home now and there's a few things we all need," she said.

"Six hundred dollars is a lot of money to be carrying around," he said. "Do you need it all now?"

"Yes, I do. My friend Mr. Redlight is with me to make sure I don't lose it and my co-signor on the account, Marc Hinn, should have called you by now."

"He called an hour ago and said it was fine with him. Yes, he's the co-signor on the account," said the manager. "How do you want the money?"

"Tens and twenties please."

The bank manager then directed the teller to count out the money for the young girl.

"We appreciate your business, Miss Galer. If there's anything we can ever do for you …"

Lilly interrupted in a voice so loud that it shocked the customers in the next line over.

"If those douche bag brothers of mine ever come around here trying to get my money, call the cops."

The bank fell silent until one of the young tellers began to laugh.

"We'll protect your money like it's our own," said the manager.

The two walked down the street to Tuller's Luncheonette, where Lilly bought lunch – a hamburger plate for both of them with sodas and milk shakes. Lilly peeled a ten-dollar bill from her wad and left a fifty cent tip.

Next, they walked to the Circle Men's Shop where she told the owner to fix Mr. Redlight up with new shirts, pants, belts, jackets and shoes.

Eddie resisted her generosity. "No, I can't let you buy these things," he insisted.

"You saved my life, and my cat's, too."

Eddie relented and spent the next hour trying on apparel. The pair laughed and joked as he slid in and out of new duds – stripes that went this way, stripes that went that way.

Growing a bit alarmed, the owner asked, "You *do* have a way of paying for this?"

After Lilly flashed the haberdasher her bankroll, he moved in double time.

"I know it's a little early, but do you need a winter coat?" he said.

It was sweltering outside and the pair laughed.

"We'll be back when it gets cold," said Lilly.

With packages in hand, they moved onto Penny's Department Store where Lilly bought Sisters Agnes, Imelda and Russell the most expensive hand creams, soaps and shampoo the store had. At

Sears Roebuck, Lilly bought ten of the biggest fans she could find. She paid cash and asked that they be delivered to St. Joseph's Home at once.

Lilly then went to the jewelry counter where she purchased a heart-shaped pendent. "I'd like it inscripted," she said to the counter lady. "To Mom: Best Friends Always."

Turning to Eddie, Lilly said, "Mom's in county jail. I'll have the lawyer give this to her."

She also bought a collar and a rubber mouse for Leroy.

"Good, now everyone's got something." she said.

"You didn't buy anything for yourself, Lilly," said Eddie.

"I don't need anything. Just a couple of cartons of Winston's next time out."

Eddie and Lilly stood for a while on the corners of Division and South Street, the same place where he had stood every night for twelve years. Lilly had seen Eddie Redlight a hundred times standing there waving at the cars.

She also remembered her brothers yelling out the car windows, "Hey, you fuckin' retard."

"Ya miss your old spot?" asked Lilly.

"Nope," he answered.

Lilly flagged down cabbie Vinnie Sereno, who tooled by in his beat-up station wagon.

"Where ya going?" yelled the cabbie

"Over to St. Joseph's," said Lilly. The pair hopped in with all their packages. The car lurched forward, as the cabbie engaged the gears.

Pushing his porkpie hat back on his head, the cabbie said, "Hey Eddie, how ya' doing? Haven't seen you since you got beaned a while back."

"It's okay, Vinnie. I'm working at the Home now and staying in the dormitories."

"That's what I hear. It's lonely out here at night without you, my friend. There's no one to wave to anymore."

"I miss you too, but I have a lot of responsibility at the Home now," said a very officious Eddie.

"Good for you," answered Vinnie, genuinely happy for his old buddy.

"The Sisters treating you okay?" he asked.

"Everything's fine."

The cabbie knew who Lilly was. He also knew Lilly's family.

"How's your mother doing, Hon?"

"She'd be doing better. Thank's for asking," said Lilly. "Mom's in county right now for killing the old man."

"Yeah, I heard," said the cabbie. "Your mom's a nice lady, and we wish her the best."

"She's got a good lawyer, and he thinks she can beat some of the charges," said the young girl.

"That's great. What about your brothers?"

"The cops are after them, and they know it. Probably hanging out over in Vermont or maybe up near Lake George."

"I see everyone in town and I haven't seen them in quite a while," he said. "I'll keep my eyes out for 'em."

The cab moved through Peekskill down along South Street and past Lil' Trenton Jackson's lady's place. They drove past where Cookie Reams lived, then down along the Hudson River and over to St. Joseph's Home. Vinnie Sereno refused to take any money for the ride.

As the pair arrived, men were unloading the big fans from the Sears' truck. At first, Sister Agnes thought the monsignor had sprung for them, as he knew about the sweltering conditions at the Home. But upon examination of the delivery slip, she realized that Lilly had bought them.

"A very nice thing you've done for us," said the head Sister.

Lilly then handed her the gifts of shampoos, soaps and lotions.

"Thank you so much," said Sister Agnes. "Personally, I can't accept gifts. With your permission, I will give my things to the other Sisters. But I'm very grateful."

"That's fine," said Lilly.

"I've taken these personal vows," said Sister Agnes. "Someday, I'll tell you about them."

It was late afternoon, and Lilly hurried off to assist Sister Russell with dinner. Since it was Eddie Redlight's day off, he placed his new clothes inside his wall locker and walked out to the ball field for a smoke.

On the side of the Home, young kids were playing basketball, kicking soccer balls and skipping rope. In the small cemetery, a few men were weeding while others were digging and cleaning up around the gravestones. A heavy blanket of humidity that was summer's calling card was being chased away by cool breezes coming off the Hudson River.

A southbound freight train was making its way across Annsville Creek, blasting its horn as it approached Peekskill. When it got closer, Eddie Redlight counted the locomotives. If there were three or more, then the freight train was a long one.

Eddie would guess at the number of cars it was pulling – twenty, thirty, forty or fifty. Always a guessing game. But he was pretty accurate. Eddie could guess the number of railroad cars in a freight train with the best of them. He had practiced this for over twenty years while working for the railroad. It's what you did when you were alone.

The Los Angeles Coliseum

and the Bear Mountain Ridge

Along with the best distance runners in the world, France's Michel Jazy arrived in Southern California early in order to see the sights, get a suntan and prepare for his major West Coast debut. Jazy was entered in the 5,000- meter run, which was a change of plans that his team devised on the way over from France.

Jazy had thought about running the 1,000 meters and maybe setting a world record. It was a soft record and Jazy knew he could surpass it. But there wasn't much talent in the field, and this distance was sort of a non-event for Americans. It was too damned hot to run the ten-thousand so he decided on the 5,000 meters – three and one tenth miles – because he had already run his share of other distances this season and this would be a good change. The race would take place in the historic Los Angeles Coliseum, which was the site of the 1932 Olympics.

His good friend and world record holder, Ron Clarke of Australia, and few other top distance runners from Down Under joined him for tours of Disneyland, Hollywood, the La Brea Tar Pits, and Beverly Hills. The international distance runners couldn't get over how many "things" Americans had.

There were two cars in every driveway, sometimes three. Houses were big enough for eight people, instead of the usual four-person family. At the grocery store, there were seven brands of soup, twenty brands of toothpaste, dozens of different kinds of beer and a hundred types of cookies and candies.

American consumption was off the charts, they figured. In Australia, the supermarkets carried one or two brands at the most. And in France, except in the major cities, there was even less. But these American had it all, they thought.

Jazy ran along the beautiful grass median on San Vincente Blvd., the Pacific Palisades, the Coliseum and University of Southern California. What great weather, he thought. Sunny and mild every day. If I had this weather, I could dribble a football (soccer ball) for a mile in under four minutes, he thought.

At five feet nine and 145 pounds, Michel Jazy was a lithe, graceful, running machine. His dark, combed hair seemed to stand straight up when he was in full gallop. He was a great competitor. Always first or second and always close to, or exceeding, world marks. Great endurance and speed off the charts.

Jazy would also face America's top distance runners who had proved their mettle at the last Olympic Games. One of them was an Olympic champion. But the race would be between Jazy, Clarke and a Kenyan named Kip Keino.

Back on the East Coast, no one knew for sure why CBS dropped its demands for a championship American field in Peekskill's Midnight Mile, but Fraggo said he knew.

"I threatened to shut down CBS, and they listened," he told everyone.

Peekskill's mayor thought it was the town's impassioned plea to continue on with the meet that swayed the network.

France, of course, said it was their threat to pull out of the meet altogether that changed the course of events. And, it truly might have been.

No one knew for sure. Because just when things looked like they were irretrievable broken, CBS issued a communiqué stating that the race would be carried live in its original format. No further details were provided.

Meanwhile, Mike Carroll's conditioning was approaching peak form. After a week or so of serious training, he had reached his former healthy state and told Honey and Cookie that he was ready for faster and harder workouts.

With a week left before the race, Cookie thought this was a bad move. As a matter of fact, Cookie decided to stop timing Carroll altogether, letting him run his distance and do his sprints at his own cadence.

Cookie explained to him that sometimes runners became slaves to the stopwatch, when what really matters is competing against other athletes.

"I know how fast you run, Boy. Old Cookie will tell you if you're slowing down."

Mike Carroll continued long runs through Blue Mountain State Park. He'd run through the wooded area and then onto Washington Ave. through downtown Peekskill and on home.

There was a ten-mile route, a five-mile route, the hill run, the flat speed run, and his secret workout – the one route he never advertised or showed anyone, not even his brother whom he competed against. It was three-quarters of a mile around a small series of summer cabins way back in the woods. Carroll would run this loop five to six times as hard as he could. It was the toughest workout he ever did.

He ran his secret workout all times of the year – during cross-country, indoor and outdoor track. It didn't matter whether he was prepping for a three-mile race or a fast 880. The secret workouts always did the trick.

Honey and Cookie tried to follow him one day to see what he was doing, but he gave them the slip in the woods. He didn't show up until a couple hours later and was totally exhausted.

Back at home, Marie was standing tall for the family. She cooked, cleaned, shopped and ferried the kids back and forth to summer camp and always left a little gas in the car for Mike to use on his dates.

Mickey however, was beside himself, making everyone a wreck.

"How do your legs feel?" he'd ask Mike like he was some kind of quarter horse. "Are you getting enough to eat? Are you getting enough steaks? Are you getting enough honey?"

"I never get enough Honey," Mike said, laughing.

"You know what honey I'm talking about."

The Depew Park track was now totally surrounded by bleachers. It was estimated that ten to twelve thousand people could see the race inside the oval. Huge cranes and trucks began to form a circle around the venue. Trailers were towed to the park for production crews.

Fraggo set up a special seating area for the town's Gold Star Mothers who had lost their sons in the war. He painted all the seats in the section gold and arranged for cushions for the women to sit on. He cordoned off the area with beautiful red velvet. It was located right at the finish line – the perfect seats.

Mayor DiGregorio spent hours each day at the War Memorial on Division Street, not only prodding and pushing the workers but also backslapping and shaking hands with supporters.

Cookie had arranged an easy assignment for Mike Carroll at the post office, as the race drew near. Instead of loading and unloading heavy mail trucks, Carroll now sat for three to four hours counting out stamps for the next day's shift.

"Gotta get ya off yo' wheels, Man," said Cookie. "Now, you can grow a fat ass like everyone else in the post office."

Mike Carroll liked his new job. When reporters showed up unannounced to do interviews with him, the postmaster gladly showed them the door.

"This is the United States Post Office!" he reminded everyone in his stern manner.

On this night, one of the mailmen carried a special package over to Carroll.

"Hey kid. I have to give you this, but I wish I didn't," the mailman said with his hat in his hand. "We all loved your brother. He was a lot of fun to work with."

With those comments, the mailman handed Mike a large manila envelope.

It was heavy and beat to shit like it had come from the other side of the world, which it had. The return address read:

Commanding Officer
November Company
3rd Battalion, 5th Marine Regiment, 1st Marine Division
FPO, San Francisco

Up in the right corner of the envelope was scribbled the word, "Free."

It was addressed to "Parents of: Cpl. Jackie Carroll, USMC."

Mike Carroll was speechless. It was Jackie's mail and personal effects from his unit in Vietnam.

His brother's big green sea bag had come home from Vietnam some months earlier, containing his uniforms, books, camera, sunglasses, trinkets from the Philippines and the like. The family had suffered much grief going through his personal effects. It was like a second funeral. Now, there was more.

Mike Carroll held the envelope in his hand for a long time. He rubbed the paper and squeezed the contents. He smelled it. It smelled awful. Mike didn't open the package; it was addressed to his parents, and after all, he did work for the post office.

He put the package in his backpack and decided to show it to Mickey when he got off his shift later that night. He didn't want his mother around when they opened it. Mike feared it would push her over the tipping point.

At ten o'clock, Mike Carroll finished his shift at the Peekskill Post Office, and said goodbye to his fellow workers. He changed into his running shoes and threw his brown penny loafers into his backpack.

He looked at his wristwatch before scooting through town just like his brother had a few years earlier. Actually, their lives were so similar. They ran track, worked at the post office and ran the same routes home in order to get in a few extra training miles.

Mike Carroll thought about his brave Marine brother all the time. What happened out there to November Company? What had the battle that took his brother's life, really been like? Letters from Jackie's commanding officer and fellow NCOs had arrived after the funeral, telling the family about his brother's courage in battle. His fellow infantrymen all loved his good humor and affinity for playing pranks – like the time he added extra gasoline while burning the shitters and exploded them all over camp, or when he placed his commanding officer's photo over a nude Playboy centerfold and **used** monopoly money in the village to buy black market goods from the Vietnamese.

"You numbah ten motha fucker," yelled the village chief over the barbed wire perimeter fence.

What was combat truly like? Was it glorious? Was it sickening? Who did my brother think of when he was dying? Was it me? Was it Mom? Was it the saints?

In Catholic school, the nuns said one would think of Jesus of Nazareth, resurrecting from the grave and floating off to heaven on a cloud. Is that what it was like?

Mike Carroll made a hard turn onto Division Street then moved on towards Route 202 and up the darkened hills. He was moving at about a four-minute, thirty-second per mile pace — fast for most people, but just cruising for him.

The car behind him, however, was moving much faster. In an instant, the Galer brothers had their prey right in front of them, and Carroll didn't even know it. The car pulled directly in front of Carroll and the Galers slammed the brakes, to cut off his escape route. He was locked in between a 10-foot high retaining wall and their vehicle, foxtail and all.

"So you little prick, there's nowhere to run, is there?" Robert shouted, as be jumped from the car. Richard, the driver, threw the vehicle into park and ran behind Carroll. He caught up with him and pinned Mike to the wall.

The Galers had been drinking, and their breath smelled of alcohol.

"I thought you guys were on the 10 Most Wanted List?" asked Mike. "What are you doing around here?"

"Shut up, Carroll."

"What do you think we should do to him?" asked Richard.

"How about drowning him in Lake Mathews?" asked his brother.

Carroll surveyed the scene, and it didn't look too good for him. Neither one of the Galers appeared to have a weapon, but one was probably nearby, he guessed. Maybe a gun, or certainly a knife, was under the car seat or in the glove box.

"You carrying any money?" asked Richard.

"Not enough for you guys."

"Let me see your wallet and toss the backpack over here," Robert ordered.

Carroll handed them the wallet. They took a ten-dollar bill out of it and dropped it on the ground.

"Now, the backpack."

Carroll knew he had his brother's Vietnam envelope was in it.

"There's nothing in the pack, only shoes and a newspaper."

"Gimme the fucken' backpack," shouted Richard, who pulled up his shirt to reveal a .38 caliber pistol in his waistband.

Carroll handed it over and the brother threw it in the back seat of the car.

"Now, get in," Richard said.

Robert Galer objected. "I don't want to take him anywhere. That's more kidnapping. Let's just cut his Achilles tendons right here."

"He's coming with us!" screamed Richard, as he pulled Carroll towards the vehicle.

Robert blocked his path. "He's not coming with us, gimme the gun."

As the two brothers began to scuffle, Carroll broke free, vaulted over the hood of the car and began running down the street.

"Look what you did now, you stupid fuck," yelled Richard.

Robert took the gun from Richard's belt and fired off a half dozen shots at the fleeing Mike Carroll who was now running faster than anyone on earth.

"Let's get outta here," yelled Robert as house lights came on across the street.

The Galers jumped in their car and roared off as fast as they came. They drove mostly down side streets, knowing the cops would be arriving shortly. Carroll would probably call the cops as well.

The Galaxy 500 turned north heading out of town. The brothers headed for Harriman State Park across the Bear Mountain Bridge where they had been hiding out. The park was big enough for them to blend in and hide the car. Plus, park rangers didn't have two-way radios and didn't bother checking license plates in the parking lots.

The Galers had picked the perfect hiding place. They could eat with the park tourists in the restaurant and shower by the lake, which is what they had done for the past two weeks. That, and drink cases of beer.

"Step on it," Richard yelled to his brother who was now driving.

"Shut the fuck up, and gimme a beer," answered Robert.

The Galers were in need of some serious suds, but had no church key to open them with.

"Shit, where's the can opener?"

"Look in the back."

Richard found the opener on the back seat along with Carroll's backpack.

"Look what we got here," he said, as he pulled the backpack to the front seat.

The brothers opened the beers while they were tooling along Route 6, as Richard scrounged through the pack. He pulled out Carroll's penny loafers and threw them out the window.

"He won't need these anymore."

Richard then grabbed the manila folder holding Cpl. Jackie Carroll's last effects.

"What's that?" asked Robert as he rounded the corner.

"Some bullshit with a lot of writing on it – FPO addresses, 3/5 Marines, please forward... "To the Parents of Corporal Jackie Carroll.""

"Anything valuable?" Robert interrupted.

Richard began to tear open the envelope. "We got some letters, dog tags, some pictures and this manual."

"What's it say?" asked Robert.

"It says, uh, Abco Study Guide."

"What the fuck is that?" asked Robert.

"Abco Study Guide ... dunno."

"Junk. Shit, there's nothing in here," he said, as he threw the envelope in the back seat.

It was near midnight and few cars were on the curvy road. The Galers were smoking and joking, as their Galaxy 500 worked its way to the Bear Mountain Bridge – a formidable structure hundreds of feet above the swift-flowing Hudson River. The bridge, a true work of structural art, ran from the cliffs on the east side of the river to a turnabout on the western side. It connected two very scenic parts of New York.

The posted speed limit was thirty miles per hour, but the Galer vehicle was doing over fifty-five when it reached a sharp turn near the bridge. Overcorrecting at first, Robert Galer tried to steer the big car back to center when his front tire hit a curb. The car zoomed onto the bridge out of control, hitting one rail, bouncing off another, and flipping over the side to freefall hundreds of feet through the air.

The Galaxy was turning upside down and backwards as Robert continued to turn the wheel and hit the brakes on the big car.

Fishing below the bridge for river catfish, Jimmy Gentile guided his little 12-foot boat out of the main shipping channel and dropped anchor. He popped a beer and turned on his transistor radio. There were a lot of good songs out now, and he enjoyed listening to them at nighttime when there was no atmospheric interference.

He loved all the new British bands that hit America's pop charts – The Beatles, The Dave Clark Five, and the Rolling Stones. He like them all – even The Monkeys and Peter and Gordon – though some of his friends accused him of being a sellout.

The Galers' car hit the water roof-first. The brothers were crushed instantly when the roof caved in on the seats.

Gentile, who worked as a base maintenance man at West Point, thought a 155mm artillery shell had gotten away from one of the young officers during nighttime firing maneuvers. He swore to himself that it was an artillery shell that hit near his boat. It was that loud.

Gentile never saw the Galers' car. It quickly rolled over and sank in the deepest part of the Hudson River. Two weeks later, a fisherman pulled Richard Galer's severed head out of his net while trolling for baitfish near Iona Island. Robert was never seen again.

The Midnight
Mile

The peacocks knew something was wrong when Depew Park caretaker Tony Abalone layed out a perfect trail of feed from the edge of the lake to the newly fortified Stalag-like birdcage.

When the peacocks attacked the mayor and Irish Brigades during the big softball game, Abalone got his ass chewed out. After all, he was in charge of the big birds. He cleaned their stalls, fed them and called the veterinarian when they got sick. There were twenty peacocks, and they were featured in all kinds of local tourist literature and bird magazines.

Abalone was afraid of them. They had attacked him so many times he couldn't keep count. The Depew Park peacocks were beautiful and everyone loved them, but they were "mean as hell" if you messed with them. And getting them in their cage when they didn't want to go was messing with them.

"Have you rounded up the big birds yet?" demanded the mayor's secretary in an early morning phone call.

"Not yet; still working on it," said Mr. Abalone.

"We got reports of peacocks biting network people. Please call the mayor when they're locked up," she said.

The peacocks didn't want any part of this new cage and weren't falling for the old Goldilocks trick.

"Ah, fangoule," said the caretaker.

Honey brought a copy of *The New York Times* with her to track practice. Mike Carroll was loosening up, running pick-up sprints at half speed.

The article focused on Michel Jazy's upcoming race in Los Angeles against the best distance runners in the world. It mentioned that he would be coming to Peekskill to run a benefit race for a slain Marine. The article made it sound like Jazy was going to jog around the track for a few laps then put this upstate high school kid away with a withering sprint. It was a condescending article, and Honey and Cookie decided not to show Carroll. Even executives at CBS were pissed off at the *Times* for running this trashy article.

Some local runners were allowed in the race to fill out the field. West Point's Jimmy Wagner, who had run 4:00.1, was entered. Iona College's Phil Karpinsky was entered. He had a personal time of 4:05 seconds. Two club runners from the New York Athletic Club were invited to compete. Both were former college runners who had mile times between 4:05 and 4:10.

Mike Carroll had the slowest time going into the meet, having recorded 4:10 when he won the New York State high school championships.

But that had been some months ago – a world ago, according to Carroll. He thought he could now run a 4:10 mile dribbling a basketball around the track.

Honey Sanders wasn't doing as well. Her parents had split up, and her father had moved in with his girlfriend in Poughkeepsie. Susan Sanders was down for the count; she was drunk all the time and depressed. The most beautiful in-ground pool in Peekskill was full of green slime and not fit to swim in.

"I'll be in college and out of that house in one year," Honey cried one day. "And I'm counting the days."

The Sisters of St Joseph' Home began praying in earnest for Mike Carroll's victory about a week before the race. They said morning and nightly prayers, always asking St. Joseph, their patron saint, for a special burst of wind to carry their boy to victory. They were unsure whether Jazy was a Catholic, but assumed he was, as France was a Christian country.

"Have the wind blow them both around the track, only Carroll a little faster," Sister Imelda prayed.

Eddie Redlight, who had seen the Carroll boys running through town for years, told everyone at the orphanage that Mike Carroll could beat anyone, Olympians included.

"Jackie Carroll was the fastest person I ever seen run, until his brother Mike came along. He's even faster."

The kids at the Home were all excited about the upcoming race. Fraggo had provided tickets for them and arranged transportation to get them there. Rumors circulated around the Home that Mike Carroll was an orphan from St. Joseph's who was later raised by the Carroll family. It wasn't true, but it gave all the kids a sense of connection to the young man and his upcoming race.

Mayor Di Gregorio was pulling out what was left of his hair. There were not enough hotel and motel rooms in the Peekskill area to accommodate all the out of town guests. Michel Jazy and his entourage would have four rooms at the Peekskill Motor Inn and media were already booking the remainder.

There were a dozen or so motels in the area, including the "world famous" Union Hotel (that is, famous in 1915). Spectators would be put up in motels from Croton to West Point and from Verplanck to Yorktown Heights.

Peekskill Military Academy agreed to house spectators at a nominal fee, but there would have to be two persons to a room and everyone would be using communal bathrooms.

Now that all the Galers (the bad ones) were either dead or in jail, the Peekskill police department had extra deputies to free up for crowd control and parking duties.

Peekskill's volunteer fire departments, the catalyst for the first fund raising event, were front and center for the big race. Fire trucks would be stationed all around Depew Park, and fundraisers would be held in conjunction with the meet.

"We have to hit the long ball on this fundraising," said the fire chief.

The town asked meteorologists from West Point and New York City to help predict the weather for the big race. It was well known that thunderstorms could hit any time during the late summer months, but with two days to go, clear skies were predicted.

Michel Jazy won his big 5,000-meter race in Los Angeles, upsetting Ron Clarke and the newcomer from Kenya, Kip Keino. Jazy won the race by sprinting by Clark and Keino with 300 meters to go. The time was close to a world record.

Jazy was photographed with the mayor of Los Angeles. He was photographed with the cast of "The Munsters" and the

Mouseketeers. He also had his picture taken with the USC football team that was preparing for their season opener.

After an all-night flight from Los Angeles, the French entourage arrived at LaGuardia airport early in the morning. They were whisked away by special police conveyance to their hotel in Peekskill. The race was a day and a half away.

Monsignor Healy, who had been at a big Catholic confab in St. Louis, arrived back in town a few days early to make sure Mike Carroll had his race strategy down cold.

"How are you going to run him, Son?"

"Monsignor, this is new territory for me. I'm going to stay with him as long as I can and do my best."

The monsignor scratched his chin and thought about it for a while.

"Perfect answer. Give it your best, and God bless."

On race day, Mickey Carroll woke up with a splitting headache.

"I'm sure it's the tension," he declared.

Since the race wasn't until midnight, Mike Carroll slept in until almost noon – a full twelve hours of sleep. Mickey and Marie had ordered his younger brothers and sisters to stay away from his room and keep the noise down, which they did. It was a warm morning and Mickey hoped the fan he put in Mike's room would keep him cool. When the kids wanted to go swimming about mid-morning, Mickey said no. The grabass in the backyard would wake up their older brother.

Marie was sitting in the living room reading magazines and newspapers, cutting out articles that pertained to the family. So much had happened in such a short time. There were two scrapbooks, one for Corporal Jackie Carroll USMC, and the other for "The Midnight Mile."

There were so many news articles about both boys, and lots of pictures. Marie knew she was blessed with such talented older sons, and she hoped all the publicity they received didn't negatively affect their younger brothers and sisters.

Marie knew she had many more years of child rearing left and hoped that she and Mickey wouldn't be burned out when the little ones came to bat. She worried about how much energy she and her husband had left for the family. It was if she had already lived a lifetime.

People began pouring into Depew Park Stadium about three hours before race time. All the Peekskill players were in attendance. The entire Knights of Columbus sweltered under their heavy cloaks and hats. Monsignor Healy and Mayor Di Gregorio sat with the VIPs. The Irish Brigades, including the Fighting 69, were angling for seats nearest the johns so they could continually drink and drain. The St. Joseph's kids, hundreds of them, ran wild all over the place; the nuns had given up containing them. Eddie Redlight and Lilly sat in the last row so they could smoke. The West Point coaches sat front and center. Thrown out of his house by his wife for being a miserable bastard, Gus the conductor smuggled a six-pack into the stadium and was sharing his beers with cabbie Vinnie Sereno.

There were high school bands, cheerleaders, and enough snow cones to ice a hockey rink.

Earlier in the day, Michel Jazy had jogged around Depew Park's oval. He was impressed and liked the way his spikes dug into the track. Consular General Claude Lambeau and his staff, who provided for all his needs, had accompanied him since his arrival. During the day, Lambeau had taken Jazy to see Peekskill's war memorial. The media photographed Jazy and Lambeau placing flowers at the memorial.

After eating a steak and a grilled cheese sandwich, Mike Carroll dressed and prepared to leave the house. It was still a few hours until race time, and Honey and Cookie were picking him up.

Marie Carroll asked to be alone with her son for a few moments, and everyone cleared out of the living room.

Marie spoke first. "The day your brother Jackie left for Vietnam we said goodbye in this same room. I made a mistake that day," she said, trying to keep her composure. "I told him, 'I'll never see you again.' That was a mistake that I can't take back." A wave of emotion gave her pause. "Son, Michael my Archangel, I'll see you tonight at the finish line."

Mike wiped his tears away. "You've got the best seats in the house," he said, kissing his mother.

The TV lights had turned little Depew Park into a major league stadium. Thirty minutes before race time the track and bleachers were bright enough to take photos without flash. Large CBS cameras were stationed at every turn, and miles of black electrical wires seemed to run everywhere. For two hours, the local bands played music. An hour prior, Joey Dee and the Starlighters sang a number of popular songs. Marci became the perfect Beach Blanket Bingo Annette Funicello. When the Irish Brigades belted out "Garryowen" the peacocks roared in defiance but couldn't escape Tony Abalone's new cage.

With much fanfare, the Gold Star Mothers were seated; each received a bouquet of red roses. There were eleven mothers in attendance, but not Louise Alforni, who had since been institutionalized.

Sal Fraggo had stationed himself next to the announcer and would chime in from time to time about local gossip. Up in a booth, a professional announcer from CBS would call the race.

Claude Lambeau and Michel Jazy walked up to Mike Carroll, who was putting on his spikes in the infield grass. Jazy was an older looking man, deeply tanned with tight lines in his face. His blue uniform contained the flag of France. His legs were thin, but powerful. They reminded Carroll of two pistons.

Lambeau and Jazy kissed Honey and shook hands with Cookie, whom Mike introduced as his coach.

"Good luck, mon ami," said the Frenchman.

"Good luck to you, Sir, and thank you for coming to America," said Mike Carroll.

The consular general hugged the American athlete.

Carroll jogged around the infield grass. He was approached by his West Point friend, Jim Wagner.

"I'll take out the pace," said Wagner. "I'll try to go a minute, fifty-eight seconds at the half. Stay behind me and relax for as long as you can."

Honey walked over to Mike, kissed him on the lips and wiped the sweat off his face.

"You're already sweating. That's a good sign," she said. "One other thing mon ami."

"Yeah?" he asked as he jogged away.

"I love you."

Mike smiled and waved.

Producers for CBS seemed to be in charge of the meet as the athletes approached the starting line. Each runner was guided to the track and placed in lanes for introductions. Jazy was in lane one; Wagner, lane two; Carroll, lane three, and Karpinsky from Iona, in lane four. Runners from the New York Athletic Club, NYAC, were in lanes five and six.

Commercial breaks seemed to keep the runners on the track for a long time between introductions.

The starter, a serious man with glasses, faced the runners and said, "I'll give you two commands. Set. And then the gun. Good luck."

The runners walked back to their lanes and waited for CBS to give them the signal. There was no breeze at all, and the temperature about 70 degrees. Perfect running weather.

Carroll looked around Depew Park and saw 15,000 people – about 10,000 more than ever attended a sporting event in this stadium. What a show. He saw the nuns and kids from the Home and thousands of local people. Everyone was here.

Were they coming to see him, or Jazy? Didn't matter.

Mike looked over and saw his family, smiling and laughing. Marie was sitting with the Gold Star Mothers, proud as a peacock.

The red lights on the big CBS cameras suddenly went on, and a network wag yelled, "Ready to go!"

Carroll and Jazy took a long look on each other, then, stared straight ahead.

The starter raised his pistol and fired the gun.

Jimmy Wagner sprinted to the lead ahead of the pack. Mike Carroll tucked himself in behind Wagner, followed by Jazy, Karpinsky and the rest of the field.

Unlike the earlier 880 in Yonkers, there was no bumping and pushing. It was a gentlemen's race so far. Following Wagner as he was, Carroll forgot about Jazy for a moment. He had run against Wagner a lot when he was a high school sophomore. Mike had been outclassed by both his brother and Wagner during those early races, but that was when he was younger.

The pack of runners – still in the same order – passed the quarter-mile mark in 58 seconds, a good, swift pace. The crowd was screaming so hard Carroll couldn't hear his first split. (He got the time from the big, new scoreboard.)

Jazy's coach was screaming in French, and Mike wished he were a better student so he could understand what was being said.

They passed Honey at the 660-yard mark, and she yelled and screamed for Mike to stay relaxed.

"You have a beautiful girlfriend, mon ami," said Jazy, who was on Carroll's shoulder.

"Merci beaucoup," answered Carroll.

Jazy then sprinted past Carroll and Wagner, catching them both by surprise and opening up a five-yard lead. Mike Carroll didn't panic.

It was a beautiful night and Carroll kept looking up in the stands as he rounded the turns. Could this all be possible?

As they approached the 880 mark, Carroll heard the timer call out 1:58 seconds. He also heard his father yelling, "Close the gap! Close the gap!"

Jazy had a good ten-yard lead when Carroll went around Wagner.

"See you at the finish line, Bro," he said to his West Point friend.

Cookie Reams had a good feeling at the half-mile mark. He knew that Mike Carroll was relaxed and running within himself, but he gave his standard yell just the same: "Go motha-fucker! Go!"

George Pataki, who would later become mayor of Peekskill and then governor of New York, saw the sparks flying from Mike Carroll's spikes.

"Holy Christ!" he yelled to his friends. "Did you see that, did you see those sparks?"

Coming into the last lap, Mickey and Marie were all screamed out; the noise around them was deafening. Carroll had closed the gap on the Frenchman to a single stride.

Jazy's coach was now screaming, "Allons! Allons!" (Let's go, let's go.)

And then, when it couldn't get any louder, it did. Carroll flashed by world record holder Michel Jazy with 440 yards to go. One more lap.

The time at the three-quarter mile mark was 2:57 seconds.

The Frenchman was caught sleeping, as Mike opened up a five-yard lead, then a ten-yard lead. The high school kid from Peekskill roared around the track with thousands of people screaming in his ears. Cookie was comatose, and Honey was crying.

Two hundred-twenty yards to go. Half a lap more.

Jazy was back on Carroll's shoulder now as the two raced down the track far ahead of the field. This Olympian was a true champion, not giving one inch. Sparks flew from both their spikes. Carroll was tired, but his legs were still pumping, and that's what counted.

The Frenchman pulled ahead around the last turn. Carroll ran him wide like a pro. The two entered the final straight dead even.

The big scoreboard was ticking 3:40, 3:41, 3:42. Carroll surged past Jazy as the crowd erupted. Then, the Frenchman caught back up. They drove their arms as hard as they could towards the finish line. Thirty yards, twenty yards. They hit the tape together.

Carroll looked up at the clock. It had stopped at three minutes, fifty-two seconds, 3:52.

The runners hugged each other.

After they met to compare stopwatches, officials were shouting and screaming: "A new world record!" "A new world record!"

"You are a great champion," said Michel Jazy.

"Thank you again for coming to America," answered an exhausted Mike.

The race was too close to call. Officials waited for a photograph to determine the winner and this took a few minutes. Mike was staggering and weaving on heavy legs. He could barely speak. His tongue licked his lips.

Honey ran up and kissed him and wiped sweat from his eyes.

They looked over to see Cookie, who was nearest the judges. He was screaming and jumping around in a combination of disbelief and glee. And that's when they knew who had won the race.

Reporters jammed around Carroll, as the police cordon collapsed.

Carroll looked for his mother in the stands.

"Mom, Mom!" he yelled.

He wiped the sweat from his stinging eyes. She wasn't there! Marie wasn't with the Gold Star Mothers. Where was she?

A reporter's strobe light blinded Mike.

"She's not with the Gold Star Mothers!" he yelled to reporters.

"I want to ask you a few questions," said the newsman, pushing a microphone into his face.

Mike Carroll was being blinded by both the sweat in his eyes and the bright television lights. He swatted his hands again and again towards the light, trying to block it out.

The Running Man of
Charlie Med

As the mid-afternoon rain subsided, nurses and orderlies of Charlie Company's 1ˢᵗ Medical battalion opened the flaps on their big green recovery tent to reveal thirty or so badly wounded Marines.

With only a single fan to circulate the hot air, the tent was sweltering. Opening the flaps allowed a breeze from the South China Sea to wash over the patients, but it also permitted a bright sun to shine on the men.

Medical personnel were in a constant frenzy of changing dressings, adjusting IV bags and administering morphine. Some of the men were still unconscious from operations that had saved their lives. Some were in terrible pain and woke to find gaping gunshot wounds in their extremities. They screamed in pain until the morphine was applied. Some were missing limbs. A chaplain would be called when they woke up.

"No! No! Please God, No!" the amputees screamed again and again. "No!" they cried.

The reaction was always the same.

The recovery tent, one of ten in the U.S. Navy's 1ˢᵗ Medical battalion at Chu Lai, Vietnam, was filled to the brim with broken men. It smelled like antiseptic. Medical personnel said it smelled like the floor of an X-rated movie theater.

Over in a far corner, a corpsman yelled, "Get the doctor. This one is coming out of it!"

A wounded Marine was waving his hands in front of his face, trying to block the fierce sunlight from his eyes. He was perspiring and mumbling to himself and had a bad case of the "Jimmy Legs." After a long, long sleep, he was now awake and looking around, slightly frightened.

He lay half naked on a cot with an IV bag suspended on a pole above him. He had a bandage on his right flank with some drainage tubes connected to a pan that sat on the wooden floor. The right side of his head was bandaged with heavy white gauze. His eyebrows and crew cut were seared off his skin and a gob of salve covered a large burn mark on his center chest. His lower lip was shredded where he had bitten through it, and his tongue was moving around searching for water.

"Can I get a drink?" were his first words.

A Navy corpsman brought a plastic cup of water and helped the wounded Marine drink it down.

"Are you in any pain?" asked the corpsman.

"No. I'm okay," said the Marine.

In a moment, the ward's chief medical doctor arrived. He was a twenty-five-year-old dark-haired, razor-thin lieutenant.

"Welcome back! We were beginning to worry about you," he said. "Who are you?"

"I'm Jackie Carroll, Corporal. November Company," he said with perfect clarity.

The doctor looked into his eyes with his small light, and felt his pulse. Using a damp sponge, he wiped sweat off Carroll's face and chest, carefully avoiding the burned area.

"He's still hot," he said to the corpsman. "How do you feel?"

"I feel okay, but I'm real thirsty," Jackie answered.

"You've been unconscious for three days. Welcome back."

"What happened?" asked Jackie.

The doctor studied his chart.

"You were medivaced here on Saturday and came in fully conscious. I was on duty. Shrapnel wounds, right side. Some minor burns on head and chest, and shrapnel wound, head. We cut out the shrapnel from your stomach and flank. A piece of shrapnel about three inches long was sticking out of your head. I know it hurt like hell because you were screaming and in pain," said the doctor. "We x-rayed your noggin, then removed the metal from your head. You were still awake and cursing at everyone."

A number of medical orderlies had gathered around Corporal Carroll's bed as the doctor spoke to him. They waved and smiled at Jackie, and he waved back as best he could as the doctor spoke.

"You were just exhausted so we put you out, also gave you medication for pain."

Eyeballing the chart and getting serious, the doctor then stroked his forehead.

"But you stayed unconscious for a full three full days. We tried to wake you, but couldn't. The neurologist came in this morning to examine you. He didn't know what the problem was. He studied the x-rays. The shrapnel didn't pierce your brain, but it sure gave you a bad concussion and a fractured skull."

There was a long pause, as the gathered medical personnel stared at Jackie. Off in the distance, muffled cries of the wounded could be heard. Then, the doctor spoke.

"Corporal, where have you been?"

A few days later, Jackie was doing much better. The drainage tubes were pulled from his wounds and most of the bandages had been removed from his head. He was beginning to look somewhat normal.

A Marine general made the rounds one evening, passing out Purple Hearts to the wounded. Jackie, who had gorged himself on macaroni and cheese, was sick to his stomach throwing up in a bedside pan. The general pinned the Purple Heart on his pillow. "Congratulations, Son," said the one-star. "Your country is proud of you."

A staff officer from his rifle battalion came to visit with Jackie and filled him in on the battle. He told the wounded man that despite heavy Marine casualties, the enemy had lost an entire regiment, which forced the NVA Division back into Laos.

"You guys did a great job. Superb job. Your company commander and all your lieutenants were wounded, some very seriously. All your machine gunners were killed, as were your mortar men. Two of the three radiomen were killed, and of course, a lot of grunts.

"You guys fought like hell. We estimate about two thousand NVA on the field. Your little group held off over a thousand enemy soldiers. This is the biggest battle for the division since the Korean War. They'll be talking about this fight at Camp Pendleton when you're an old man."

A few days later, Jackie Carroll, USMC was sitting up in bed. He still had a fever because his body was fighting off various infections.

"Still, no mail?" he asked the orderlies, as they distributed letters and packages to the wounded men around him.

"November Company is out in the boondocks. It takes a while to get your mail re-routed."

Jackie didn't know any of the other wounded Marines in the beds around him. Because of his head wounds, he was moved out of the general patient population and into a special ward where he could be constantly observed.

Medical personnel who had watched over Jackie when he was unconscious ribbed him about being out of it for so long.

"Dude, you were the running man of Charlie Med," said Doc Steele, a 20-year-old corpsman 2nd Class from Newark.

"What do you mean?" asked Jackie.

"Your legs were moving, arms moving, head moving, but you wouldn't wake up. And when Lieutenant McCann wiped you down and changed your bandages, you moaned like you was bangin' a 'ho, in Shit City," Doc Steele said, cracking himself up. "You were a trip, Man. After that, she wouldn't come in here no more. Everybody was pissed at you 'cause she's only the best-looking nurse in the division."

Doc Steele was applying salve to Jackie's chest burns with a wooden tongue depressor.

"About a day after you came in we tried to wake you up. One of November Company's KIAs was all tore up and nobody could make out who he was. They needed you to identify him."

"Who was it?" asked Jackie.

"Don't remember, but they got him ID'd."

The neurologist visited with Jackie each day. He was told that his wounds were healing and he'd be returned to his rifle unit in a month or so.

"Sorry, Son," said the Navy captain. "I'm sure that's not the news you wanted to hear."

"It's OK, Doctor. It's what I expected," the corporal answered.

The doctor sat down on the edge of his bed and began to talk in earnest.

"You were unconscious for so long with this type of wound. We didn't think it was that serious. After we took the metal out of your head, we thought you'd be up the next morning, but you stayed out of it for three full days. You just wouldn't wake up. Get some paper when you get a chance and write down what you remember. Might mean something one day."

The Navy captain said he was on-call for an operation and excused himself.

"Good luck to you," he said.

Jackie had small burns on the tips of his thumb and index finger on his right hand that the medical personnel had missed. He thought it was from gripping the hot barrel of the M-60 machine gun. So when he tried to write, just like the doctor said, his hand hurt and he had to stop.

A few days later, using writing paper from the PX, Jackie wrote to his father about the battle and his vivid dreams after his head injury. He apologized for the agony he had caused the family by joining the Marines and hoped he could rectify it some day.

A staff clerk from battalion visited him one day, offering to ship the Purple Heart medal home to his family.

"It'll get lost or stolen, if you leave it in the rear," said the clerk.

The letter was three pages long and Jackie folded it numerous times before placing it in the Purple Heart box. So it wouldn't obscure the beautiful medal, he pulled out the velvet tab holding it in place and put the handwritten note behind it and out of view.

The orderly then mailed the Purple Heart to Peekskill, N.Y.

Afterword

On A Cold Winter
Day

The train to Peekskill was only sparsely filled during the mid-morning hours. Everyone had already gone to work in New York City and only a few students and workers on the late shift were returning at this hour.

I'm an old man now, and I know that for sure because the other day while driving along, a young girl gave me the finger and yelled, "Fuck you, old man!" after I blew my horn from the car behind her. I had interrupted her cell phone chat, as she was oblivious to the changing traffic light.

We rounded the big Buchanan Curve and the conductor yelled, "Next stop, Peekskill. Peekskill will be your next stop."

The train stopped and a few stragglers debarked into a cold, overcast morning. A new platform had been built and one could walk off the train without having to jump three feet to the ground. Across the way, white caps appeared on the mighty Hudson River.

The train station appeared as it had forty years ago – exactly the same, except for one small change. The north end of the station had been turned into a pub, and on this morning a half-dozen men were drinking beer and reading *The New York Daily News* and *The New York Post*, while music played in the background.

Sorrento's Italian Restaurant where my family ate Friday night meals, and my parents sang songs, is no longer there. It's a parking lot now. Up on the hill above the train station overlooking the Hudson River is a huge condominium development. St. Joseph's Home for Orphans went away and only a chapel and convent remain near the site.

My cabbie friend, with the porkpie hat and busted up station wagon who gave me a free ride home when I came back from

Vietnam, is long gone, murdered by a fare late one night. There is now a fleet of taxis cabs and commuter vans where his old car used to be.

My sister is picking me up today. I've been gone for almost thirty years, living in California.

We drive first to Assumption Cemetery to visit my parents' grave. It's high on the hill and overlooks a beautiful valley that today is bitterly cold and wet.

John J. Flood	Eleanor P. Flood
Born: Oct 3, 1918	Born: October 22, 1922
Died: Oct 11, 1989	Died: June 20, 1990

My father died a long time ago, and my mother shortly after. I'm wondering if he ever showed her that special letter from Vietnam. It was something he wouldn't be inclined to do. The letter contained quite a story, but parts of it would be painful, especially to her.

I was the wounded Marine in Vietnam. During a fierce battle, I was wounded first in the right side with shrapnel from a mortar that practically fell on top of me. Later that evening, after hours of fighting and struggling to stay alive, another mortar hit nearby, sending shrapnel into my head. I remember the head wound hurt and the stomach wound burned.

I was evacuated at first light, flying to the medical outpost on a CH-34 helicopter, which was loaded with wounded and dying men. The floor was covered with blood and spent shell casings from the door gunner's machine gun.

When I arrived at the hospital fully conscious, shrapnel was taken out of my stomach. It was bedlam at the hospital, with casualties stretching out to the helicopters' landing zone. The doctors tried to x-ray my head to determine if the shrapnel pierced my brain, but the x-ray machine was broken. They then loaded me into a van and sent me to another location where the x-ray machine was working. I was okay.

They sent me back to the first place and removed the shrapnel by pulling it out with a pair of pliers. (I don't think there was another way to do it.)

It hurt like hell, and I screamed and made a pest out of myself.

I'm sure the medical personnel thought I was the biggest baby in the Marine Corps.

Then, they gave me a bunch of medication, and I went out like a light.

I woke up a couple of days later. Whether I was unconscious, or in a coma or just totally exhausted, I'll never know. It was never explained to me. But I do remember the doctor asking, "Where have you been all this time?"

Soon after, I wrote a letter to my father – which was unusual, because I always wrote "Dear Mom and Pop." But this time I didn't. I addressed the letter to my father, and placed it in the back of my Purple Heart box, which was mailed home by clerical personnel. I wrote about the battle (I skipped a lot of gory details) and about my battlefield dream, and I was surprisingly articulate.

I apologized to him for the agony I had caused the family by joining the Marines. It simply put them through hell. I was sure my absence had contributed to my mother's severe depression and alcohol problems. It pushed her over the tipping point, and the family was clearly imploding.

But my dreams in that field hospital were about other things as well. I was a terrible student in high school, who valued jumping naked off the school roof into a pile of snow more than studying for a key examination. I was a decent athlete and found most of my success running track at Depew Park in Peekskill. Most girls in high school regarded me as an average unknown, but in my dream, the prettiest girl in the city loved me like no other.

I was always in summer school, having to repeat some class or the other. Our assistant principal referred to me once as a "summer school commando."

I failed French one year and had to repeat in summer school. Knowing I ran track, the French teacher brought in an article about Frenchman Michel Jazy, who had just broken a world track record. I had never heard of Michel Jazy. My real hero in high school was Kansas's Jim Ryun, who had broken the four-minute mile. His pictures were all over my room.

Eddie Redlight was a man my father often waved to while driving through town. When I called him a "retard" once for standing on the street corner the way he did, my father became angry with me. "He's one of God's children," he said.

The Sisters of St. Joseph's Home taught me in grammar school and beat the crap out of me when I screwed around, which was fairly often. I also played baseball at the Home, and worked there as well. When I was wounded the last time in Vietnam and finally shipped home, one of the Sisters came to the Navy hospital to see me. They will be the first ones in heaven, if there is such a place.

My running pal who went to West Point was always a better runner than I was, and he was a brave lieutenant in Vietnam as well. And I did use his Sunday school class drawings as a battlefield dressing.

During school breaks, I unloaded mail trucks at the Peekskill post office, and often ran the two miles home, since I never had a ride.

I worked at Indian Point Nuclear Power Plant as an accountant for the company, but fell in love with the crazy antics of the unionized labor force. When a powerful shop steward drove up one time in his stretch limo, his workers literally threw down their coats so he wouldn't have to walk in the mud.

Our family did have the biggest above-ground pool in the neighborhood and Leroy our cat was the undisputed champion of late night screeching and screwing. The Galer family was imagined. I knew no family like that in our town, although I do remember running like hell from a certain Galaxy 500.

When my father died of cancer, it was the saddest event of my life and of my brothers' and sisters' lives as well. He was such a kind and gentle man. We were going through his personal effects one day, trying to get insurance and pension information for my mother. We cried as we went through his junk drawer, which contained mementos from his life: old coins, matchbooks, collar stays, pictures and photos from his own childhood, watches he never wore, eyeglasses, car titles, tie clips, mass cards, playing cards, Coast Guard insignias from World War II, certificates of baptism, communion and confirmation. And then, under all the stuff, a plain blue box. Nothing much. It looked like it held a watch or bracelet, but there was nothing in it.

I held it for a moment, opened and closed it a few times and then pulled the box apart, revealing the letter I had written to my father years ago from Vietnam. It was still there in the Purple

Heart box, and I hadn't seen it since the day I mailed it from the hospital. Unlike the newer medals, which say Purple Heart on the outside of the box (my second one has this insignia), the old World War II medals sit in a plain, unmarked box with no writing on it.

And that's the one I got.

Upon returning from Vietnam, I found my Purple Heart medal pinned to a small display my father had set up in the living room, together with track trophies, miniature flags and my boot camp photo. My brothers and sisters called it a shrine. It was one of the many nice things he did.

The box the medal came in and the letter it contained were never thought of again. Soon after, I left home for good, first to college and then onto the world.

I don't know if my father ever read the letter. I don't know if he even found it. My guess is that he read it and put it back, not showing it to anyone, as it contained some painful remarks.

That letter became the basis for this book.

When I was wounded in Vietnam and floating around in space reserved for the nearly departed, I dreamed of a track stadium late at night, away from the harsh glare of the sun. It was in my own hometown. A family that was torn apart so badly, was now happy and healthy, and cheering from the stands. Everyone was at the track meet. There were no more tears and heartaches for this family. It was a calm, clear night as I walked to the starting line to run the biggest race of my life, "The Midnight Mile."

About The
Author

Photo by Caroline Orford

Denis Flood was a high school track champion who was wounded fighting with the Marines in Vietnam. After recovering from his injuries he went on to become the U.S. Marine Corps champion in track. As a walk-on at the University of Tennessee, Flood then earned a scholarship, became team captain and Southeast Conference (SEC) champion and record holder. He went on to serve almost forty years in the active and reserve military, retiring as a Navy Captain in charge of NCIS reserve forces on the West Coast. He lives with his wife and family in California. For more information on Denis Flood you can visit his web site: www.denisflood.com.

WA